POUTI[illegible]GIN

Steve Rhinelander

Savant Books and Publications
Honolulu, HI, USA
2022

Published in the USA by Aignos Publishing LLC
An imprint of Savant Books and Publications LLC
2630 Kapiolani Blvd #1601
Honolulu, HI 96826
http://www.aignospublishing.com

Printed in the USA

Edited by Helen R. Davis
Cover by Daniel S. Janik, Steve Rhinelander and Helen R. Davis
Background cover image by Şahin Sezer Dinçer from Pixabay with permission; foreground cover image "Photo 81163113" © Sergey Bogomyakov | dreamstime.com with permission.

ISBN/EAN: 978-0-9994633-5-2

First Edition: January 2022
Library of Congress Control Number: 2021952999

Dedication

For Laurie–I love you.

Acknowledgements

I owe a debt of gratitude to countless people who assisted me while I was writing this novel. I conducted much of the research for this novel on Wikipedia and other similar online resources. Because those research materials were generally written anonymously, I regret that I cannot thank those authors by name.

The novel includes a discussion of the Battle of the Plains of Abraham, represented as an excerpt of a fictional history textbook published in 1940. I based the style of that excerpt on *A Basic History of the United States*, by Charles A. Beard and Mary R. Beard (Doubleday, Doran & Co., 1944).

In the alternate history of this novel, the Louisiana Purchase of 1803 did not occur. Instead, that area of about 828,000 square miles remained a French colony known as "French North America." For the brief discussion of law administration in French North America in this novel, I relied heavily on background I learned from *France and Britain in Africa*, Prosser Gifford and Wm. Roger Louis, Eds. (Yale University Press, 1971) and *West Africa under Colonial Rule*, Michael Crowder (Northwestern University Press, 1968).

I am also indebted to Mr. Christopher Scoggins, my Creative Writing teacher at Hartford Union High School in Hartford, Wisconsin. In addition to helping me develop as a writer, he gave me advice on writing novels that would prove indispensable decades later.

In addition, I must thank Kathy Olenski and my sister-in-law, Lisa. They read early drafts of the novel and gave me very helpful comments and edits. In particular, I appreciate all the time and effort Lisa took to teach me everything I will ever need to know about the pluperfect tense.

Finally and most importantly, I thank my wonderful wife, Laurie. She gave me constructive criticism when I asked for it. She gave me encouragement and support when I needed it. I am unbelievably fortunate that she is a part of my life and nothing I say here could fully convey how much I love her.

Prologue

September 13, 1759

My Dearest Marie-Thérèse:

I have little time now, but I may never have another opportunity to tell you how much I adore you, more than any mere earthly possession, more than the very life-sustaining air I breathe on this cool but sunny morning, with the beauty of the sunrise surpassed by nothing save my memory of your visage and our lovely children.

The British are assembled at our doorstep. How they arrived there, I dare not venture a guess. General Montcalm's meeting with myself and his other advisors just ended. The others advised attacking the British before they become entrenched, but I fear their bravery is misplaced on this occasion. I counseled caution. The Enemy cannot successfully storm our battlements and they cannot besiege us before the fall of winter. The General has left us to consider his options. I cannot predict his decision. I can only endeavor to ensure that, whatever fate lies ahead, History will show I performed my duty to the best of my ability.

Forever Truly Yours,
Your Affectionate Husband,
Pierre-François

Chapter I

La Baie des Puants, Stinkwater Bay, was the name French explorer Jean Nicollet gave to Green Bay in 1634. Over 300 years later, Samuel de Champlain Le Pelleteur thought the name was also an apt description of his life—like a sad song when you're on your fifth glass of gin, or the bad break you get as soon as you think it can't get any worse.

Le Pelleteur contemplated the nature and quality of his life's stench, along with various other weighty issues, while sitting in his 1927 forest green Chevrolet sedan at 3:00 in the morning. Like him, the car was several years past its prime. It was one of six cars in the parking lot of a cheap motel about five kilometers north of Neenah, a Menominee town about 60 kilometers southwest of Green Bay. Neenah was familiar to many in Québec because the name of the town was emblazoned proudly on manhole covers on city streets throughout the country. Unlike the dome-shaped houses seen elsewhere in the town, the motel was shaped more like an Iroquois long house: twelve rooms, side-by-side, under a roof with gables on each end, running parallel to a parking lot. Each room had its own door and a view of a cross-section of the parking lot and Highway Q41 beyond. The roof was completely covered with snow. Grotesquely huge, undulating icicles hung from the roof halfway to the ground.

Le Pelleteur was careful to park in a spot that gave him a good view of the motel room his client's husband had checked into earlier that evening. He had his Graflex Speed Graphic press camera balanced on the dashboard, with the flash bulb in the middle of a silver parabolic dish only slightly larger than a pie plate and the bellows extended towards his quarry's motel room door. Le Pelleteur bought the camera in a second-hand shop on *La Rue Laurier* for seven *livres* in 1936, after nine months of frustration taking photographs in dark motel parking lots with a 20-year-old Brownie camera and using his car headlights for lighting.

His night was unfolding as many of his nights had over the past five years. Hours earlier, he had finished reading by flashlight the previous day's *Journal de Green Bay*, Sunday, February 4, 1940. He spent some time wondering why they call it "News" when all the stories seem so old. President Duplessis promises that the Québec national economy will emerge from the Depression any time now. Nazi Germany invades another Eastern European country and is rumored to be planning an invasion of France. The Green Bay Packers lose another hockey game (this time to the Fort Duquesne Penguins, 4 to 1).

The business card in Le Pelleteur's pocket identified him as a private investigator, but in the long, dark night, cold enough to make time itself seem thick and sluggish, he fought his boredom by thinking of more descriptive terms for his chosen profession. One possibility was executioner of marriages that have overstayed their welcome on Death Row. Alternatively, he could be a tool that women use to make their sad, bitter lives sadder and bitterer. More colorful, although somewhat macabre, he could be some kind of demon who derives his nourishment from the misery of jealous women and confirms their worst fears for ten *livres* a day plus expenses. These musings did not exactly swell his chest with pride, but then again, as he often reminded himself, giving a damn generally isn't worth the effort.

The highlight of the evening came about five minutes later, when a pair of love birds as charming as the roaches under Le Pelleteur's refrigerator scurried out of their motel room. He was a nervous man in his 50s, scanning the horizon for unwanted witnesses. Twenty kilograms overweight, his grey suit and cloth overcoat matched his hair. He wore a red and white sash tied around his waist, a *ceinture fléchée*, a fashion accessory unique to *La République Québécoise* that evolved from the arrow-patterned sashes worn by the *voyageurs* in the 1700s and 1800s. She was a thin blond woman in her early 30s. Her skimpy-but-pricey black dress and skimpier-but-pricier fox fur coat seemed woefully inadequate for a Green Bay winter night, although it seemed unlikely to Le Pelleteur that the weather was high on her list of priorities when she was getting dressed that evening. The fur coat and diamond bracelet suggested that she might be taking advantage of him just as much as he was taking advantage of her.

The detective shifted his fedora to the back of his head so the brim would not interfere with his camera, focused quickly through the windshield and snapped a picture of the lovely couple gingerly making their way from the motel room door through the icy, slushy parking lot to the Nervous One's dark red 1938 La Salle. Light from the flash bulb temporarily flooded the parking lot, then faded as Le Pelleteur tried to start his car, only to hear the sickly growl of a dying battery.

This gave the Nervous One a choice: slink away in shame or erupt in a fit of anger. Le Pelleteur hoped for the former, but was not surprised when Nervous chose the latter. He marched towards Le Pelleteur's car with all the righteous indignation of someone who knows he's been caught red-handed and started pounding on the driver's side window with the bottom of his fist. Le Pelleteur locked the door and stared straight ahead, fully intending to exercise some restraint, maintain some dignity, until cracks started to spider across the window. His eyes darted to the site of the impact and he growled. Before Nervous could shift from anger to fear, Le Pelleteur threw his door open, scattering shards of glass. He knocked Nervous off balance. As Nervous started to fall backwards, Le Pelleteur grabbed the front of his coat, precariously in mid-plummet, pushed him to the middle of the parking lot, slammed him to the ground and socked him in the face. He was about to fire off another punch, but he caught himself and stood up when he realized that the man had stopped moving.

Blood crawled like a worm out of the man's left nostril across his upper lip. Le Pelleteur felt like the guy who stole candy from a baby, then bragged about how easy it was at his favorite bar only to find himself surrounded by a roomful of shocked, horrified faces. The detective could tell as soon as he saw the guy emerge sheepishly from the motel room that he didn't know his way around a fistfight. He fully intended to go easy on the guy, but let him get under his skin anyway. Then he noticed the thin woman looking on, mouth agape but silent, like the cold winter night had frozen her scream. This mortified him further. Not only did he lose control, he lost control in front of a witness. Her revolted gaze was like a fire hose spraying embarrassment and shame, extinguishing the final embers of the rage Le Pelleteur felt a minute earlier. When he could stand it no longer, he turned away and asked himself, "Why do I never see this kind of thing coming?"

After he had regained some of his composure, he looked back at the woman and asked, "If I get him to the car, can you get him home?"

As she shook her head no, the detective found a note pad in his car and drew her a map to the home address of his client, the wife of the man on the ground. He knelt down and fished the car keys out of the no-longer-nervous man's pocket and tossed them to the bleach-blond witness to this grisly scene. Then, recalling one of his *Sûreté* training classes from a million years ago, long before he was kicked off the force, he grabbed an arm and a leg and induced the dead weight to roll up onto his shoulders. As he staggered to the red La Salle, she ran mincingly ahead to unlock the car door. Le Pelleteur deposited his load in the back seat. As he watched the love birds drive away, he suddenly drove the palm of his hand into his forehead. He forgot to ask her to help him jump-start his car before she left.

He went to the Manager's Office to find someone who could give him a jump. He found the door locked. No one answered the doorbell, thereby maintaining his perfect record for bad breaks for the evening. He checked the door to the love birds' former room, hoping just for someplace warm to wait for morning and found that it was locked. He could try to start his car by popping the clutch, but in the dark *Ouisconsin* night, with his luck, he figured he would push his car into a ditch before it started running. Left without options, he trudged back to his car, rolled down the driver's side window to prevent more glass shards from falling out. He kept several XY Company Four-Point Blankets, broad multicolored stripes on a white background, in his back seat, as this was not the first time he ended up sleeping in his car after a stakeout. He used one blanket to block some of the wind from the open window and huddled in the back seat under the rest, hoping that the morning would be warm enough to bring his battery back to life.

Chapter II

Le Pelleteur opened his left eye to see the dawn oozing peach-colored sunlight across his face. He closed it again for a time, hoping but not really expecting that the sun would go away and he could go back to sleep. Eventually he gave up and crawled out of his car, cold and stiff, like a perch that had just been pulled from an ice fishing hole. After scraping the frost off his car windshields, he got in, tried to convince the engine to turn over and failed. Then he pounded on the motel office door to rouse the manager and failed again. He marched back to the Chevrolet across the -10°C parking lot, rubbing his arms, trying to feel less cold and stiff, but that didn't work, either. He noted silently that his record for the morning had quickly become 0-for-3.

He leaned against the fender and rubbed his whiskered cheeks. He looked east and saw that the sun had almost cleared the horizon. It could be a couple of hours before the motel manager would stumble out of bed and rejoin the living. In that kind of cold, two hours is a long wait for a telephone. He could always kick the motel office door in, but with his luck, that would finally wake the manager and interrupting his beauty sleep would piss him off enough to call the police and have Le Pelleteur arrested for breaking and entering. While the detective tried to think of something else he could do, he began to stare into space. His mind started to drift like the snow in the field across the road, while steam blasted from his nostrils like a locomotive. The snow was smooth, flat and a meter thick. The pink light of the sunrise was fading, leaving the field an endless bleak expanse, glaring an eye-piercing white, like the vacuum that nature was supposed to abhor. It threatened to swallow up anything that came near it, like Lake Michigan swallowing a pebble, but without the evidentiary ripples showing briefly that it used to exist. For a moment, Le Pelleteur couldn't decide whether that kind of oblivion would feel repellent or inviting. He concluded that it really didn't make any difference. Few things in his life did.

A sudden freezing gust of wind refocused Le Pelleteur's attention to the problem at hand. In the morning light, he noticed a slight downward slope in the desolate early morning highway a short distance from the motel parking lot. Now that he could see where he was going, he decided that popping the clutch was worth a try. Pushing the car out of the lot wasn't easy since the car was as cold and stiff as he was. Nevertheless, he was eventually able to build up a little speed. He jumped into the car, popped the clutch and after the car lurched and shuttered to life, he headed towards Green Bay.

This stretch of Highway Q41 was a two-lane road cut through maple and spruce woods, roughly paralleling the gentle curves of the *Rivière Renaud*, or Fox River. The low morning sun through the tangle of leafless winter branches cast narrow patches of light and shadow. Driving through those patches reminded the detective of the flickering of a dying florescent light. A mild wind blew wisps of snow across the road like the spirits of giant white snakes. Occasionally, small drifts began to creep across the highway like giant white fingertips reaching across the road. Between the tree trunks, one could catch glimpses of the river, at some times sun-speckled and dazzling, at others a frozen grayish white veneer of ice.

Le Pelleteur was not particularly interested in the scenery, being as alert as you would expect him to be after three and a half hours of sleep in a car as cold as a meat locker. He was also distracted by a headache that felt like a monkey wrench starting to clamp down on his temples.

He had already turned up the 1927 Chevy's heater full blast, but it was fighting a losing battle with the arctic wind barreling through the open driver's side window. He rummaged around his inside coat pocket for a Du Maurier cigarette and found he had crushed the pack in his sleep. When he finally worked a coffin nail out of the pack, it was twisted like a pale white arthritic finger.

Le Pelleteur began to notice occasional bicycle tracks cutting across the snow drifts. Those tracks were the only signs of human life he had seen since the fight last night. Suddenly, Le Pelleteur saw the edge of a bicycle wheel poking over the ditch on the left side of the road, just before a little bridge over a creek flowing into the river. He pulled over, got out of the car and left the engine running while he walked to the bike. He identified it as a blue Schwinn boy's bike. The detective thought the bike looked pretty old, beat up and deduced that it could be a hand-me-down. If so, this kid could have an older brother. He climbed a few meters down the hill on the side of the road leading to the creek, knelt down next to the bike and used his forearm to measure the distance from the seat to the pedals. "Looks like he's about 170 to 175 centimeters tall," he thought. "A fairly good job of hiding the bike, but he could have done better." He scanned the horizon and immediately focused on a set of footprints along the creek, ducking into the woods about 50 meters away. He could not imagine anyone over 16 coming this far out of town on a bicycle and he could not imagine anyone under 16 up at this time of the morning and running around in the woods in this kind of weather doing anything other than poaching pelts from someone else's trap line. He also noticed that the snow was drifting across the prints. They would be erased in less than five minutes, making the kid a lot tougher to track. "If he planned that, he's pretty clever."

The fur trade remained the biggest source of jobs in most native towns in *La République Québécoise*, as it had been for the previous 300 years. In the early 20th Century, the industry shifted from beaver, which was used to make top hats throughout the 1800s, to mink, ermine and fox for fur coats. However, in 1933 when the fur industry declined due to the Depression, President Taschereau tried to bolster it by subsidizing top hats. As a result, a few men started wearing top hats, primarily elderly gentlemen in Native communities, and the resurgence in beaver trapping was still going strong in 1940.

Le Pelleteur scowled at the landscape as a gust of wind blew needle-like shards of ice into the side of his face, almost like a Saharan sand storm. He disliked his poaching insurance defense work almost as much as he disliked his unfaithful husband investigations, even when he was in a fairly good mood. Poaching someone else's trap line is almost as much work as running your own. No one gets rich poaching. It is something people resort to when they are struggling to get by. So, Le Pelleteur could not help having a little pity for the kids he tended to catch poaching. If they were really bad kids, they would come up with a better scam.

As a result, he would not have been thrilled over the thought of tracking a kid through the woods, even if he wasn't tired and sore and cold from sleeping in his car, even if the wind wasn't driving through him like a power drill through soft butter. Nevertheless, he resigned himself. The Mutual of Duluth Fire and Casualty Insurance Company had him on retainer to investigate poaching claims. He signed up for the job and he did not see himself as having any option now.

Le Pelleteur doused his cigarette in the snow, climbed back up to the road and jogged back to the car. He kept a Smith and Wesson .32 caliber handgun in the glove compartment, even though his work following cheating husbands didn't call for a gun very often. He put the gun in his coat pocket, then waded back into the knee-deep snow, following the poacher's trail as it was drifting in. He paused for a second and placed his hand next to a footprint. It was more than twice as long as his hand from the base of his palm to the tip of his middle finger. "Size 12 or 13," he thought. "Practically clown shoes. Kid can't be too graceful. He's at that awkward age." Le Pelleteur also noticed that they were sneaker tracks, the kind with the white rubber toes and shuddered at the thought of snowmelt soaking through canvas.

As he followed the trail into the woods, the maple trunks seemed to surround him. The snow was only 30 centimeters deep here, much easier to navigate. The leafless canopy let in enough sun to make the snow twinkle as he marched through it. The forest partially shielded him from the wind along the creek, reducing the howl of the wind to a whisper, almost drowned out by the rhythmic crunching of his footsteps. The trees swayed in the wind, creaking like an 18th Century sailing vessel crossing the Atlantic. After five minutes, he found a set of beaver traps, uncamouflaged and tripped. The tracks showed that the kid was running, but was weighted down. He must have heard Le Pelleteur coming. He must be close.

The tracks led to a stand of pine trees. Le Pelleteur followed the trail, squeezing between the intertwining pine branches. Suddenly, before he could reach for his gun, his rib cage felt crushed, like it was hit with a wrecking ball demolishing a skyscraper and he found himself flat on his back in half a meter of snow with a burlap sack full of beaver carcasses on his chest. He was dazed for a few seconds. Then, in a panic, he screamed "My car!" He left it running on the side of the road, practically begging the poacher to steal it. Le Pelleteur grabbed the sack and sprinted through the woods like a toy poodle struggling for traction on a linoleum kitchen floor, wondering what he ever did to deserve all this aggravation.

Chapter III

While Samuel de Champlain Le Pelleteur had developed a habit of asking himself what he did to deserve the frequent less than spectacularly fortunate episodes of his life, he was aware on some level that the question was rhetorical. He knew what he did. It happened five years earlier, June 3, 1935, to be precise. The *Brigade financiere*, or "Bunko Squad," of the Green Bay Bureau of the *Sûreté du Québec* was already oppressively hot at 9:30 in the morning. It was the kind of a morning when breathing felt like inhaling Jello; when people who overestimate their wittiness ask if it's hot enough for you; when sweat would glue your shirt to your back and suck your soul out through your pores.

The inspectors of the Bunko Squad had independent authority to conduct criminal investigations and interrogate suspects. In this way, it was like the *Brigade criminelle*, which was responsible for homicides and other major crimes and unlike other divisions of the police force that conducted investigations under the supervision of an Investigating Magistrate. The Squad was housed on the fifth floor of a nine-story Romanesque Revival building on *La Rue La Salle Sud,* with brown rough-hewn stone blocks on the corners and fake columns supporting fake arches around the windows. It was the height of architectural style when it was built 50 years earlier, but on that day the building's various ledges and design elements merely served as nesting sites for pigeons and collection points for their droppings.

The Bunko Squad office was a reflection of the men on the Bunko Squad themselves. It looked neglected and resentful that it was not someplace else. No one knew what color the cement walls were painted originally, but they were a stained and faded beige now. Long florescent light fixtures hung from the four-meter-high ceiling, struggling to illuminate the room through a permanent blue haze of cigarette smoke. Ten dented grey metal desks were scattered throughout the room between four big square columns supporting the ceiling, partially buried under heaping mounds of manila file folders. Six men sat at the desks poking at typewriters with their index fingers and wearing sweat-stained dress shirts and shoulder holsters, cuffs rolled up, collars unbuttoned and ties loose enough to fit around their waists. Someone else was reading the newspaper and another was giving himself a hernia trying to get one of the windows to open wider. The white noise of electric fans almost drowned out the clacking of typewriters and the occasional wooden chair squeak.

In a back corner of the room, a three-meter by four-meter space was blocked off by a cheap partition, to give the impression of a private office. The impression was heightened by stacks of paper lining the cubicle. Chief Inspector François Dombrowski, Polish *Québécois*, the grandson of one of the millions of Southern and Eastern Europeans who immigrated to North America in the late 1800s, emerged from his lair. He had wavy blond hair and deep blue eyes, a barrel chest and ham fists sticking out of his rolled-up shirt sleeves. He needed to keep the top two buttons undone to fit his collar around his neck. "Anyone see Marleau and Le Pelleteur? Them lazy bums ought to be at work by now."

"What's the matter, Chief? You got a hot date with one of 'em?" La Pointe was the self-appointed comedy relief of the Squad. Chief Inspector Dombrowski asked, "Jealous, La Pointe? I told you before, you're not good enough for me, you know?" The Chief Inspector's joke got a bigger laugh.

Another detective offered, "I thought I heard them grilling someone in one of the interrogation rooms when I got coffee this morning."

Dombrowski exclaimed, "My God, they've been grilling that bastard for twelve hours now." That bastard was Big Jim MacTavish. He was the head of an oil company in Edmonton, in the Dominion of Oregon. He had spent the previous six months spreading lies about a big oil field that had just been discovered in Huronia and selling millions of *livres* worth of phony stock. He had spent the previous week telling reporters that it was all his geologist's fault.

Suddenly, Marleau and Le Pelleteur appeared in the squad room, escorting MacTavish in handcuffs and announced that their suspect had confessed. The office erupted in cheers. As they proceeded to lead their suspect down to a holding cell in the basement of the building, Chief Inspector Dombrowski told Marleau to take care of it while he had a word with Le Pelleteur in his office.

Dombrowski excavated a chair from a stack of paper and offered it to Le Pelleteur, while he leaned against the corner of his desk and crossed his ankles. The effect was both casual and imposing as he loomed over Le Pelleteur in the chair.

"So, I found your report on the Maisonneuve case on my desk last night."

"Have you had a chance to read it?"

"It's forty-seven pages long, typed single spaced, Champ." Dombrowski called most of his employees "Champ" from time to time. "It ain't exactly a page turner, you know? I read enough to see you threw quite a few accusations around. Bribes, numbers rackets. I was surprised to see you name two detectives in this office, you know? Jean Lemieux and Claude Bigturtle? Most would try to cover for their buddies on the force."

"I didn't enjoy naming them, but our job here is to try to clean up the streets and they're making the job harder."

"Isn't this the case I told you not to work on, Champ?"

"You told me not to spend too much time on it. I worked on it only when I didn't have anything else to do."

"For someone who is supposed to be so smart, big-time college kid and all, you're kind of stupid, ain't you?" Le Pelleteur graduated *magna cum laude* from the *Université de Green Bay* and attended a year of law school before he decided that he would rather work for the *Sûreté*, where he thought he could do more good. After eight years on the Force, he was still the "college kid."

"Since taking hints is not one of your talents," Dombrowski continued, "let me spell it out for you. I did not want you working on the Maisonneuve case, at all, at any time, period."

"But I just started to figure this thing out."

"Not quite. It's not just Lemieux and Bigturtle, you know? I also earn a very nice supplemental income ensuring that certain people are not ensnared by the long arm of the law unnecessarily. And that's the problem. I have developed a very comfortable lifestyle because of my close working relationship with Mayor Maisonneuve and too much attention could become inconvenient for me. You're getting too close and I can't trust you to back off and be reasonable. Of course, if you become inconvenient for me, I could become inconvenient for you, you know?"

Le Pelleteur struggled to make sense of what was happening. Eventually Chief Inspector Dombrowski filled the silence. "When you've been around as long as I have, you end up with a lot of friends who can do a lot of favors for you. I could arrange for you to be framed for bribery. Discredit you and take some heat off of Lemieux and Bigturtle, you know? I could also arrange for you to trip down a flight of stairs and break your neck. But again, arranging such things can be inconvenient, so today is your lucky day. All I'm going to do is fire you. No frame-ups, no jail time and no painful accidents, unless you start poking around again in things that do not concern you anymore, you know?"

Le Pelleteur still could not comprehend what was happening. Dumbrowski explained, "Just to be clear, the alternative is you make a big fuss, you end up dead and you still lose your job."

The shocked, puzzled look on Le Pelleteur's face eventually faded to an expression you might have if a hundred pounds of bricks had just been dropped on your stomach. "So, this is it?"

"Afraid so."

"I'm off the Force?"

"Afraid so."

"This is two weeks' notice?" Le Pelleteur asked hopefully.

"This is get your ass out the door and don't look back."

Le Pelleteur felt like the chair had been pulled out from under him, but instead of simply falling to the floor, the floor collapsed under him and he tumbled wildly and uncontrollably into some incomprehensible nightmare world. He could not believe that his career had been destroyed because he did his job too well. He had dedicated himself to protecting and serving the City of Green Bay and the City was giving him the bum's rush. His feeling of shock and confusion competed with the abject hopelessness of finding another job in 1935. He came from a wealthy family and he could ask his father for a job, but that idea horrified him more than the prospect of starving to death unemployed.

Dombrowski winced, as if to say destroying Le Pelleteur's life "hurts me more than it hurts you." "Look, I like you, you know? There is something kind of refreshing about someone who hangs around here for eight years and still thinks he can make a difference. Maybe I can get you two weeks' severance pay. I'll see what I can do."

Two weeks' severance pay was Le Pelleteur's contractual right, not a favor to be bestowed upon him by the grace of Chief Inspector Dombrowski, but Le Pelleteur decided not to point that out. The former rising star of the Green Bay Bunko Squad saw that the Chief Inspector held all the cards and there was nothing else he could do. He got up to leave the office, when he saw Marleau back from the holding cells and celebrating with the rest of the guys. He realized that, although it was too late to save himself, it wasn't too late to do something for his partner.

"What about Marleau?"

"What about him?"

"Like I said, I wrote that report on my own time. He doesn't know anything about it. He has 26 years on the Force. He doesn't need to lose his job. Besides, he has a wife and kids to support."

"He was your partner. He must know something."

"Have I ever lied to you before?" Dombrowski started to think about that. "Besides, as we were discussing a few minutes ago, I can fight this and try to make your life inconvenient. How much do you want to avoid that?"

"You're pushing your luck, you know?"

"Am I really asking for that much?"

Dombrowski heaved a frustrated sigh. "All right. I heard there's an opening on the *Brigade criminelle* for someone to work murder investigations. I'll move him there. That should keep him out of my way. Now get the Hell out of here before I change my mind."

Marleau was still downstairs dealing with MacTavish and everyone else had resumed hunting and pecking on their typewriters, so no one noticed Le Pelleteur when he emerged from Dombrowski's office. He shuffled unsteadily past the rows of metal desks and out of the building, trying to make sense of the emotions swirling in his head. When he reached the sidewalk, he realized he felt like a mark. While he felt stupid for letting himself be suckered, part of him felt like he deserved to be suckered for being so stupid. Part of him also felt sick, like he had a deep, gaping hole in the pit of his stomach. Finally, at the base of his brain, he had a small, hot ember of anger, vowing never to let anyone sucker him again.

Chapter IV

Le Pelleteur emerged from the woods on the side of Highway Q41, immensely relieved to find his car still running on the side of the road and the bicycle gone. Le Pelleteur muttered, "Either the kid can't drive or he hasn't graduated to Grand Theft Auto, yet." It was his first lucky break in a long time, but not lucky enough to make up for the previous 12 hours.

He dumped the sack of beavers in the back seat and drove off towards Green Bay. In 15 minutes, the city skyline, in the *Département* of Green Bay, in the Region of *Ouisconsin* in *La République Québécoise*, rose up in the distance; tall, powerful buildings filled with tall, powerful people. In the penthouse offices of the skyscrapers, hundreds of meters off the ground, one could find millionaires running factories manufacturing lumber or liquor or chewing gum, effortlessly earning more money than they knew what to do with. Meanwhile, on the street, one saw regular people rushing to their regular jobs, struggling to earn enough money to finance their regular lives. Just under the surface, lurking in the alleys and the shadows, Green Bay also had a full spectrum of the criminal element, ranging from two-bit hoods to half of City Hall.

By the time he reached the city, the Monday morning rush hour was slowly crawling towards its inevitable decline. As he drove to his office, Le Pelleteur waved to the statue of his namesake, Samuel de Champlain, erected in the middle of town in 1908 during Québec's 300th anniversary. Governor Champlain always looked a little undignified at this time of year with his head and shoulders buried in snow. His mother claimed descent from Champlain's cousin, a great source of pride in her family. His father's pedigree was also very impressive, to people who tended to be impressed by such things. One of his illustrious ancestors was Colonel Pierre-François Le Pelleteur, Vicomte de Chardonnay, one of Montcalm's advisors during the Seven Years War. According to family history, he was the brains behind Montcalm's brilliant tactical maneuvers that defeated the English at the Battle of the Plains of Abraham. His grandson, General Louis-Phillipe Le Pelleteur, is credited with keeping the British from establishing more than a toehold on the Gaspe Peninsula in the North American Theater of the Napoleonic Wars. At that time, the United States joined the war and with their help, the French pushed the British out of the Gulf of St. Lawrence and took and held the west half of Newfoundland, although they gave it back to Great Britain in the Council of Vienna in 1815. Louis-Phillipe's son, Jean-Luc Le Pelleteur, led a regiment in Louis Papineau's army in the 1837 War of Independence. Each of these heroes was granted land south of Lake Superior, over 8000 *arpents* in total. The family used the trees on that land to develop a maple syrup company that had grown into the second largest in the North American market by 1900.

At the beginning of the 20th Century, Sam's grandfather, Adélard Le Pelleteur, decided to enter politics and served as a Member of the National Assembly for the Green Bay – North *arrondissement* from 1904 to 1919. Although he was the Minister of Finance for eight years in the Lomer Gouin administration, Adélard considered the high point of his career to be his opposition to the 1911 trade agreement that President Laurier had negotiated with the United States – the agreement that led Laurier to lose the election to Gouin later that year. Defeating the agreement allowed several protectionist measures to remain in place, which endeared Adélard to Green Bay's industrial interests, but didn't exactly swell Sam's heart with pride. He thought Laurier's trade agreement would have led to less expensive consumer goods and a better market for *Québecois* farmers, making the country as a whole better off. As a result, he saw his grandfather's accomplishment as one of many historical examples of the rich getting richer at the expense of the working class.

His father had served as Chief of Staff for a Member of the National Assembly and now sat in the *Ouisconsin* Regional Council. His Uncle Edouard worked for some administrative agency in Montréal. Although he spent a great deal of time with his uncle while he was growing up, going on camping trips during the summer and going to hockey games during the winter, his uncle had never explained to him what exactly he did from day to day.

Le Pelleteur spent no time contemplating his family history, however, as he continued driving through town towards his office, in Marquette Hall, one of the oldest buildings on the campus of the *Université de Green Bay*, located on the Left Bank of the Fox River. When Le Pelleteur left the *Sûreté*, the University President agreed to lease office space to him at very reasonable rates, because in 1931 Le Pelleteur recovered most of the 250,000 *livres* from the Endowment Fund that the President had invested in a Ponzi Scheme and saved the President's reputation.

Most of the people living in this section of the Left Bank were university students. At times, they seemed to roam the streets in herds, like bison on the Great Plains of French Missouri. It was also a working-class neighborhood, descendants of Germans and Scandinavians who came to Québec for farmland in the 1800s and Negroes who came from Mississippi in the 1920s, looking for a decent job. Some found work singing the Blues in small bars catering to students.

While Le Pelleteur was crossing the Fox River over the *Rue Michigan* Bridge, his secretary, Sophie Marleau, was sitting behind a battleship grey desk in the center of a room on the first floor of Marquette Hall that was once the Bursar's Office and now served as Le Pelleteur's outer office. Upon entering the outer office, one was immediately confronted by a counter about waist high. The area beyond the counter was about five meters square. This room was originally white, but had since faded to a yellowish gray. The walls and the ceiling were decorated with retrofitted electrical wires, like rectilinear varicose veins. Along the left wall was a row of 12 wooden filing cabinets, 90 percent filled with students' financial records, some of whom had graduated almost 100 years earlier, when Louis-Hippolyte La Fontaine was President of Québec.

Around her shoulders, Sophie wore a red buttoned sweater with some kind of snowflake pattern; the room was always too cold for her in winter. Her big blue eyes were obscured by her bigger horn-rimmed glasses. She liked to wear her dark brown hair shoulder-length. She kept a small jungle of potted flowers and ivy plants on top of those filing cabinets. Behind her was a pair of pointed-arch windows. Along the right wall was the door to the inner office and an old table with a coffee pot. Revealing the school's Jesuit background, that wall sported a poor reproduction of the Last Supper and a Crucifix with an unnecessarily gruesome Jesus nailed to it.

Sophie was the daughter of Philippe Marleau, Le Pelleteur's partner when he was in the Bunko Squad. He thought she was a great kid. He was aware at some level that she was 22 and could not be called a kid anymore, but he had known her since she was ten and old habits were hard to break. He hired her in 1935, after she asked him for a job for the summer between her junior and senior years at Honore Mercier High School. He kept her as his part-time secretary when school started in the fall. The next year, shortly after she graduated first in her class, he talked the monks running the *Presse* into letting her try to edit one of the college textbooks they were about to publish. After they saw her work, they agreed to hire her as a part time editor and let her review textbooks while she worked as his secretary. At that moment, she was editing a history textbook:

Excerpt from
Québec: The Noble Patrimony of an Independent Nation
by Prof. Jean-Marie Schneider, 5th ed., 1940:

Most historians consider the Battle of the Plains of Abraham to be the turning point in the Seven Years' War and many consider it to be a major turning point in world history.

The British tried and failed to break through the French fortifications at Beauport, downstream from Québec City, on July 31, 1759. Subsequently, the British spent August bombarding Québec City from across the St. Laurence River and also attacking the isolated farming settlements scattered through the surrounding area. They hoped, ultimately in vain, to draw the French out of their defensive positions. By September, the British were becoming desperate. They knew that, unless they could consolidate their gains before winter came, they would risk forfeiting those gains.

The British General, James Wolfe, devised a bold plan to cut off the supply lines to Montréal of the French Army, under General Louis-Joseph, Marquis de Montcalm. Early on the morning of September 13th, Wolfe led his army upstream on the St. Laurence River, past Québec City. Wolfe sent Colonel William Howe and 24 men to climb up a steep cliff, thought by the French to be unscalable, to dispatch the small detachment guarding the road to the Plains of Abraham outside Québec City. This cleared an easy access path for the main British forces, 3300 men, to climb to and deploy on the Plains outside the Citadel by dawn.

Upon seeing the British army assembled, General Montcalm's first impulse was to attack before the British became entrenched. However, one of his advisors, Colonel Pierre-François Le Pelleteur, persuaded Montcalm that the British could not take the Citadel by siege before the onset of winter. By mid-afternoon, the British were entrenched, as Montcalm expected, but were harassed by French regulars and Québec Militia, redeployed from Beauport and led by Colonel Louis Antoine de Bougainville, from the cover of the forested area on Wolfe's left flank.

Eventually, the French strategy was successful. The British were not prepared for the cold and winter that year was early and uncommonly harsh. Within a month, by October 15th, the weather had become intolerable for the British, forcing them to sail back to Great Britain before the pack ice at the mouth of the St. Laurence would block their retreat. During the winter of 1759-60, for budgetary reasons, the British decided to concentrate their efforts in Europe, thus ceding victory in North America to the French.

Questions for Further Discussion:

1. Assume that the French had joined the British in battle on the Plains of Abraham on the morning of September 13, 1759, before reinforcements from Beauport had arrived. Although the French had superior numbers, the British troops were, on average, better trained in Eu-

ropean-style open field warfare than the French troops. Who do you think would have won such a battle?

2. Assume that the British had won the Battle of the Plains of Abraham. What would have been the results of that victory?

3. While General Montcalm's defensive strategy was ultimately successful, it resulted in allowing the British to cause considerable damage to *Québécois* land and property. Do you agree or disagree with historians who argue that General Montcalm's strategy reflected an unwarranted disregard for *Québécois* interests? To what extent, if any, did reactions to this strategy contribute to the motivations underlying Québec's declaration of independence from France in 1837?

Chapter V

While Sophie reviewed her history book, Le Pelleteur completed his drive to the *Université* and was now marching across the Quad on a narrow path between two parallel elbow-high snowbanks towards Marquette Hall, a tall, thin, square, Gothic tower built of the cream-colored brick typical of Green Bay architecture. It had pointed-arch-shaped windows and a spire like a cross between a crown and a dunce cap. It looked like the kind of place that should have a damsel-in-distress imprisoned on the top floor or some kind of torture chamber in the basement. It was built when the University was founded, during the reign of Charles X, in 1823. In Le Pelleteur's opinion, the building looked like it was constructed in 1323. He thought that was fitting, because the Jesuits who ran the place could have been born in 1323. Originally, the structure provided offices for the Dean and the College Administrators. They abandoned the building about 50 years later, in favor of one with more modern facilities at the time, gas lights. The Administrators debated whether to tear down the building for ten years, until they gave it to the *Presse de l'Université de Green Bay*, who needed more space for its textbook editors, in 1896. Almost forty years after that, when Le Pelleteur started working as a private detective, he was given the only otherwise unoccupied room in the building to use as his office.

As Le Pelleteur stomped the snow off of his feet in the building lobby, he saw *Père* Jean-Luc O'Shaughnessy come out of Le Pelleteur's first-floor office. *Père* O'Shaughnessy was the head of the editorial staff and Sophie's boss for her second job. *Père* O'Shaughnessy considered the work she did for Le Pelleteur to be her second job. O'Shaughnessy, as usual, looked at Le Pelleteur like he had just bitten into a wormy apple.

"*Monsieur* Le Pelleteur." The priest marched up to him and growled. The balding cleric was in his early 50s. At 150 centimeters, he was about 35 centimeters shorter than the detective. His long, narrow, pointy nose always seemed to Le Pelleteur like an index finger silently pronouncing "*J'accuse*." *Père* O'Shaughnessy would disagree if you suggested that he had never forgiven the University President for allowing Le Pelleteur to invade his turf. He would argue, disingenuously, that he was still adjusting to the new arrangement. In either case, *Père* O'Shaughnessy tended to make Le Pelleteur the brunt of his displeasure.

Most days, Le Pelleteur would make an effort to tolerate O'Shaughnessy and he would last a good five minutes before he ran out of patience. On that morning, however, he felt as much tolerance towards the cleric as he would a sharp pebble that had been in his shoe for three days. He decided to try a sarcastic preemptive strike.

"*Père* O'Shaughnessy, ordinarily, I look forward to your daily whiny disparagement, because it brightens my morning *so* much. However, today, I've had it pretty rough and it's only quarter to ten. So, if you would be so kind, perhaps you could shove a sock in it. Tomorrow, you could spend twice as long cataloguing my sins, if you so desire."

The priest ignored the detective, as usual. Le Pelleteur saw that O'Shaughnessy was soft and round, like an overripe tomato and knew that he could defend himself about as well as an overripe tomato in any kind of physical confrontation. Le Pelleteur never knew whether the priest was extraordinarily brave and did not care when or if he pushed Le Pelleteur too far, or extraordinarily stupid and never considered the possibility.

"Just look at you," *Père* O'Shaughnessy sputtered while he examined Le Pelleteur. The detective's night in his car left dark brown hair sticking up at various angles. His blue eyes were slightly bloodshot and the stubble on his unshaven face looked like 60 grit sandpaper. The beige camel's hair coat and blue pinstripe suit he wore were wrinkled and dirty from his morning adventures. As his hands thawed and lost their numbness, they started to tremble with shooting pain.

"You are a disgrace," O'Shaughnessy continued. "Drunk at this time of day. I have warned you about the evils of demon rum."

"First, my demon of choice is gin. Let's give credit where credit's due. Second, I am not drunk. I spent all night working. In fact, my client last night was a victim of adultery and this morning I prevented a theft. When you think about it, I have been enforcing the Sixth and Seventh Commandments. I have been doing God's work, the job you signed up for. When was the last time you broke a sweat doing God's work? When was the last time you broke a sweat doing anything?" Le Pelleteur punctuated his last sentence by jabbing his finger into O'Shaughnessy's chest. Then, he walked away, ignoring O'Shaughnessy's rejoinder.

As usual, as soon as Le Pelleteur set foot in his office, he found Sophie reading a manuscript and holding a red pencil. She immediately shooshed him and continued to study her manuscript. He leaned against the counter for 15 impatient seconds, until she finally looked up at him. "Would you be so kind as to pour me a cup of coffee?" he inquired. In addition to answering the phone and taking messages, Sophie made coffee every morning. It was one of the few things she did less than excellently. Her brew was usually about half-way between 40-weight motor oil and pine tar, but the private eye thought it was better than no coffee at all and a lot better than the slop he could make. As she got up from her desk, he asked, "So, what are you reading today?"

"It's a history book. It mentions someone named Pierre-François Le Pelleteur. Any relation to you?"

"No." Samuel de Champlain Le Pelleteur lied.

Sophie changed the subject. "You look like Hell. No, you look like Hell after it was in a bad fight. You look like Hell the morning after it got drunk. You look like ten miles of bad road in Hell."

"Very funny. You should have your own radio show."

Le Pelleteur often ended up sleeping in his car after a stakeout and usually came out looking like a crumpled piece of paper. Sophie made fun of Le Pelleteur's rumpled suit as a reflex action, but grew concerned when she did not hear the usual sarcastic, tongue-in-cheek tone in Le Pelleteur's response. "Are you OK?"

"Yeah, I'm fine. I heard that the Packers lost last night." Le Pelleteur offered by way of explanation for his lack of chipperness. She noticed he gritted his teeth as he began to gingerly remove his coat from his sore, beaten body and she noticed the knuckles of his right hand, still blood-stained from the previous night's parking lot fight. She lifted the gate in the counter and ordered him to sit down. As she got the first aid kit from the bottom drawer of her desk, she explained, "I got news for you. They figured out that infections are caused by leaving dirt in open wounds, not by evil spirits like they thought in the Middle Ages." She took some rubbing alcohol and a cotton ball from the kit and started to clean his hand.

"When you're done playing Dr. Kildare, I have some actual secretarial work for you. You know, the stuff I pay you to do?"

"Do you mean that you're going to pay me some time in the near future?"

"Any time you think you can find a better job someplace else, give it your best shot."

While he was usually a month or two behind in her salary, he knew she wouldn't leave. First, her part-time textbook editorial work paid her enough to get by on and was more intellectually interesting than any other job available to a 22-year-old woman in 1940 Québec. More importantly, for her entire life, she had longed to be a cop like her father and three older brothers. She knew the *Sûreté* would never hire a woman, so a private investigator's secretary was the closest that she could get. While she finished bandaging his hand, she pretended to consider leaving, then said, "You would never survive without me. I couldn't let you suffer like that. What would you like me to do today?"

"First, send a bill to Mutual of Duluth. I caught a poacher in the act. Charge them for a day of work."

"You did? When did that happen?"

"It's been an unusually productive morning for me. I'll tell you all about it some time when I'm more than barely conscious." Sophie glared at Le Pelleteur and threatened to stab his newly bandaged hand with a red pencil. He relented, polished off his coffee and poured himself another cup. Then, he regaled Sophie with his exploits of the past six hours, including his embarrassingly one-sided boxing match in the motel parking lot and getting ambushed in the woods by a poacher with a bicycle.

"Is that the same poacher you said existed only in Indian radio commercials to scare people into buying insurance?"

"One and the same," he replied, ignoring her smirk. "When you call the insurance company, tell them we have the pelts and can return them as soon as they get a claim and can tell us the rightful owner. After that, call Druillette." Henri Druillette was a Chevrolet dealer based about five kilometers from Le Pelleteur's office. "Get an estimate for replacement of a driver's side front window and a new battery. Bill it to Mrs. Gratiot."

"Why?"

"These are expenses that I incurred while working her case. Besides, she is probably going to get that money from Mr. Gratiot in her divorce and Mr. Gratiot did break my window."

"OK, that explains billing her for the window, but not the battery."

He stared at her for a few seconds with a look of disgust on his face. "Alright, Little Miss Goody-Goody Pain in the Ass, just bill her for the window. The next time I can't start my car, you're pushing."

"Anything else?"

"No, that should do it. Thanks. If you need me, I will be in my office sleeping."

Chapter VI

Le Pelleteur awoke with a start. For a disoriented second, he thought that he was bitten by some kind of spider, but in fact Sophie was poking him in the shoulder. He had been sleeping on the sofa, an outdated, 60-year-old, overstuffed Victorian monstrosity with freakishly gigantic needlepoint roses faded to an anemic shade of pink. When he moved into the office in 1935, it had been unused for a few years. He found a few pieces of abandoned office furniture and schoolroom equipment, three centimeters of dust on the floor and that sofa. Its origins were something of a mystery to Le Pelleteur. It was clearly not the standard-issue, institutional couch one would expect to find in a large organization like the *Université de Green Bay*. It may well have been considered in style when it was manufactured, during the Franco-Prussian War and purchased at that time by a bursar with an easily offended sense of interior design. It could have been brought in more recently, perhaps as recently as the Great War, by a publishing house employee who inherited it from his grandmother and thought it was too ugly to keep in his house. In any case, as the result of either inertia or apathy, or both, the sofa remained in place through successive occupants of the office, including Le Pelleteur, growing more outdated and uglier with time.

"What?" Le Pelleteur asked Sophie, still groggy.

"We have a new case," she announced as he slowly sat up and rubbed his eyes. "I told her you were on the phone with another client," she explained, handing him a note. "When you are sufficiently conscious, buzz me and I'll let her in."

"What's your guess, another cheating husband surveillance job?"

"I don't know what this one's after. My guess is she's trouble."

Sophie went back to the outer office while Sam stretched. He then made an effort to straighten his hair as walked to the wooden swivel office chair behind his grey metal desk and called Sophie back on the intercom.

The sight of this client sauntering into his office briefly stopped him in his tracks. She was nothing like his usual clients. She was much younger, late 20s, platinum blond, perky red lips, big blue eyes the color of the ocean as seen from some tropical island paradise. Her legs made him glad her polka-dot dress stopped above her knees. He was certain that this was not going to be one of his usual cheating husband cases. Any guy who ran around behind her back was too stupid to deserve her.

She made his office look different, better, although he was not certain why. It was the same oblong room that he remembered. At the back of the room was the olive-grey metal desk he had always had, the same two matching metal chairs sitting in front of it and the same upright, wooden-framed chalkboard on wheels behind it. The dark wood paneled walls were still devoid of decoration except for the huge map of *La République Québécoise* and a photograph of some graduating class from 1911 that were in the office when he moved in and his autographed photograph of Curly Lambeau that his Uncle Edouard gave him for his 15th birthday. In the opposite end of the room from his desk was the same ugly overstuffed couch that he was sleeping on a few minutes earlier.

As she came up to his desk, he introduced himself and offered to shake her hand. The afternoon sun from the window back-lit her, almost like a halo in a medieval painting. She looked like Carole Lombard might, if she died, became an angel and came back to Earth to seduce him. When he was younger, what felt like 100 years ago, a dame like her would have made his jaw drop, ricochet off his foot and skitter across the floor into the corner. Now, he knew that, whatever else happened, Sophie probably was right about her. She was going to be trouble. On the other hand, her kind of trouble had a certain undeniable appeal.

"You look like someone who likes to get right to the point, *Monsieur* Le Pelleteur?" she observed cheerfully as she sat down, displaying just the right amount of leg.

"We can certainly get right to the point if you prefer. I like to please my clients if I can," Le Pelleteur replied, as he circled his desk and took his seat.

"That doesn't surprise me at all. If I hire you, will you please me?"

"I can't make any promises, but I can tell you I haven't had any complaints yet."

She started to examine him, size him up. He let her. At first, he figured that it was the least he could do if he wanted the job. However, he soon realized that she was fighting some kind of battle of wills, to see who would break the awkward silence first. After another 30 seconds of silence while he tried to guess why she wanted a battle of wills, he gave up and inquired, "So, what can I do for you?"

She suddenly became slightly annoyed. "I am Nathalie Juneau. I run the Solomon Juneau Shipping Company. We specialize in transporting valuable articles, usually artwork. We have suffered a series of losses and I want you to investigate."

The name "Juneau" meant that she was not simply gorgeous, but rich as well. In the 1830s, Solomon Juneau came into the *Ouisconsin* area as a *voyageur*, married into the Menominee tribe and amassed a small fortune over the course of his lifetime. During the late 1800s, many of his 13 kids and their descendants built their shares of his fortune into financial empires, rivaling the Rockefellers and the Carnegies. They controlled downtown real estate developments, newspapers and later radio, lumber, manufacturing and other enterprises. Various branches of the Juneau family owned some of the biggest mansions lining Bayshore Drive.

"What was lost?" Le Pelleteur asked, while rummaging through a desk drawer and finding half a pack of Du Maurier cigarettes. He held the pack up to offer one to her.

"Generally, Indian-related artwork." Nathalie Juneau explained, while taking a cigarette and leaning towards the silver butane lighter that Le Pelleteur had just pulled from his pocket. "Frederick Remington bronzes, portraits by George Caitlin, prairie landscapes by Charles Russell, Albert Bierstadt and Chief Joseph Light-Catcher. Each of these pieces is worth at least a hundred thousand *livres*, some are worth millions. There were also a lot of valuable Indian artifacts. Blankets, buffalo robes, saddle bags, a few pairs of moccasins, all from the 1870s or earlier."

"When did this start?" He asked through the side of his mouth while lighting his own cigarette.

"About a year and a half ago. At first, the losses were once every four or five weeks, but it has been happening more and more often. Now it's about twice a month."

"Why don't you go to the police?"

"We couldn't stand the publicity. We're often hired to ship priceless articles and we depend on an unblemished reputation of reliability."

"And your insurance company?"

"They're also investigating. However, these are difficult times, as I'm sure you know. One suspects they are searching primarily for an excuse not to cover my losses. I would prefer to have an independent investigation."

"Do you suspect anyone in particular?"

"No. I have no idea how these thefts keep happening."

"So, it could be an inside job."

"Yes, I suppose it could."

The detective pondered for a moment. "If I accept this job, you would be my client. In other words, I want you to hire me, not the Solomon Juneau Shipping Company."

"What's the difference?"

"I want to be the one to decide when or if to let others at your firm to know that I'm a private investigator and so I don't want my fee to come from the firm's accounts."

"That's fine, then."

"I would also expect your cooperation in conducting an independent investigation. I would expect complete access to your personnel, your records and your clients."

"I can assure you, *Monsieur* Le Pelleteur," she smiled playfully, "I can give you all the access you will need."

"You seem very confident for someone who does not know how much access I will need."

"As you put it, *Monsieur*, I haven't had any complaints yet."

He leaned forward and stared into her eyes. "I get ten *livres* per day, plus expenses."

She took an unmarked white envelope out of her purse and tossed it onto the desk, nonchalantly pronouncing, "That should be enough to get you started." He glanced inside and found 100 *livres* in crisp new bills. He liked what he saw. He was late with the rent, his last three clients' bills were overdue and getting them to pay up was like extracting blood from a block of ice. On the other hand, he didn't trust her. There was something fishy about her story—there was no reason to throw that kind of money or innuendo around if she wasn't hiding something. He suspected that he was getting set up. The question was whether he could take the job and her money while avoiding her trap. He was not certain he could, but he thought that finding out would be more enjoyable than any other job he had taken for a while.

Chapter VII

Le Pelleteur took a drag on his cigarette, exhaled and watched the smoke dissipate through the office for a few moments. "I'll take the job," he finally announced. "I'll start posing as one of your drivers tomorrow morning and see if I can get a handle on what goes on."

"You may be a fine private investigator, but I don't know if you know anything about handling fine art. I would feel much more comfortable if you approached this situation some other way." She emphasized "comfortable" in a way that sounded vaguely sensual. At that moment, however, his attraction towards her was almost outweighed by her interference in his investigation.

"OK," he replied, trying unsuccessfully to avoid a tone of voice suggesting it really wasn't OK. "I could work in your head office and get the lay of the land from there."

"We really don't have enough work for another office employee in our headquarters. I'm afraid a new hire would raise suspicions." She was subtle but manipulative, masking her demand with carefully calibrated charm, adjusting her feminine wiles like the fine-tuning on a radio.

He ground out his cigarette, pushing ashes out of the ashtray and onto his desk, growing less interested in hiding his frustration. "What do you suggest, then?"

Mademoiselle Juneau tapped her chin a few times in contemplation. "Why don't you pose as an auditor from Arthur Andersen and start by reviewing shipping records and calling the customers whose art was stolen?"

"I can usually learn more from interviewing someone in person than a telephone call."

"Why don't you use telephone interviews to develop preliminary theories on the thefts and follow up with in-person interviews later?"

He desperately wanted to find some flaw in her proposal, but couldn't. Although he knew he would bristle at any other client who tried so hard to insinuate themselves into his work, Le Pelleteur found himself agreeing with Nathalie's suggestion. He felt himself falling under her spell—not so hard that he didn't hear the alarm bells in his head, but hard enough to ignore them.

Mademoiselle Juneau stood up and shook the detective's hand. It was a reasonably firm handshake, like she had to prove she belonged in the business world, not like some women who limply touch your hand with their fingertips like it was a rag you had just used to wipe something off the bottom of your shoe. Sam followed her to the outer office, watching her hypnotic hips sway as she left. Sophie looked up from the textbook she was editing. When *Mademoiselle* Juneau was gone, Sophie announced, in a voice that fully reflected her lack of enthusiasm, "It looks like we have a new client."

Sam, still distracted, agreed.

"I still say she's going to be trouble."

Sam snapped out of his entranced state. "You think every woman under forty who sets foot in this place is going to be trouble."

"That's not true."

"Besides, you may not be the most unbiased observer in the world on this particular subject."

Sophie blushed. "If you are referring to the crush I once had, I've told you a hundred times that I got over it when I was thirteen."

"If that's so, then why do you swoon every time you see me?" Le Pelleteur asked, sarcastically.

"If I swoon, that should be a hint it's time for you to take a shower."

"A clever retort. You sure you're not still thirteen years old?" He chuckled a little as he poured himself a cup of coffee and returned to his office. Sophie tried to return to editing the history textbook on her desk, found it difficult to focus and decided to get some coffee for herself. She couldn't deny that, when she was a little girl, she had a slight infatuation on Le Pelleteur. But she grew out of that a long time ago. Now it was something that Sam would drag out only to embarrass her, like the baby pictures her mother would occasionally drag out when she was in high school and one of her friends had come over to study.

She knew Nathalie Juneau would be trouble the second she stepped through the door. In fact, Sophie gasped when she saw Juneau, because for a second she thought she was Celeste de Rocher. The resemblance still amazed Sophie as she watched the new client leave. Celeste was Sam's girlfriend for three years and his fiancée for another two, until she left him and broke his heart. This was in the summer of 1935, shortly after she started working for him. He had just left the *Sûreté* and started his private investigation business. She never heard the details of what happened. She just saw the results. He would stumble into the office half-drunk every morning, drink more until noon and pass out by mid-afternoon.

His first potential client showed up about a month after Sophie started working, a middle-aged woman with too red lipstick and a hat with royal blue feathers sticking out in every direction, flouncing up and down as she walked. Sophie never learned what the woman wanted. Instead, she watched the blue feathers as the woman went into Sam's office and stormed out in a disgusted huff five minutes later. Sophie ran into Sam's office to find him vomiting into a grey metal waste paper basket. Five hundred reactions hit her at once, like a proverbial ton of bricks. Part of her wanted to sit down with him and explain rationally how bad his life could get if he didn't straighten up. Part of her wanted to slap him in the face. Part of her just wanted to run away. Part of her felt ashamed, as if some of the shame he must have felt in being seen in such a debauched state had rubbed off on her.

Instead of doing any of those things, she sat down on the big ugly couch and cried. Sam wanted to say something, but quickly realized that there was nothing he could say. He left. She did not see him for the rest of the day. The next morning, first thing, he walked up to her desk and promised her that she would never see him in that condition again. "I better not," she insisted and poured a cup of coffee for him. Sam kept his promise, limiting his drinking to after business hours. Neither Sophie nor Sam talked about that day again, but it was a day she would never forget. Even though Sam didn't talk about Celeste, she knew he still missed her. She also knew what could happen if he fell for this new woman and had his heart crushed again.

Chapter VIII

Le Pelleteur showed up at Nathalie Juneau's office at 9:30 the next morning, after dropping his car off to get the window repaired. Although he had not slept in the grey business suit he wore that morning, it still managed to get wrinkled by the time he got downtown.

He took the *élevé* commuter train to the XY Trading Company Building in downtown Green Bay. The XY Company, formally known as the North West Company, was one of the oldest corporations in North America. It started as a loose collaboration of *voyageurs* canoeing from Montréal into the wilderness in the 1700s to trade rifles and copper pots to Natives for beaver pelts. The Company quickly grew into the dominant fur trading operation in North America, buying out its only serious competition, the Hudson's Bay Company, in 1821. The "XY" nickname was derived from the *voyageurs*' practice of marking their bales of furs with "XY" before shipping them to Paris.

The company eventually evolved into a department store chain, competing with Macy's and Marshall Field's in the United States and Dillard's in Texas. The "XY Company" nickname survived into the 20th Century, although the department store bore little resemblance to anything the *voyageurs* would have recognized. The flagship of the chain was the 80-floor Art Deco centerpiece of the Green Bay skyline, the tallest building in the world for eight months, until the Chrysler Building in New York City was completed in 1930. The first six floors of the building supplied the finest in fashion and home decor to the city's high society, the people who care about whether they get invited to "the" social event of the season, those who live beyond the reaches of the business cycle.

As he entered through the gold-framed revolving doors, Le Pelleteur was overwhelmed, almost assaulted, by the glitter and opulence of the main floor. He considered the trappers and *voyageurs* who had provided the foundation for this monument to conspicuous consumption. If they were to try to set foot in this place, thought Le Pelleteur, security would immediately throw them back out onto the street. His musings over this injustice were interrupted when he passed the perfume counter on his way to the elevator, noticed an exorbitant price on a tag and pictured a young debutante preparing for her cotillion negotiating the number of beaver pelts she would need to trade for 50 milliliters of Chanel No. 5.

The rest of the XY Building was office space, over half-empty for most of the past decade. The world headquarters of the Solomon Juneau Shipping Company was a small suite of offices on the 17th floor. The outer office was small and fairly non-descript. It could have been Le Pelleteur's dentist's office. A couch lined the left wall, behind a coffee table with old magazines. A receptionist sat at a desk to the right, near a hallway leading to more offices.

The receptionist, Claire, reminded Le Pelleteur of somebody's grandmother, the kind of person you might find in an apron baking cookies. As he introduced himself, she exclaimed, "Oh, yes, of course, dear. *Mademoiselle* Juneau told me all about you. You're the man from Arthur Andersen." She stood up and motioned him to follow her.

"Where are we going?" Le Pelleteur asked, curious.

"*Mademoiselle* Juneau said you wanted to review some of our shipping records. I have a place set up in the file room for you to work."

"Thank you very much, but if you don't mind, I would like to talk to *Mademoiselle* Juneau for a few minutes first."

The request seemed to take Claire by surprise. She sat down at her desk, picked up her telephone and pushed a button. In a few seconds, she announced, "You can go right in," and motioned towards the office door behind her. It was the office of a middle-aged business executive—oak desk big enough to sink an ocean liner, dark wood paneling, a panoramic painting of a canoeist paddling across a lake hung over a leather couch.

"*Monsieur* Le Pelleteur, I am so glad you came. Please sit down. I asked Claire to help you get set up. Is there a problem?"

Le Pelleteur sat in a leather chair in front of her desk. "Not at all. I just thought it would be helpful to ask you a few questions, first."

She hesitated, then responded too enthusiastically, "But of course. What would you like to know?"

"Well, let's start with why are you 'so glad' I came?"

"Excuse me?"

"When I sat down, you said you were 'so glad' I came. Why? Did you expect me not to come?"

"Is there some reason why I shouldn't be glad you came?"

The detective asked the question to see if it would throw her off balance. When it didn't, he was impressed. To Le Pelleteur, she became a little more attractive, but also a little more likely to be trouble. He went on to ask several routine questions: How do customers place shipping orders? How do shipments get routed? How do the customers get billed? Then he made a more personal observation.

"If you don't mind my saying, you seem rather young to own a company."

"Actually, I don't own this company. I have a minority interest in a number of shell corporations that own this firm and about a dozen other businesses, together with about twenty cousins and uncles."

"Then, you seem young to be running a company."

"My father started this company in 1907. Unfortunately, he died unexpectedly just before *Le Fête de la Saint Jean-Baptiste* in 1938. I was told it was his dying wish that I be appointed president, but I think I got the job because no one else wanted it."

Le Pelleteur glanced at the office decor again and guessed that it was selected by her father and she hadn't redecorated after he died. Like her handshake, he read the office as a sign of a woman trying hard to fit into a business world occupied by men. He also noted to himself that the art thefts started shortly after she took over the company.

Nathalie Juneau suggested they start reviewing the shipping records, unless Le Pelleteur had more questions. She led him to Claire the receptionist, who appeared to scurry away from her desk towards the file room, although Le Pelleteur had to walk unusually slowly to keep from bumping into her.

The file room was a sterile, grayish white room about three meters wide and ten meters long, with a row of filing cabinets along one of the longer walls. At the far end of the room sat a darker grey table accompanied by an old heavy wooden chair, a telephone, a lamp and a green ceramic ashtray that appeared to have been stolen from a hotel in Atlantic City, New Jersey. On the table rested 26 file folders representing 26 stolen masterpieces or rare artifacts. Claire smiled, told him to let her know if he needed any help finding anything and left him alone.

He skimmed through each file. Other than the items that were supposed to be shipped, nothing struck him as out of the ordinary. As Nathalie had informed him, Le Pelleteur found that the shipments occurred at random intervals over the previous eighteen months. Some shipments were for relatively short distances, while others were cross-continent. The shipments were not made on any particular day of the week, nor during any particular time of the month. He did not see any particular pattern in the buyers or the sellers. Among other things, they seemed evenly distributed throughout North America: Montréal, Detroit, Sault Saint Marie and Green Bay in Québec; Boston, New York and Atlanta in the United States; Houston, San Francisco and Los Angeles in the Republic of Texas; and Portland, Seattle, Vancouver and Calgary in the Dominion of Oregon. There were even two or three people on his list located in St. Louis in France's Missouri Territory.

He proceeded to telephone each of the buyers and sellers listed in the files. Most of these were long distance, operator-assisted calls which took three or four minutes to connect. He finished at 6:30 PM. Again, none of these interviews turned up anything that appeared out of the ordinary. He asked Claire about arranging interviews with the drivers of the trucks carrying the stolen shipments. She apologized, called him "dear," and explained that all the drivers were on the road and could not be contacted. He asked for their personnel records and Claire obliged. Finally, Le Pelleteur called Sophie to tell her he was not returning to the office that afternoon, collected the files and his notes from each telephone call, left the building and headed home, trying to figure out his next step.

Chapter IX

For Le Pelleteur, home was 1638 *L'Avenue Frontenac*, Apartment 2C, a walk-up, one-room efficiency on the cheap side of town, two floors above a pawn shop. The furniture was utilitarian—not much more than a tan leather armchair, a kitchen table and chairs and a couple of lamps. The rent was affordable and the roaches tended to keep to themselves.

Next to the apartment door was a week-old newspaper, grey, wrinkled and brittle, like ancient parchment. Sam took his shoes off and put them on the paper and draped his cold, wet socks over the radiator. He dropped his briefcase on the Murphy bed that he did not bother to fold up on most mornings and peeked out the window to confirm that the sack of beavers that he confiscated from the poacher was still frozen and tied to the fire escape. He proceeded to make himself dinner, a venison burger and baked beans fried on a hotplate and a glass of gin. (Ground venison was on sale at the meat market two blocks from his apartment.)

He ate in his leather armchair, feet crossed on the bed, swirling the ice in his gin glass and staring at the briefcase as though his eyes could pop it open and fold the papers inside into origami flowers. Eventually he gave up, did an hour of calisthenics in his living room and went to bed.

The next morning, Le Pelleteur walked into his office to find Sophie apparently in the process of sacrificing a squirrel on her desk.

"What are you doing?" he asked, awake enough to be curious but not enough to be shocked.

Sophie explained, "I assumed the owner of the beavers would prefer it if his pelts were dressed, so I found a book in the library last night on basic trapping techniques and I set a trap and caught a couple of squirrels to practice on."

Le Pelleteur looked around the office and found a file cabinet drawer open. Inside, he found the drawer empty, except for a grey squirrel pelt stretched out within a tree branch bent into a small oval leaning against one side. "I have to say this is very nice work. However, some trappers are kind of touchy about letting other people skin their catches. I think we would be better off keeping the beavers where they are, tied to the fire escape at my apartment, until we can return them." When Sophie seemed disappointed, Sam offered, "Of course, I don't see any problem with finishing what you've started. Two squirrel pelts won't make you rich, but they might be enough to buy you lunch."

The cheerful smile returned to Sophie's lips as she finished skinning her second squirrel. She finished her history textbook by noon and spent the rest of the day reviewing a college-level engineering textbook. Sam spent the day in the office searching for some kind of pattern in the data he had collected the day before. Sam emerged from his office two or three times, like a shipwreck survivor stumbling out of the surf onto a desert island, only to pour himself another cup of coffee and dive back in. For the rest of the day, she heard occasional bursts of staccato chalk tapping, separated by long stretches of muffled grumbling.

At 1:00, when Sophie saw that Le Pelleteur had forgotten lunch, she ran to the University cafeteria and bought him a *tourtière*. He ate it standing and staring at his chalkboard. He had listed all the buyers and sellers he called the day before and drawn lines between them so that the board looked like it was covered with spider webs.

At 6:30, when he came out of his office looking for another cup of coffee, he was surprised to Sophie still working at her desk.

"You're still here?"

"Brilliant observation! The Sleuth *Extraordinaire* strikes again!"

"Let me put it another way. Why are you still here, given that the office closes at 5:00 and you could have left then, Smart Ass?"

"I'm close to finishing a book and I decided to stay until I got it done."

"What are you reading today?"

"*Electromagnetic Fields: Theory and Applications.*"

"I can't wait for the movie. Feel like taking a break? I sure could use one."

Sophie marked her place with a scrap of paper, rebundled her galley pages in order and sauntered into Sam's office. Sam poured the last dregs of coffee into his green *Université de Green Bay* Phoenix mug and followed her, like a plow horse after 40 *arpents* of rocky soil. The Athletics Program chose the Phoenix as the team mascot in the 1870s, in reference to a large but subsequently largely forgotten 1871 forest fire in the Peshtigo area northwest of the City, overshadowed by a concurrent fire in the city of Joliet near the southern tip of Lake Michigan.

Sophie sat on the couch and put her feet up. Sam pushed around the two green leather chairs normally reserved for clients so they faced each other, sat in one, and put his feet on the other. They silently stared at the disorganized scribbles on the chalkboard for a few minutes, then Sam announced, "Well, that is what I accomplished today. Impressive, don't you think?"

The detective saw pity in Sophie's eyes, the kind of pity she might feel for a stray dog with a limp, or some other generally unwanted creature that other, less soft-hearted people might consider too ineffectual to be even worthy of contempt. He found being the object of her pity more frustrating than failing to find the pattern he had been searching for all day.

"Have you ever heard of Johann Elert Bode?" Sophie asked. Sam shook his head.

"Bode was an astronomer in the 1700s. One day he looked at the distances from the Sun to all the known planets at the time, Mercury to Saturn and thought he saw a pattern. He wrote a paper and told all his astronomer friends and everyone thought he was a big deal. Coincidentally, when they discovered Uranus later, it fit the pattern and so did the asteroids between Mars and Jupiter. But Neptune didn't fit and when they discovered Pluto a few years ago, it blew this pattern out of the water. Bode went from a big deal to the answer to a trivia question."

"My sympathies to *Monsieur* Bode. I could tell you everyone who played goalie for the Packers for the past twenty years, but that wouldn't have anything to do with anything, either."

"The point is, maybe if there really was a relevant pattern in all these art thefts, you would have found it by now. Maybe, at this point, if you find a pattern in all this, it's more likely to be a remarkable coincidence like Bode's pattern than something you can use."

"What are you saying? 'When the going gets tough, give up'? I have to admit it has a certain appeal."

"No, I was trying to suggest you might be better off finding another approach to the problem."

"The problem with your suggestion is that I don't have any other leads at the moment. I need to keep looking for a pattern until another approach comes along."

"This shipping company is a family business, right? A family like the Juneaus must show up in the newspaper Society Section fairly often. I could check the newspaper indices in the University library and see if anything turns up."

Le Pelleteur thought for a second. "That's a good idea, but only if you can spare the time. I'm not in the mood to listen to *Père* Stick-up-his-Ass whine about me monopolizing you again."

"I'll make sure to keep up with the work *Père* O'Shaughnessy gives me."

"In the meantime, I'll keep working this angle." Le Pelleteur said, pointing his thumb at his chalkboard.

"Why don't you quit for today and start fresh in the morning?" proposed Sophie. Le Pelleteur's head was spinning at 78 rpm. His tiredness and frustration had grown beyond a headache. The dull, throbbing pain had spread throughout his body, like he had been trampled by a small herd of rhinos, like he had been wrestled to the ice and pummeled by a hockey defenseman twice his size. When he closed his eyes, he saw nightmare visions of the files he had been studying. They started to form patterns that disappeared when he looked directly at them. They became dots that refused to be connected. Opened, his eyes felt like moss was growing on them. Le Pelleteur thought for a second, then offered, "I will if you will." She nodded her head. They chatted about electromagnetic fields while he finished his coffee. He paid her for the lunch she brought him earlier that day while they were putting on their coats. Sam drove Sophie to her apartment building, a few blocks west of the Campus and then turned around and headed towards his favorite bar, Johnny Blood's, on the other side of the river.

Chapter X

Johnny Blood's was a block away from the Fox River, near Green Bay's loading docks and the Warehouse District. It tended to be quiet at this time of year, when the Port of Green Bay was frozen in and would remain so until the spring thaw, when ship traffic would resume and Great Lakes sailors would need a place to get drunk during shore leave. The place livened up a little on weekends, when a handful of college kids would come here to listen to the Blues, although not too many, because the vast majority of kids preferred the traditional *quadrilles* or the new Jitterbug music from the United States. During the week, however, not even the college crowd would show up at this bar or its neighbors, preferring establishments closer to campus. So, these places became favorites of a certain kind of cheating husband to take his mistress—the kind that thought being seen in this part of town didn't count as being "seen."

That was part of the reason that Le Pelleteur came here. Contrary to popular opinion, cheating husbands with their mistresses stuck out like neon signs in a coal mine shaft in this neighborhood. The bartender, a former Packer left wing colorfully named "Johnny Blood" McNally, usually heard about such sightings before too long and was more than happy to pass the gossip along to Le Pelleteur for a five-*livre* tip and his continued patronage. However, Le Pelleteur had a multitude of other reasons for coming here. It was only four blocks away from his apartment building. It was a good place to get poutine and gin when he couldn't face another hotplate dinner alone in his apartment and it was one of the few places in the neighborhood that served any food at all.

Le Pelleteur considered McNally's poutine to be the best in the city. Québec believed poutine to be its gift to the culinary world; the culinary world, to put it mildly, would prefer to give it back. Poutine in most of Québec was French fries smothered in a brown gravy, but most places in *Ouisconsin*, including McNally's bar, specialized in a variant known as "Green Bay Style," which was served with greasy blobs of cheddar the color of Hunters' Safety Orange. More often than politics or religion, the conversation most likely to turn a Green Bay Thanksgiving meal from a joyful holiday gathering to a red-faced, eye-bulging, table-pounding shouting match was initiated by a new bride who had recently married into a Green Bay family, innocently asking her mother-in-law, "Why did you have to ruin it with all that cheese?"

The Green Bay Style poutine was not the only attraction that Johnny Blood's held for Le Pelleteur. In addition, they usually put the hockey game on the radio. Moreover, when the Packers were not playing, Johnny Blood would book a live Delta Blues act, the kind that would sound like a knife wound to the stomach, the kind that could make a guy stab himself in sympathy before the end of the second set. For Le Pelleteur, it was like rebreaking a bone so that it could reknit correctly; it was painful in the short run but always made him feel better by the time it was over.

Johnny Blood's also provided Le Pelleteur with a reasonable substitute for a romantic relationship, namely Odette. Before he had met Nathalie Juneau, Odette provided him with all the romance he could tolerate. Odette was in the middle of a rough patch, one that started roughly the time she was born. She was two goals behind before the opening face-off and had been playing short-handed ever since. As a teenager, she learned she could provide certain marketable services to the sailors who didn't want to spend their shore leave getting drunk. Over the next thirty years, life had not given her many opportunities to develop other marketable skills. Johnny Blood's provided her with a convenient base of operations, particularly during winter, when dressing for the weather was not conducive for business. More than once, Le Pelleteur found himself in a mood to share her company. In addition to the years she had spent honing her craft, she shared his interests in hockey and music. In fact, earlier that evening, Odette had dropped into the bar to offer her services to Le Pelleteur. He declined, as he often did when his mind was preoccupied with a case, but he bought her a drink and a serving of Johnny Blood's poutine and they listened to the first period of the Packers game together.

More than anything else, Le Pelleteur came to this bar because, after a lot of years and about a thousand liters of alcohol, Johnny Blood had become something like a friend. After making a career based primarily on breaking up marriages, Le Pelleteur wasn't anybody's candidate for Mr. Popularity and maintaining a friendship by itself would be adequate incentive for him to continue his patronage.

The bar was a single room, about 10 meters wide, 20 meters deep. As one enters, the bar itself is on the left, shellacked dark walnut facing a row of bar stools, red leather tops, many with egg-yolk yellow foam sticking out. Behind the bar, a multitude of liquor bottles and a 10-year-old wooden "cathedral-style" Philco radio were displayed in front of a large mirror in a wooden frame. In the corner of the mirror were photographs of the bartender hoisting the Stanley Cup after the Packers won the 1929, 1930 and 1931 championships. Next to the mirror, a metal sign advertised *Jean Talon* beer and two cardboard posters announced an upcoming engagement by a new act, someone named Elmore James. On the opposite wall was a line of coat pegs. Beyond the end of the bar were five or six tables and a small stage with a microphone stand, a waist-high wooden stool and an upright piano. The side walls were exposed brick. The back wall was covered by a faded blue curtain. The stamped metal ceiling was four meters high, still coated with soot from gas lights that had been replaced with electric 30 years earlier.

Odette announced at the first intermission that it was time for her to go home. Sam slipped her a kiss on the cheek and a five-*livre* bill into her pocket before she left. During the second period, as was his custom, he listened with his feet up on a chair from the next table. He smoked Du Maurier cigarettes, snacked on peanuts and nursed his third and fourth glasses of gin. The Packers fell behind the Joliet Black Hawks four to two, giving up the fourth goal with 17 seconds left in the second period.

"What's on your mind?" Johnny shouted from the bar. It startled Le Pelleteur, because it was the first sound either of them had uttered in over an hour. An hour without talking could have been a personal record for Johnny.

"Why should anything be on my mind?"

"If you weren't preoccupied with something, you would be a lot more disgusted with the game and you would be ready for another by now."

"Been thinking about a case."

"Feel like talking about it?"

"No. I came here to get away from it." Johnny Blood's strong suits were poutine and corny jokes, not his deductive reasoning skills and Le Pelleteur doubted that discussing the case with him would be productive.

"Well, I can help you get your mind off it, then. Did I ever tell you about the time in my rookie year I chained the rear axle of Curly Lambeau's car to a light post in the City Stadium parking lot?"

"Yes."

"Well, did I ever tell you the story about the guy who came out of church with two black eyes?"

"Yes."

"Really?"

"At least three times."

Johnny went back to wiping down the bar. He looked like a scolded puppy, or a little boy who just heard that the circus changed its plans and was not coming to town after all. Le Pelleteur started to feel guilty and he found the guilt annoying. "I was trying to spare you a boring conversation, but on second thought, your insights on the case might be helpful to me." The bartender came quickly from behind the bar and sat down at Le Pelleteur's table. The private investigator mentioned that there were 26 art thefts and explained all his failed attempts to find a pattern in those thefts. Johnny inquired, "So, there were twenty-six pieces of art, with fifty-two sellers and fifty-two buyers?"

"Yes."

"I'm surprised to hear there are so many people around who can afford that kind of fancy stuff." Johnny then jerked his head towards the radio and announced, "Oh, the third period's starting," while he shuffled back behind the bar. Le Pelleteur just stared at the radio behind the bar. He cheered when Clarke Hinkle scored for Green Bay three-and-a-half minutes into the period and Don Hutson tied the game less than a minute later. However, neither team scored a tie-breaking goal and Le Pelleteur stopped paying attention to the game by the time by time it ended. He was engrossed in thought about something Johnny said, so much so that he barely noticed when that night's musical act, Big Bill Broonzy, got on stage. McNally often booked new acts on Wednesday nights and moved them to Fridays or Saturdays if they developed a following. The band captured Le Pelleteur's attention when it started playing. It turned out to be one of the better acts that Le Pelleteur had heard. There was something in the way Big Bill plucked his guitar. It sounded like a needle poking holes in Le Pelleteur's heart. There was something in his rough tenor voice that could reach down into Le Pelleteur's chest and latch onto his soul:

My baby said she loved me, but my baby was untrue.
My baby said she loved me, but my baby was untrue.
Her mouth was full of lies. She made me look a fool.

The second song was "It Was Just a Dream."

It was a dream, Lord, what a dream I had on my mind.
It was a dream, Lord, what a dream I had on my mind.
Now, when I woke up, baby, not a thing there could I find.

When the third song started, Le Pelleteur scribbled a few notes onto a cocktail napkin as he got up to leave. "Not a thing there could I find. How many people can afford fancy stuff? Is she making me look a fool?"

Chapter XI

Thursday started sunny and warm, 6° below, Centigrade, the warmest morning since Halloween. The eastern sun illuminated the XY Building like a beacon, a ray of hope on the Green Bay skyline. At 10:00 in the morning, Samuel de Champlain Le Pelleteur was striding determinedly down the hallway of the 17th floor of the XY Building. His heavy wool camel's hair overcoat streaming behind him like Superman's cape in those U.S. comic books that had recently been translated into French and imported into Québec. The detective had a glare in his eye and a scowl on his face, like a borderline psychotic bent on truth, justice and the *Québécois* Way. His left hand incongruously throttled a small bouquet of mixed flowers. In almost no time, he had marched the length of the hallway and had reached the offices of the Solomon Juneau Shipping Company. Le Pelleteur took a deep breath to help regain his composure temporarily and carefully opened the door to the outer office.

Claire exclaimed, "Well, hello, *Monsieur* Le Pelleteur."

"Hello. I brought you some flowers to thank you for being so helpful the last time I was here."

"Well, aren't you a dear."

"No, I am not."

"Excuse me?"

"If anyone asks you about this particular moment in the future, I am not a dear, I am not sweet and I am not in any way thoughtful. I am like an animal, a *Voyageur* who has been in *Le Pays-en-Haut* for three winters and has just shown up half-naked with native war paint on his face. I burst into the office demanding to see *Mademoiselle* Juneau. You tried to stop me, but I got past you before you could do anything. Understand?"

"Yes, I think I do."

"And please don't tell anyone where you got the flowers. It would ruin the reputation I'm trying to build."

"Of course, dear."

Le Pelleteur winced, like he just watched a forward for the Toronto *Feuilles d'Érable* intercept a Packers cross-ice pass and take the puck straight to the goal unopposed. Claire was briefly confused, then quickly apologized for calling him "dear." Le Pelleteur then marched to the Company President's door, threw it open, stood in the doorway and glared. The fury in his stare could have set most people's hair on fire. However, she disarmingly replied, "Well, this is a pleasant surprise." She sat behind her desk and arranged herself coquettishly. Instead of instinctively shrinking into a defensive posture, she immediately decided on a strategy to throw him off balance and implemented it very skillfully. He hesitated to admire her manipulation, but only for a second.

"Is it really all that pleasant?" He inquired innocently as he sat down, head propped up on his elbow on the arm of the chair, feet crossed in front of him.

"Yes," her brow furrowed slightly in confusion.

"Why?"

"What do you mean, 'why'?"

"Why is seeing me again 'pleasant'?"

"This again? You were so charming when I hired you. Why have you been acting so strangely ever since?"

Le Pelleteur jumped to her desk and leaned over, palms down on the green felt blotter. "Let's think for a minute about all the misconceptions that you may be harboring over there in that pretty little head of yours. First, I think a more apt description of me when we met Monday afternoon would be 'bleary-eyed' or maybe 'incoherent.' I could even see 'hung over,' but no way in Hell was I 'charming.' Second, I find myself wondering why you would call me charming when I clearly was not. The best theory I got today is that you're working under a misconception that I'm the kind of guy who would flush his brain down a toilet at the first sign of a good-looking dame and a little sweet talk. Sorry to disappoint you there, sister, but it usually takes a lot more sweet talk and a liter of gin to get me that far around the bend. Your third misconception is that I am not bright enough to figure out that all the thefts you hired me to investigate are fakes. Your fourth misconception is that I have so little integrity or self-respect that a pile of cash big enough to choke a moose might somehow make up for playing me for a chump. Wrong on all counts, although I have to admit that I'm a little surprised to find I have some self-respect that hasn't been ground into dust years ago."

"So, this game is going to play out like this," Le Pelleteur continued. "You owe me twenty *livres* for two days of work, plus I'm billing you for my new car battery because it died while I was working your case," he lied, "and I think a new battery is a fair trade for getting jerked around. Here is the rest of your retainer. The next time you get the urge to run a scam on a private dick, find some other patsy." With that, he stood up and tossed the rest of the money at her, 75 *livres* in worn fives and tens. The bills fluttered onto her desk as he started to walk out the door.

Nathalie Juneau sat stunned for a moment. As Le Pelleteur reached the door, she shouted at him to wait. He thought for a minute, marched back to her desk and snarled, "Wait for what?" He gritted his teeth, like the words left a bitter, revolting taste in his mouth.

She continued to process the information for a few seconds. "What do you mean, 'fakes'? What makes you think anyone has been faking the thefts?"

Le Pelleteur thought that Juneau's surprise was not completely believable, like a politician swearing he knows nothing about a bribe. Instead of answering her question, he sat down and chuckled quietly, "Don't tell me. Let me guess. You're hearing all this for the first time. You had no idea that the thefts were fakes, or that you were sending me on a wild goose chase, or that all your insurance claims were bogus."

The sides of Nathalie Juneau's mouth curled slightly downward and a tear began to trickle from her left eye before she turned away and hid her face. Samuel de Champlain Le Pelleteur also looked away. Part of him was disgusted by the spectacle and he could not decide what turned his stomach more, her playacting or finding himself falling for it. Another part of him wanted, almost longed for, her tears to be genuine and was scrambling mentally to cook up some reasonable justification for believing her story. He hadn't fallen for her, but he had been balanced precariously on a precipice, dangerously close to falling ever since they met. Losing Celeste ripped a gaping hole in his chest, like a hollow tree trunk and over the years, he had convinced himself that learning to ignore the hole was an adequate substitute for dealing with it. Nathalie Juneau might be just what he needed to fill that hole, or she might leave him with another gaping hole in his chest if he gave her half a chance. If Nathalie Juneau is on the level now, he thought, it might be worth it to give her that half a chance.

He wiped his hand over his face and focused back on the gently weeping woman behind the desk. "Look, I'll tell you what I'll do. I'll poke around and see if I can find out who is running this scam. But, if I find that it's you, that's it. I won't care what you say or do after that. I won't care if your eyes turn into Niagara Falls. I'm taking back the retainer," he growled, grabbing the currency he just tossed onto her desk, "and I'll turn you over to the *Sûreté*, or the insurance companies, or both."

Chapter XII

Le Pelleteur demanded to interrogate the other people working in the headquarters. Nathalie led Le Pelleteur to the next office, where her brother Denis sat leaning back in his leather swivel office chair, hidden by the society pages of the *Journal* except for the wing-tip shoes on his desk. Le Pelleteur gathered that reading the paper constituted the bulk of Denis's work responsibilities, because his desk was deserted, except for a telephone and a growing collection of scuff marks. Before long, thought Le Pelleteur, the desk would be scraped up like a hockey rink at the end of a period. Nathalie introduced Le Pelleteur to Denis, but failed to elicit any reaction. She repeated her introduction more loudly, then called Denis a brat before she left.

"Mind if I sit down?" Le Pelleteur inquired.

"Actually, I do, but I don't care enough to try to stop you."

Le Pelleteur sat in one of those new Mies Van Der Rohe-style black leather chairs and examined the office. It was almost as big as Nathalie's, but unlike her office, Denis had no artwork on his walls. The lack of paperwork or any other sign of activity on his desk made the room seem emptier—more barren. The window overlooked the downtown area and the Bay beyond, frozen and gleaming in the morning sun.

Le Pelleteur turned his attention back to sizing up Denis as he continued to sit oblivious to the man sitting in front of him. He had a pouty, childish demeanor. He looked like the kind of guy who grew up never hearing the words "no," or "sorry, not today," or "you'll have to wait your turn." In addition to looking bored, Le Pelleteur thought he looked slightly but permanently inconvenienced, as if he realized he was expected to make a contribution to society and he resented society for being too stupid to recognize that his mere existence should be contribution enough. People like Denis always reminded Le Pelleteur of a good set of china, perversely considered more valuable because they so seldom provide any useful service.

Le Pelleteur tried again to attract his attention. "So, what is it that you do around here?"

After a few more seconds of awkward silence, Denis stated casually from behind the newspaper, "I spend most of my time trying to avoid tedious conversations with tedious people."

Le Pelleteur sat quietly for a moment, thinking deeply about Denis's response, then asked, "So, how long have you been defrauding your insurance company like a common thief?"

"Common?" Denis demanded, finally lowering the paper and looking at Le Pelleteur.

"Pardon me. How long have you been defrauding your insurance company like a rich, over-privileged, upper-class twit of a thief?"

Denis Juneau leapt to his feet in a fit of pique. Le Pelleteur jumped up as well, leaned over the desk and stared menacingly into his eyes. "If you want to avoid the tedium of picking up your teeth off the floor, you better not make any more sudden moves." Denis plopped back into his chair, sulking. Le Pelleteur sat down slowly, leaned back and relaxed, crossing his legs. "Now, if you would be so kind, how long have you been defrauding your insurance company?"

"What makes you think I would bother defrauding anyone?"

"Well, I can see you don't exactly whistle while you work like a happy little dwarf. I could also see how you might have expected to be the one in charge after your father kicked the bucket and how you might resent seeing your sister take over instead. Your little caper might be your way of getting back at your family for passing you over and pulling it on your sister's watch might be your way of getting even with her for being more competent than you. Also, I can't help but notice that, in all your theatrics, you never denied the accusation."

"For the record, I have never defrauded anyone. Second, I never wanted anything from this monument to boredom except an income sufficient for someone of my social standing. I certainly never wanted to run this dump and I never really cared who did. Hell, if I were in charge, I would have to pay attention to what's going on from time to time. Also, if I wanted to get even with my sister for anything, I would just start spreading rumors about her sleeping with the gardener. Much easier and more straightforward than 'pulling a caper'."

"Let's say for the sake of argument that I buy your story. Any ideas on who might be committing this caper?"

"My guess is Jacques Cloutier. He's the only one around here who really knows what he's doing enough to figure out how to defraud an insurance company."

Chapter XIII

Le Pelleteur thanked Denis for his time and sauntered down to the neighboring office. "Pardon me, *Monsieur* Cloutier, could I talk to you for a few minutes?"

Cloutier was a balding, grey-haired man in his early 60s. He wore a white dress shirt and a black bow tie. He sat with his elbows on his desk and his forehead in his hands, scowling at accounting reports. He looked like a man who had spent his life undergoing some mild form of torture and had almost become used to it. "Who are you and what do you want?" He emphasized "you," like it was some kind of insult.

"My name is Samuel de Champlain Le Pelleteur. I'm the auditor that *Mademoiselle* Juneau hired."

"Oh, yes," he responded, in an overburdened tone of voice. "She said you might be stopping by."

"Did she say why?"

"I figured it had something to do with the shipment thefts."

"What do you do around here?"

"I do just about everything. I manage the accounts, do the payroll, route the trucks. The numskull next door is supposed to be in charge of corporate accounts. As the president, Nathalie is a supervisor, which means she stops by every week or so and tries to understand what I do."

"It sounds like you're the guy that holds the whole operation together."

"Pretty much." When he said this, the weariness of his voice only partially hid his pride.

"And yet this is not the Cloutier Shipping Company, is it?"

Cloutier exhaled an exasperated sigh. "I worked with Benoit Juneau for forty years, helping him to build this business out of nothing. Now, instead of getting some kind of reward for my service, I have to do all the work around here plus carry his dead-weight kids."

"Frustrating."

"It can be."

"What do you know about the art thefts?"

Cloutier looked annoyed for a moment. "Not much. I can get you a list of the stolen items and the times their shipments were scheduled, but I'm surprised you don't have that information already."

Le Pelleteur accepted his offer, so he could check to see if Cloutier's list matched the one he got from Nathalie. Then he inquired casually, "Did you know that the art thefts were fakes, part of some kind of insurance scam?" The accountant jolted back, like he had just touched a hot stove. Before he could react further, Le Pelleteur offered, "The reason I ask is that Denis figures you to be the mastermind of the scam."

"That bastard! It's just like him to blame someone else."

"But then again, you're in a perfect position to pull something like that off. You said yourself that you run the Company almost single-handedly. I can also see you thinking that the Company owes you something after your years of loyal service. I think the smart money's on you."

"You and that lazy-ass bum next door can think what you want. I have never lied or cheated anyone out of anything in my life and nothing you say can change that. Now, get out of my sight."

Chapter XIV

Le Pelleteur walked slowly and deliberately down the hallway from the Juneau Company offices to the elevator, contemplating the suspects and their equally questionable claims of innocence. As the elevator descended, he felt like he was standing in a worse spot than a dead end, staring at a three-story brick wall at the end of a dark alley. He also felt like a can of beer in a paint-mixing machine, his head spinning more than a little bit and ready to explode.

His head continued to spin while he marched through the Perfume and Intimate Apparel sections, on the ground floor of the XY Company department store, towards the *L'Avenue Vaudreuil* exit. He stopped suddenly when he noticed a long, thin canister speeding through a pneumatic tube along the ceiling. The XY store, like most department stores, was permeated with pneumatic tubes for carrying payments from sales counters scattered throughout the store to some secret location elsewhere in the building, where change was made and sent back with a receipt. The theory was that handling all the cash transactions in a central location prevented petty thievery at the sales counters. However, like a hammer that thinks everything is a nail, Le Pelleteur's time on the Bunko Squad left him thinking everything is a scam. He always suspected that the tubes merely centralized the thievery.

He suddenly realized that, just like the pneumatic tube system, all the telephone calls to and from the XY Building were funneled through a central point—a switchboard, probably in the basement of the building. If the art thefts he was hired to investigate were faked, then each telephone call he made on Tuesday as part of his investigation must have been faked as well. He started to look for a stairway to the basement.

The detective found the Bargain Basement tables piled with clothes considered fashionable only a year before. He walked across the floor to an unmarked door in the corner, between the bathrooms and the fitting rooms. A stairway led to a sub-basement, dimly lit with unshaded incandescent bulbs. The walls were poured concrete, part of the foundation of the building, the unseen and unappreciated structure supporting all the floors and their conspicuous consumption overhead. As Le Pelleteur reached the bottom of the stairs, a janitor crossed his path. He was an old man in old overalls, carrying a bucket of cloudy grey water as if it contained 40 years of hard labor. Le Pelleteur saw him as another part of the foundation of the building, unseen and unappreciated, supporting all the floors and their conspicuous consumption overhead.

After he watched the janitor walk away, he stopped waxing philosophical and walked quietly in the other direction. As he peered into a series of storage rooms, he started to feel like a miner looking for a vein of gold. Finally, he found an opening on the right without a door that led to a small room with a switchboard. A woman in her 50s wearing glasses and a flower print dress was connecting calls to all the offices in the building. At least 20 cords stretched out from spring-loaded pulleys into the jacks displayed vertically in front of the operator. She wore headphones and a ring around her neck supporting a shiny black horn that she spoke into.

Le Pelleteur stood in the hallway out of her sight, eyes closed, concentrating on her voice. When he was certain that she was the operator who handled all his calls from the previous Tuesday, he slid silently into the room and leaned against the wall, waiting for a break in the influx of telephone calls.

"Excuse me, my name is Samuel de Champlain Le Pelleteur and I'm a private investigator." He placed one of his business cards on the edge of her desk. "I was hoping that I could impose on you for a few minutes to ask some questions."

"That's out of the question. I am on duty now and I have to watch my switchboard." She covered her mouthpiece and stared at the switchboard while she spoke to him.

"I would be happy to talk to you some other time when you're not on duty, whenever it is convenient for you."

"I am not in the habit of talking to strange men and I do not appreciate you continuing to bother me while I am working. Please go away now." She pulled another cord and plugged it into the switchboard.

He waited quietly, leaning against the wall for what seemed like an eternity for both of them. She tried to ignore him, but grew more nervous as time trickled by. Meanwhile, he grew more impatient, but did a much better job hiding it. Eventually, she covered her mouthpiece again. "If you continue to bother me, I will call the police."

Le Pelleteur started to grind his teeth. He stepped toward the switchboard, grabbed a plug out of a jack, pulled the cord, extended it the length of his arm and let it snap back to the base of the switchboard with a loud "thwack." Then in a single, fluid motion, he grabbed the arm of her wooden swivel office chair, spun it around and leaned down. He stared into her eyes, gritted his teeth and growled, "I wanted to have a pleasant conversation about this, but since you've made it clear that we can't, we will do this unpleasantly. We both know that you spent most of the day Tuesday misdirecting telephone calls. I know because they were my calls that you were misdirecting. Now, the way I see it, you have two choices. One option is that you tell me who you directed my calls to and why and my menacing shadow will never darken your switchboard again. The other option is that I show you a new game I like to call 'getting arrested for wire fraud.' Green Bay's Finest will drag you out of the building, in handcuffs, through the Perfume and Intimate Apparel departments, provoking a scandal in front of dozens of shocked customers. Prison is at least a possibility. However, I can promise you that, regardless of how guilty or innocent you are, you will be interrogated for hours and the kind, understanding proprietors of the XY Trading Company will give your job to someone else before you see the light of day again. So, what'll it be?"

"I'll lose my job now if you don't let me get back to the switchboard."

"Perhaps then it would be in your best interest to tell me what I want to know."

"I don't know."

"You don't know if keeping your job is in your best interest?"

"I don't know who I directed your calls to or why."

"You must know something."

The operator heaved an exasperated sigh. "About three weeks ago, I found an envelope in my chair when I came into work in the morning. I opened it and found a note offering ten *livres* if I would agree to spend a day routing all the calls from a particular phone number in Suite 1722 to another suite in this building. I was to tape my answer under my chair. I agreed and on Tuesday, I got another envelope with five *livres* and instructions to route the calls to Suite 5104. This morning, I found a third envelope with another five *livres*. None of the notes were signed, so that's all I can tell you."

"You find an anonymous note saying 'commit wire fraud' and you just do it? You don't question who or where the money is coming from? You aren't even a little curious about why this mysterious letter writer wanted you to do this?"

"Take a look in the paper someday. You might notice that times are tough. Ten *livres* can go a long way."

"It never occurred to you that you might be getting set up for something?"

"Sometimes you gotta throw the dice, even when the odds are with the House."

Le Pelleteur concluded that he was unlikely to get any more useful information from the operator. "Thank you," he replied and spun her back to the switchboard. He walked away with nothing more than confirmation of his theory on how the fraud was done and more than a little embarrassment over strong-arming a respectable, middle-aged woman.

Chapter XV

Le Pelleteur left the XY Building a little before 11:00, oblivious to the carefully and artistically arranged jewelry in the display windows facing the sidewalk on the ground floor of the building. He continued the four blocks through the downtown *Boucle* or "Loop" area to the closest *élevé* station, on *L'Avenue Vaudreuil*, contemplating his conversations with the Juneau Company employees and the XY Building telephone operator. Over the course of the morning, clouds had erased the sun. The dirty grey sky was now the same color as the dirty grey streets and the dirty grey buildings. Wind funneled between the skyscrapers, numbing his face and driving the cold into his bones. His pants legs flapped like flags behind his ankles. As he climbed the stairs to the platform, it started to sleet. The platform crackled with the pelting of tiny ice chips.

The train finally showed up. Le Pelleteur rode back to the *Université de Green Bay* campus watching a white haze envelope the Green Bay skyline. He slogged back to his office, pausing briefly to have an argument with *Père* O'Shaughnessy in the lobby of his building and invited Sophie to join him for lunch in the school cafeteria. She looked outside at the weather and made a sarcastic comment about his timing while putting her coat on.

They walked across campus to the cafeteria as the sleet grew stronger, like raining needles. As they joined a line slightly shorter than those at the Department of Motor Vehicles, Sophie mentioned she called the insurance company again that morning and no one had filed a poaching claim.

"Somebody will, sooner or later," Sam replied.

"You said you found these pelts near the highway outside of Neenah. I was thinking it might be a good idea to head down there and do some detecting."

"Unfortunately, my car is still in the shop. Besides, I'm in the middle of this art theft case and I don't really have the time right now."

"I was thinking it might be a good idea for me to go to Neenah."

"How would you get there?"

"I can borrow my parents' car for the afternoon."

"It's snowing pretty hard. It might not be a good idea to go today."

"It's just lake-effect snow. It won't be snowing outside of the city limits."

Sam was about to tell her she couldn't go, simply out of force of habit. Then, he considered the idea for a moment and could not see how letting Sophie play "private eye" in Neenah for an afternoon could get her into any trouble. "Sure, why not," he replied, as Sophie beamed.

They bought platefuls of some substance purported to be a tasty and nutritious lunch and walked to a cavernous room filled with rows of long tables and harsh fluorescent lights. They sat down at one of the small tables along the sides of the room, near the windows that showed the city filling up with snow like sugar being poured into a kitchen canister, and he recounted the events of the morning.

"How did you figure out all the thefts were fakes?" Sophie enthused.

"The lack of pattern was too perfect. You pointed out that there would probably be some pattern that fit some of the thefts, even if they were completely random. It eventually made me wonder why I wasn't seeing any patterns at all. Also, last night, my favorite bartender was surprised to hear that there were so many high-end art collectors active in these economic times. Put the two together and you begin to wonder whether all these people really exist. So, I made a few phone calls this morning before I left the apartment. Five calls in a row, I got a recording that said the number was not in service. That struck me as more than a little suspicious."

"There's that razor-sharp intellect in action again. Who do you think did it? Any hunches yet?"

"I don't know. It could be anyone who works at the shipping company. They all seem to have a decent motive."

"Especially that Nathalie Juneau. I could tell she was trouble the moment I met her."

"Well, believe it or not, I don't trust her, either, but I won't let that stop me from working for her or billing her." He did not tell Sophie that he would also be more than willing to sleep with her if he got the chance. He knew she would accuse him of letting a good-looking dame cloud his judgment. He was not in the mood for arguing with her, especially because he wasn't 100 percent certain she was wrong.

"So, what's next?" Sophie inquired.

"Did you get a chance to research the Juneau family like you wanted to?"

"Nathalie is the second youngest of six children…"

Sam cut her off. "Hang on to that thought for a while. What can you tell me about Zoe Juneau?"

"Nathalie's mother? Why?"

"It just so happens that I have the afternoon free and I thought it would be nice if we could talk to someone who could tell us something useful about this company and these people. Since Benoit Juneau isn't too talkative anymore, being dead, *Madame* Juneau might be worth a shot."

"OK. Zoe and Benoit Juneau were married in 1902 and had six children. She was born Zoe Dorion in 1884, into a fairly typical high-society family; wealthy but almost upper-middle class when compared to the Juneaus. *Madame* Juneau does volunteer work for the Green Bay Opera Society, the Historic Preservation League, the Art Institute of Green Bay, maybe half a dozen others."

"Sounds like a busy lady, not like the kind who would have time for uninvited guests, even if they ask their secretaries to call for an appointment first."

"I have another idea for you," Sophie announced and started to explain while they walked back to the office.

During her research, Sophie learned that Evangeline Juneau, Nathalie's grandmother, was still alive, 88 years old and living with her daughter-in-law. As soon as they reached the office, Sophie gave Sam the Juneaus' home telephone number. Sam called and asked the butler who answered the phone for an appointment to meet with Evangeline, explaining that he wanted to talk to her about Green Bay high society in at the turn of the century. After a long wait on hold, the butler came back on the line and, in a tone of voice that sounded like he was telling a grubby five-year-old not to touch the furniture, instructed Le Pelleteur to come at 2:00 that afternoon.

Chapter XVI

Le Pelleteur took the *élevé* to the Bayshore Drive stop at the end of the line and had to take a taxi the rest of the way to the Juneau mansion. He was in the land of chauffeured limousines and live-in help. No bus routes ran through that neighborhood. Le Pelleteur noticed that Bayshore Drive had already been plowed, even though the snow had been falling for only two hours, rendering superfluous the snowchains on the checker cab's tires. By contrast, the snowplows would not reach his neighborhood until midnight.

The Juneau mansion was an oversized French provincial nightmare, festooned with gables and dormers, as was popular among Gilded Age Robber Barons at the time it was built. It would have covered more than half a city block if it were downtown. It was built for Nathalie's great-great-grandfather and handed down through the generations. The doorbell sounded like the third movement of some baroque symphony that was performed only for elite art patrons with sufficiently illustrious pedigrees.

The detective was greeted by a barrel-chested man dressed like the conductor of the orchestra performing the doorbell symphony. He looked at Sam with an expression halfway between disdain and apathy that made Le Pelleteur feel like a door-to-door vacuum cleaner salesman.

"May I help you?"

Le Pelleteur recognized the condescending, slightly disgusted tone of voice from his telephone conversation with the Juneaus' butler earlier that afternoon. He stood up a little straighter and announced he had an appointment to see Evangeline. The butler somewhat reluctantly invited him in.

The butler never gave his name. Le Pelleteur decided not to ask, getting the distinct impression that the butler was not interested in idle small talk that particular day. As Sam was led through one opulent room after another, each a more extravagant tribute to conspicuous consumption than the last, Le Pelleteur half-expected the butler to have the grounds fumigated later, to remove any trace of his presence.

Eventually, the butler delivered the detective to the library. The ceiling was three meters high and the walls were lined top-to-bottom with dark-stained oak shelves, packed with Voltaire, Descartes, Dumas and other French classics. The only wall space not devoted to such weighty tomes was the back corner of the room, where there was a large window pouring afternoon sunlight onto a caramel-colored leather chair, flanked by a large potted fern and a small round table perfect for a cup of tea. Also basking in the sun was a small white-haired woman in a black sweater and pearls, with half-moon glasses perched on her nose. She looked fragile, like she was made of glass. She sat in a rattan chair on a small wheeled platform that looked like a portable throne. A heavy XY Company four-point blanket covered her lap, which caught Le Pelleteur's attention because the room was uncomfortably stuffy to him.

"*Monsieur* Samuel de Champlain Le Pelleteur," the butler announced, as if he were accompanied by a flourish of medieval trumpets.

"*Monsieur* Le Pelleteur, it's so nice of you to visit," Evangeline Juneau exclaimed, or rather, would have exclaimed if she had the strength. Her voice sounded like a cork reluctantly extracted from a wine bottle. "Would you like a cup of coffee? Perrault, coffee for *Monsieur* Le Pelleteur," she creakily commanded. Perrault the butler bowed his head slightly and left the room.

Evangeline invited Le Pelleteur to sit by gradually, almost imperceptibly, moving a gnarled hand generally in the direction of the leather chair, like any sudden movement might cause her muscles to shatter. Le Pelleteur sat, thought about asking to smoke and thought better of it. A stray ash accidentally flicked in her direction might break a bone.

"You want to talk about the golden age of Green Bay society, you said?" Evangeline Juneau croaked.

"Yes."

"What are you really after?" She tilted her body forward slightly and looked over her glasses. Her eyes were piercing in a way that Le Pelleteur had not noticed previously.

"What makes you think I'm 'really after' anything?" Le Pelleteur was surprised and a little amused by her subtle show of force.

"Let me tell you a little story, young man. When my husband died in 1904, I went from the charming hostess of the most prestigious balls of the 1890s to a woman ignored by Green Bay society. The only place I had any social standing was in the eyes of my son and now that he's dead, I don't even have that anymore. Now, my only contact with the outside world usually comes at the mercy of that vicious little shrew who married my son. She treats me like I'm senile, but even though my body is showing its age, my mind is as sharp as ever. Sharp enough to know that, when I receive a visitor from outside my family for the first time in a decade and he tells me something ridiculously patronizing, like he wants to hear gossip that was forgotten forty years ago, it's clear he's after something and he thinks I'm a doddering old fool who will give him what he wants just for keeping me company for a little while."

Evangeline reminded the detective of a poodle with delusions of being a German shepherd. He admired her guts more than he was annoyed by her yapping. Le Pelleteur also realized that he had underestimated Evangeline and worse, had been caught without a back-up plan.

Lacking any better ideas, he decided to give the truth a try. "I'm a private investigator. I have been hired to investigate some thefts at Nathalie's shipping company and I wanted to talk to someone to see if any former employees could be suspects."

"Oh! I never got involved in Benoit's business affairs," she protested, too strongly in Le Pelleteur's opinion. Her emphatic denial suggested to Le Pelleteur that she was very much involved in Benoit's business affairs, or at minimum aware of the important details of those affairs. He suspected that, like many women her age, she considered it unladylike either to be involved in business or to admit to it.

"Even if you were not involved in the day-to-day operations, you must have a wealth of historical background information." He hoped Evangeline either would not notice or would not care that he was patronizing her again. Evangeline looked up, trying to think back. Le Pelleteur thought he heard her neck squeal like a rusty door hinge in a horror movie.

After a few minutes, Le Pelleteur entreated, "I am sure that anything you could tell me would be helpful."

"There was that affair Benoit had with his secretary. I've always said that horrible woman who married him drove him to it."

"Do you know her name?"

"Oh, no. After a while, all his mistresses' names ran together for me. I am sure there were some I never heard about."

Le Pelleteur waited to see if *Madame* Juneau would think of anything else. In his experience, awkward silences were a very effective tool in getting people to talk. He had trouble reading her, however. He could not tell if she felt any awkwardness.

Eventually, *Madame* Juneau offered, "Do you know how he was murdered?"

She surprised Le Pelleteur again. According to the newspaper article that Le Pelleteur read at the time, Benoit Juneau's death was determined to be accidental. "No. Do you?"

"Yes."

"I would love to hear all about it."

"It was June, 1938. Benoit was in the Lac du Flambeau area." Lac du Flambeau was about 250 kilometers northwest of Green Bay, on Highway Q29. "He was negotiating contracts he needed to start a new ice harvesting company. I told him it was the wrong time to start a business." He saw her point. The economy had taken another dip in 1937, although not as severely as it did in 1930 and '31. "Besides, there was no growth potential in ice. It is only a matter of time before ice boxes are replaced by electric refrigerators. But he never did listen to me."

Le Pelleteur could see electric refrigerators being all the rage on Bayshore Drive, but he couldn't imagine anyone in his part of town setting their heart on new kitchen appliances any time soon. He recognized that it was not necessary to debate that point, however and asked, "What happened next?"

"He ate dinner in his hotel room that night at 7:30. He ordered a steak and French fries from room service. The maid found him the next morning, blue in the face. The coroner said he choked on a piece of meat."

"I have to tell you, *Madame* Juneau, that doesn't sound like murder to me."

"Anyone could have found a bell boy costume, gone to Benoit's room with his dinner, strangled him and stuffed a bit of steak into his throat."

"What makes you think that was what happened?"

"He couldn't have choked. He always chewed his food thoroughly."

"OK, who do you think did it?"

Evangeline's voice was drowned out by the sound of the library door bursting open and Zoe Juneau storming in. She was in her 50s, about 160 centimeters tall. Her hair was too black and her lips were too red. She had oddly muscular arms, like a plumber in an evening gown and pearls bucking for a fight.

"What kind of crazy stories is she telling you?" Zoe demanded.

"Actually, *Madame* Juneau and I are having a very pleasant little conversation," Le Pelleteur replied coolly. "I don't think we're disturbing anyone. Perhaps you would like to join us? If not, would you be so kind as to give us some quiet and allow us to continue?"

"Who are you, anyway? Get out of my house, now."

"I have an appointment to speak with *Madame* Juneau. I did not realize that she needed your permission to receive visitors, but if that is the case, I would be happy to leave as soon as the taxi comes to pick me up. If you would be so kind as to allow me the use of your telephone, I could call and then sit with *Madame* Juneau until it came."

"The chauffeur will take you wherever you want to go, now." The butler appeared from nowhere to escort Le Pelleteur out of the house. Le Pelleteur did not think he could talk his way into staying any longer and so let the butler led him away.

Chapter XVII

Five minutes later, Le Pelleteur was sitting in the back seat of a late-model black Cadillac, bigger than his apartment, gliding along Bayshore Drive like a canoe through mirror-smooth water. The red leather upholstery was soft, almost creamy. Unlike the city, where the snow was heaped with street grime on every corner, the snow on the mansions' front lawns was as smooth as the Cadillac's ride, pristine and unsullied by human contact, glittering in the mid-afternoon sun. Le Pelleteur found the scene to be charming, but misleading; life here was no less dirty than it was in the city, but they kept the dirt buried under the snow and out of sight, instead of building snowbank monuments to it everywhere you looked.

He turned his attention to the chauffeur, who wore the standard chauffeur uniform—grey, with a double-breasted coat—that made him look like a toy soldier. From the back seat, Le Pelleteur could see only the back of his head and ears sticking out from under the grey cap.

"Hi there," Le Pelleteur tried to start a conversation with the back of the chauffeur's head.

"Good afternoon, sir," the chauffeur replied, with a slight Anglophone accent. Years ago, he learned that part of his job was knowing his place relative to his passengers. So, when he spoke, his tone was formal, maintaining an appropriate distance, like a blob of seaweed on the bottom of Lake Michigan looking up at a passing yacht.

"My name is Sam."

"You may refer to me as McSweeney, sir."

"I could use a cigarette. How about you, McSweeney?" Le Pelleteur tapped his red and white pack of Du Maurier cigarettes, causing four to stick out of the pack, extended it into the front seat and insisted that McSweeney take one. Although it was a breach of protocol, McSweeney accepted a cigarette, hoping it would encourage Le Pelleteur's arm to return to the back seat where it belonged. Le Pelleteur offered to light it and McSweeney declined, punching the automatic lighter in the Cadillac's dashboard.

"How long you been working this gig?"

The back of McSweeney's head did not betray the distaste he felt for Le Pelleteur's lack of refinement. "I have been in the Juneaus' employ for seventeen years, sir."

"Heck of a long time."

"Yes, sir."

"When you started working for the Juneaus, Nathalie and Denis were still living at home, right?"

"That is correct, sir."

"How long did you drive for them before they moved away from home?"

McSweeney briefly looked upward, calculating the years. "It must have been about seven years for Nathalie and nine for Denis."

"I'll bet you could tell some pretty good stories."

"Regretfully, no, sir."

"Do you mean that you don't have any good stories, or that you're holding out on me?"

"I would prefer not to discuss the matter further, sir."

Le Pelleteur leaned up, folded his arms and rested them on the top ridge of the front seat. He rested his chin on his arms. He observed McSweeney's profile, like a marble statue beginning to crumble with centuries of wear. "Why not?" Le Pelleteur inquired innocently. "It's not a trick question. I'll bet you could figure out the answer if you thought about it. Do you mean that each and every day of each and every year that you spent carting those kids around was a cakewalk and neither of them ever took you for granted, or treated you impolitely, or dismissed you as low-class Anglophone scum? Or that there was never one day in those long, grinding years when you wished you didn't have a wife and kids to feed, so you could afford to quit and try to find a job where you were treated with some small, trivial measure of respect? Or do you mean that all those things happened, but you don't want to talk to me about it out of some kind of noble but undeserved sense of loyalty to those rotten brats?"

Le Pelleteur saw discomfort in McSweeney's right eye, like he just finished eating something starting to go bad, and recognized a crack in McSweeney's defenses. "I'll make you a deal. You answer just a couple of questions and I'll sit back and let you drive the rest of the way in peace."

The look on McSweeney's face went past indigestion and started to approach food poisoning. Le Pelleteur pressed further. "Look, I'm a working stiff trying to do a job, just like you. I'm a private investigator on a case that involves Nathalie and Denis. I'm not a reporter or anything like that, so nothing you tell me will end up in the paper. I'm not asking you to betray any confidences or to start any scandals. I'm not asking you to say anything that will cost you your job. I'm just asking for a little background information. Just a little help from an unbiased observer, to get me pointed in the right direction." As he pleaded his case, Le Pelleteur took a five-*livre* bill from his wallet, folded it lengthwise and dropped it in the front seat. "Anything you tell me will stay between us and would really help me out."

McSweeney instinctively checked his rear view mirrors, like he was checking to see if anyone was eavesdropping on them. Le Pelleteur repeated, "Just a couple of questions and that will be the end of it."

McSweeney lowered his voice and slipped out of his chauffeur formality. "No promises, but kick in another fiver and tell me what you want to know."

Le Pelleteur fished his wallet out of his inside suit pocket again. "What if I told you that Denis was involved in some kind of embezzlement? How would you react?"

"If it were just a question of whether he would be willing to dip into the till, I can't see him getting too troubled by any pangs from his conscience. But if you said he was involved in something that might take more thought than getting drunk at a fancy party, I don't think he'd be up to it."

"What about Nathalie?"

McSweeney thought about the question for more than half a block, with that indigestion look back on his face and then pronounced, "No. I can't imagine Nathalie getting mixed up in anything like that." Le Pelleteur thought that he was trying too hard to sound convincing and wondered what he was trying to hide.

Chapter XVIII

McSweeny dropped Le Pelleteur off at the Bayshore *élevé* stop and Le Pelleteur started the long ride back into town. In the industrial district, brick smokestacks spewed clouds that turned from charcoal grey to rosy pink in the setting sun. In the frigid late afternoon air, the factory fumes did not rise and blow away, but rather dribbled down the side of the cream-colored chimneys. It reminded Le Pelleteur of gigantic blobs of some kind of exotic mold that had grown on something left in the refrigerator too long, crawled out into the kitchen and now wanted to go cruising in the living room looking for trouble.

By 5:30 that afternoon, Le Pelleteur had returned to the XY Building. The department store closed at 6:00 the rest of the week, but on Thursdays, it stayed open until 9:00. Outside, the sky was black by this time and the bright florescent lights suspended from the high ceiling made the exterior seem blacker. He milled around on the first floor of the building, pretending to look for something, trying to blend in with the other customers. He hated his job the most at times like this, when he was alone waiting for something to happen. That is why he usually brought a newspaper with him on stakeouts and why he wished he could read the paper there without looking out of place.

He gravitated to a table displaying several Green Bay Packer hockey sweaters, navy blue with a mustard yellow circle displaying the player's number in the middle of each chest. The team's founder, Curly Lambeau, chose those colors because they were the colors of the *Université de Notre Dame*, where he played college hockey for a year before dropping out and founding Green Bay's NHL franchise. Le Pelleteur remembered debating with Sophie the previous October, at the beginning of the hockey season, about the Green Bay Packers' uniforms. She thought any team based in Green Bay should have green uniforms. Although she had a good point, he did not admit it to her at the time. It was more fun to tell her that she clearly didn't understand sports.

While he continued to inspect the sweaters, he also thought back to when he was twelve years old, when he was one of the many kids proudly wearing Curly Lambeau's Number 1 on one of the many outdoor rinks that sprout up in back yards and school playgrounds across Québec every winter. Suddenly, from the dark blue sea of Packer sweaters jumped out a red and white sweater of their arch rival, the Sault Saint Marie Greyhounds, like a spy that had infiltrated the Packer sweaters and had been lying in wait for the right moment to strike. He pitied the poor, humiliated boy whose mother would buy that red Greyhound sweater and expect him to wear it in public.

Meanwhile, he kept one eye on the elevators on the other side of the floor, beyond Ladies' Formal Wear. He was waiting for everyone at the shipping company to leave for the day, so he could let himself into their offices with the key that Nathalie Juneau gave him that morning and search the offices. After 15 minutes, the last employee, Jacques Cloutier, emerged from the elevators in a beige trench coat, dark brown fedora and matching brown and beige *ceinture fléchée* and carrying two large heavy-looking books, possibly ledgers. Le Pelleteur strongly suspected that those books were the evidence he wanted to find and started to squeeze past the other customers towards the exit.

Cloutier beat Le Pelleteur to the revolving door by about 30 seconds. By the time the detective reached the street, Cloutier had melted into the throng of top-hatted businessmen streaming in the direction of the elevated train stop four blocks away. Le Pelleteur followed the crowd, hoping that Cloutier was among the multitude heading for the *élevé* and that he could catch up with Cloutier before he got onto a train and was lost.

While Cloutier was waiting for the light to change on the corner of *L'Avenue Vaudreuil* and *La Rue Mercier*, Le Pelleteur gained enough ground to locate him in the crowd, but could not get close enough to stop him. On the next block, as the streetlights and the steel supports of the elevated train tracks cast black shadows into the street, swallowing cars whole like an evil jellyfish gulping plankton, Le Pelleteur inched imperceptibly closer to Cloutier as the glacier of commuters inched along the sidewalk. They crept past flashing marquee lights of the Rialto Theater, showing *Melody Ranch* with Gene Autry, the most recent example of a Hollywood cowboy movie dubbed into French. While Autry's movies were tremendously popular where they were made, the Republic of Texas, and making inroads into the United States and the Dominion of Oregon, they had not gathered a huge following in Québec. Le Pelleteur thought that the problem was the dubbing process, which made Autry sound like Le Bolduc, the *Québécoise* folk singer, choking on half a kilo of prairie dust. While Le Bolduc's folk songs were a little out of place coming from a cowboy's mouth, the accompanying violin and accordion music seemed more incongruous coming from Autry's guitar.

Cloutier continued to be swept along with the crowd down *L'Avenue Vaudreuil* towards the *élevé* station, past the St. Francis Xavier Cathedral, where, in spite of the newspaper stories proclaiming that the economy was turning around, young men in worn coats still lined up for some hot soup and a couple slices of bread. On the next block, Cloutier floated past the *Dupuis Frères* department store, where there was a polished oak cabinet floor radio receiver on display in the window. During this time, Le Pelleteur made steady but painstakingly slow progress on

Cloutier, fighting through the current of the crowd, like swimming upstream in the Menominee River during spring thaw.

Seconds before Cloutier turned into the station, Le Pelleteur grabbed his arm and pulled him out of the torrent. "Jacques, my old friend," the detective shouted as a train rattled overhead. "It seems like years since I've seen you. How long has it been?"

Cloutier was not sure whether to be confused, annoyed, or terrified. "We met for the first time this morning."

"And I've missed your witty repartee all afternoon." Le Pelleteur glanced briefly further down *L'Avenue Vaudreuil* and noticed an illuminated blue and white sign promoting *Jean Talon* beer hanging over the door of a tavern at the end of the block. "You have to let me buy you a drink. You can tell me all about the new books that you're reading." Le Pelleteur poked his finger at the ledgers Cloutier was clutching tightly to his chest. Cloutier's worst fears had come true. He considered running, but he had nowhere to go and besides, Le Pelleteur was still firmly clutching his bicep. "All right," he shouted in frustration and then whispered, "just keep your voice down and I'll tell you everything."

Chapter XIX

Le Pelleteur escorted Cloutier past a block of dark, nondescript storefronts. The streetlights, or at least the ones that worked, turned the snowbanks into some kind of extraterrestrial landscape from a *Flash Gordon* serial and cast black shadows on the cracked sidewalk. The tavern was on the corner under the electric beer sign, a brown, windowless cinderblock cube. That short walk contrasted with the previous three blocks between the XY Building and the *élevé* station, choked with white-collar workers trying to go home. Here, on the other side of the tracks, the street was empty, except for a handful of men in suits who for various reasons were heading towards the *Jean Talon* beer sign to avoid going home that Thursday evening.

They stepped into a square, utilitarian room, occupied by a horseshoe bar in the middle and a few small tables around the edges. Clearly, the clientele came here to drink, not for the sophisticated or unique atmosphere. The place was almost devoid of decoration, as if buying artwork might divert resources away from the liquor supply, or visual stimulation might distract someone from drinking. The only exception was a small painting of some kind of stylized art nouveau peacock. Its neck was too long for its body and was twisted and contorted to keep the bird's head in the frame. Le Pelleteur thought the bird might be the last remnant of a valiant but misguided and futile battle fought 20 years previously by a forgotten bartender's wife who wanted to "class up the joint a little bit."

Le Pelleteur led Cloutier to a corner table. A middle-aged waitress asked what they wanted, in a way that made it clear she really wasn't paying attention to anything they said. She had already had a long night and the evening was just getting started. Le Pelleteur asked for gin. Cloutier ordered a *Jean Talon* lager, one of Québec's most popular beers. It was named in honor of the *intendant de la Nouvelle-France*, who, according to the ads, started producing Québec's first commercial beer in 1664 to quench the thirst of grateful *Habitants*. In fact, he did it to improve the colony's balance of trade by discouraging the *Habitants* from buying imported wine.

After the waitress left, Le Pelleteur started grilling Cloutier. "An accountant sneaking out of the office after everyone else has left, carrying two ledger books. My guess is one book is real and the other is fake. That looks to me like a picture in the dictionary next to the definition of 'embezzlement'."

"Do you have children, *Monsieur* Le Pelleteur?" Not waiting for Le Pelleteur's reply, Cloutier announced wistfully, "I have four, all grown up. Ten grandchildren. Used to be eleven."

When he was with the Bunko Squad, Le Pelleteur heard at least a hundred suspects claim they had to perpetrate whatever fraud they were caught committing because they needed food for their poor starving babies. Those "poor babies" were never really in danger of starving. Most of the time, if they existed at all, they were teenagers running scams of their own. Cloutier's reference to children almost completely obliterated any chance that Le Pelleteur might feel something resembling sympathy towards him. Then, the accountant did not launch into some harrowing tear-jerker of a story, as the detective expected. Instead, Cloutier became silent. Le Pelleteur assumed that the silence was another ploy, intended to grow awkward until Le Pelleteur felt compelled to break it, thereby losing a point in some trivial power struggle. Le Pelleteur decided not to play the game and waited for Cloutier to resume his little melodrama.

Eventually, Cloutier pronounced, "Polio." One word. He did not fabricate a long, tortured, melodramatic story. He spoke with authority, like the weight carried by that word needed no embellishment. Le Pelleteur started to grow impatient. "My granddaughter died of polio," Cloutier explained.

"I'm sorry for your loss," Le Pelleteur offered, still doubting that he ever had a granddaughter, "but I still don't see how any of this relates to your shady accounting practices."

"I know all grandparents think their grandchildren are special, but my Marie stood out. You remember what it was like a few years ago. You read the newspaper. It was full of unemployment stories. You look out the window and all you see were breadlines and Taschereauvilles." "Taschereauville," named for President Duplessis's predecessor, was Québec's answer to "Hooverville" in the United States, vacant lots where men who had lost their jobs and their homes struggled to survive. "It was like a gigantic vacuum cleaner kept sucking all the light out of the world, year after year after year," Cloutier continued. "But it didn't matter when Marie was around. She created a little oasis of brightness that followed her wherever she went. Without even trying. Without even knowing she was doing it. Her mother was my youngest daughter. She and her parents lived with us after they got married, until they could afford a place of their own. Because of the Depression, they stayed with us a lot longer than they planned, so I was lucky enough to have Marie brighten my life every day she was alive.

"In December 1934, she was six and a half. At the beginning of the month, she still believed in Santa Claus. Her oasis grew a little bigger, burned a little brighter. All the glitter and sparkle of the decorations seemed old-hat and boring until you saw them reflected in her big blue eyes. She was wound up like toy car speeding along the floor and bouncing off the walls. I got a kick out of just watching her go. It was almost like I was six and getting to see her was my Christmas present.

"A week and a half later, she was in a wheelchair, like a ball of jelly. By Christmas Eve, she was in an iron lung. The oasis that followed her was snuffed out like a little candle. She took it like a trooper. Never complained about anything. But you could see she was in pain. It was hard to watch, seeing how much she hurt and knowing that you couldn't do anything about it. I just felt useless, like nothing I ever did in my life mattered anymore. When my kids were growing up, I was fixing their broken toys constantly. Each time, they acted like I had just walked on water or fed the multitudes, but all that was meaningless when I was standing there looking at Marie in that iron lung.

"She died on January 4, 1935. As hard as it was to see her in pain, it hurt more to have her gone. It was even worse to see her mother hurting and not being able to do anything to help. No matter how many times you say you're sorry, it isn't going to bring her back.

"So, when I heard that they were testing polio vaccines in New York City, I said 'This is my chance to do something.' I didn't have much in savings, but figured I could take out a loan. I talked to a few banks, with no luck. I talked to Benoit Juneau and he told me to take a hike. Said I should be grateful I still have a job. But, I had been doing the books for that jerk's shipping company for over thirty-five years at that time and I knew he was stiffing me. So, I shifted some funds around and came up with 2000 *livres* to help finance the vaccine tests."

"Let me guess," Le Pelleteur interrupted. "After you saw how easy it was, you decided to make a little donation into your own bank account and you've been, shall we say, supplementing your disposable income ever since?"

"No. I have been shifting three and a half *livres* out of my paycheck every week back to the company. In five more years, I will have repaid the money."

Le Pelleteur was stunned. In his years on the Bunko Squad, he had heard of dozens of schemes for stealing money, but he had never heard of anyone employing such a scheme to give money back. He stared at Cloutier for a long time, looking for some slight shiftiness in his eyes or some fine mist of sweat on his palms; something to confirm his suspicions that he was lying. He studied Cloutier long enough for three tired-looking men in business suits and loosened ties to come into the bar, mount their stools and start gazing sullenly into small tumblers of whiskey and ice, but Cloutier didn't crack.

Eventually, Le Pelleteur stopped waiting for Cloutier to tip his hand and started looking for holes in his story. Suddenly, Le Pelleteur was overwhelmed with horror and disgust, like someone had snuck up behind him and belted the side of his head with a rotting lake trout. "Wait a minute. Did you say polio vaccine tests in New York in 1935?"

Cloutier looked away and nodded.

"Were those the tests I read about in the *Journal*?" Le Pelleteur grew incredulous. "The tests at Temple University that ended up spreading polio instead of curing it? The tests that ended up killing half a dozen kids? You spin this fable about your noble cause that's supposed to justify your felonious embezzlement and instead you bankrolled a child-slaughtering operation?"

Cloutier did not say anything in response. He just started sobbing quietly. Le Pelleteur saw that the tears were real. Le Pelleteur's shock melted into embarrassment. He awkwardly muttered his thanks for Cloutier's time, threw two *livres* on the table and walked briskly past the contorted peacock to the door, leaving Cloutier weeping by himself. He told himself that this was an act of kindness, that offering any sympathy to the accountant would merely draw more attention to the situation, which would be the worst thing he could do to him at that moment.

Chapter XX

After Le Pelleteur left Cloutier at the bar, he took the *élevé* home and had a dinner composed of a hotplate venison burger and three glasses of gin. Then, he listened to the Packers on the radio, losing to the Detroit Red Wings, 5 to 1, while he did calisthenics in his living room. He spent too much of his time most days sitting behind a desk or sitting in a car in motel parking lots and exercising whenever he was at home was the only way he could burn off the extra energy.

The next morning, Friday, was bright and sunny and surprisingly warm, only 10° below, Centigrade. The wind on the *élevé* platform cut through Le Pelleteur's coat like it was tissue paper. When he arrived at the office, after the obligatory theological debate with *Père* O'Shaughnessy, Le Pelleteur poured himself a hot cup of coffee and invited Sophie into his office. While she sat on the ugly floral couch, he sat on the corner of his desk. "So, what did you find in Neenah?" Le Pelleteur inquired.

"I haven't gone yet. When I talked to my mom yesterday, she had to run a few errands, so I couldn't borrow the car until this afternoon. How were things at *Le Chateau Juneau*?"

"There was a lot of running around, but not a lot of progress," he began. "McSweeney the chauffer simply confirmed our suspicions about Denis. He had to think about it for a long time before deciding to defend Nathalie. Is he hiding something about her? Did McSweeney overhear Nathalie hatch some adolescent plot years ago? If he did, would it be relevant to anything going on today? On the other hand, maybe he is keeping quiet because Nathalie has something on McSweeney? When you add it all up, McSweeney simply confirmed my opinion of Nathalie as well. I have my doubts about trusting her, but I promised her I would trust her until I had a good reason not to and I don't have a good reason yet."

Sophie was about to suggest a few reasons not to trust Nathalie, but then thought better of it. "What about Grandma Juneau?"

"That was a bigger waste of time. She insisted that she wasn't suffering from some kind of senile delusions as her family claims. I didn't get the impression that she was, but she was kind of brittle and hard to read. In any case, let's assume for the sake of argument that she was lucid and that she was wasn't lying for some reason. She said that Benoit Juneau had an affair with a secretary. He probably had several secretaries over the years. The affair, if it occurred, was either with Claire, now Nathalie's receptionist, or some other secretary. If it was another secretary, I can't see how it would be related to the insurance fraud we're investigating now. If it was Claire, what would that tell us? If she expected to get something from Benoit's will, or to get more than she got, maybe it would give her motive, but it tells us nothing about whether she actually is or isn't behind the art theft scheme we were hired to investigate.

"The other tidbit of information that Evangeline bestowed upon us," Le Pelleteur continued, "is a claim that someone murdered Benoit, grounded on an assertion that he was a diligent chewer. I think it's a lot harder to assume that this is not some kind of senile delusion, or perhaps a grief-stricken mother who can't accept that there is no one to blame for her son's death. But, if we make that assumption anyway, for the sake of argument, we have no idea who she thinks did it and no reasonably easy way to talk to her again to find out. Unless you have some brilliant insight that you would be willing to share, it looks like a dead end to me."

"Didn't Nathalie tell you the alleged art thefts started to happen shortly after she started running the shipping company, which was shortly after Benoit died?" Sophie observed. "If the death was murder, it wouldn't be too surprising if it were tied in some way to our case. Besides, if Benoit was murdered, shouldn't we care about that regardless of whether it is related to our case?"

"The short answer is that I like to save my investigative talents for paying clients. The longer answer is that I don't have much faith in Evangeline's murder theory, but to be on the safe side, let's give your father a call. Philippe can give the Lac du Flambeau *Sûreté* a call, maybe take a look at their police reports and if he thinks there's anything fishy, either he'll get to the bottom of it or we'll follow up."

"What do you think about the accountant?"

"Cloutier? He looked pretty squirrely to me at first. For the past five years, he claims he's been repaying money he stole in 1935 without getting caught? A story like that seems too good to be true. On the other hand, if you were going to make a story up, why wouldn't you make it more plausible than that? Also, if you were the master of accounting slight-of-hand that he has shown himself to be and you decided to steal some money, why wouldn't you just embezzle it, instead of complicating things with insurance fraud? And why would he admit to being involved with that polio vaccine fiasco if that wasn't true? The more I think about it, the less I like him for this caper."

"So, what's your next move?" Sophie inquired.

"Well, I have one idea left. I have a theory on how the scam was done. We know that the telephone operator in the basement of the XY Building was in on the scam, because she admitted to rerouting all my calls. So, who was on the other end of those calls? I heard fifty-two voices. They could have brought fifty-two people into the scheme, but I doubt it. The more people you have working on your con, the more chances for something to go wrong. So, it would've been better for them if they could've found someone who can do different voices – ideally, all fifty-two voices. There can't be too many people like that around and I remember meeting someone back in my Bunko Squad days who might fit the bill. I was trying to avoid looking this guy up. According to the rumors I heard, he still blames me for his most recent visit to the *Ouisconsin* Penitentiary, which happened to last two years less a day. But right now, I don't see any other options."

Chapter XXI

As Le Pelleteur started to arrange a meeting with his Bunko Squad associate, Sophie caught the Number 31 bus to the neighborhood where she grew up and walked five blocks to her parents' sky blue bungalow to borrow their car, a charcoal grey 1934 Hudson Terraplane. For what felt to Sophie like the 500th time since she learned to drive, she had to convince her mother she was not five years old, nor was she asking for permission to play hopscotch in a minefield. After Sophie explained she was just running an errand for Sam that would not be dangerous in any way, *Madame* Marleau relented. Sophie kissed her mom on the cheek and pointed the car towards Neenah.

Sophie reached her destination a little after 1:30. Neenah's iron foundry and its associated industrial blight were limited to the south side of town. The neighborhood Sophie drove through, however, looked like a typical *Ouisconsin* small town: streets lined with winter elms, their leafless winter branches dappling the sunlight, white picket fences, geodesic dome houses based on Buckminster Fuller's design and reminiscent of the wigwams of the 19th Century. She headed to the town hall. It looked like a public library, a one-story brick building with the *fleur de lis* flag of Québec flying from a pole that in warmer months was surrounded by blue and white petunias that matched the flag, but at that time was surrounded by snow like everything else within a thousand kilometers. She scampered through the cold parking lot to the front doors and then walked slowly through a granite-lined hallway looking at dark wooden doors with pebbled glass, searching for the Department of Records.

The previous day, Sophie had called the records department to ask if they could look up who was licensed to run a trap line off Highway Q41, where Sam was attacked earlier that week, only to be told that licensing information was not publicly available. She thought she might get around that policy if she asked for the information in person, while looking nonchalantly into the distance and holding a five-*livre* bill folded lengthwise between her index and middle fingers. The desk clerk told her in no uncertain terms that the information was still unavailable, like a nun who had been propositioned by a drunken sailor on shore leave, the kind of nun who made ten-year-old boys cower in Catholic grade schools. Sophie left the records office surprised that the desk clerk hadn't hit her with a ruler. She was even more surprised to find a city employee with integrity, because in Green Bay, like a wooly mammoth on a unicycle, it's not something you see every day.

By the time Sophie walked back to the car, she had thought of another line of investigation. If she couldn't identify the trapper, maybe she could identify the thief. He might know whose traps he poached and he might be willing to tell her for the five *livres* rejected by the desk clerk. Sophie's watch said 2:00. She found a little diner downtown and stopped for a warm cup of coffee. At quarter to three, she drove to the high school and found a parking spot on the street with a good view of the bike rack. She counted four blue Schwinns among the 20 in the rack. Soon after the 3:00 bell, a boy in tennis shoes as long as her forearm grabbed one of those bikes, strapped his books to a rack behind his seat and rode away. Sophie started her car and followed. She caught up to him almost immediately, slowed to match his speed and leaned over to roll down the passenger's side window.

"Pardon me," Sophie yelled while the car crawled along beside the bicyclist. He ignored her.

"Pardon me," she yelled again. "I just want to talk to you for a few minutes." He continued to ignore her. Sophie suddenly realized she was talking to a teenaged boy, the kind that was hormonally predisposed to view any request from any adult with sullen resentment. She suspected his feet were painfully cold, like a polar bear was gnawing through the canvas of his tennis shoes, but he refused to wear anything more practical because it would entail conceding to his mother's wishes. She knew the type well, growing up watching each of her three older brothers go through this phase, but she was a little surprised to find herself the adult being resented.

"I only need five minutes and I can make it worth your while if you're on the level."

"WHAT?!" he shouted impatiently into the car window, like Sophie had used the third degree on him a dozen times before.

"My name is Sophie Marleau. What's yours?"

He thought for a moment, as though it might be a trick question. "Matthieu," he finally offered.

"It's nice to meet you, Matthieu." Sophie replied, determined to be pleasant. "Would you mind giving me your last name?"

"Wapekeniew," he spat out, like it was another way to tell her to go and commit a vulgar act.

"Could you tell me where you were Monday morning before school started?" Sophie was about to explain she was working for a private investigator, not for the police and that answering her question would not get him in trouble, when his eyes lit up and he interrupted her excitedly.

"I was resetting my father's traps, when I noticed some weird old man starting to sneak up on me in the woods. He stole the pelts. I just barely got away." A chance to complain about another adult's behavior was definitely worth his time.

"Where was this, exactly?"

"Near Q41, about fifteen kilometers north of town."

"Can you tell me anything about this 'weird old man'?"

"He was French," meaning not native, "and he drove an old car from the 1920s."

It started to make sense to Sophie. Sam did not rescue the pelts from a poacher; he stole them from their rightful owner.

"Do you know if your parents filed an insurance claim for the theft?"

"I don't know. I think they said filing a claim would make their premiums go up, so they were just going to file a police report instead."

"I think your pelts might be mixed up in my case and I might be able to get them back to you, if I could talk to one of your parents."

Matthieu's disposition began to sour again as the topic of conversation shifted away from himself. He said his mother was at home and gave her directions, with an expression that suggested that the words tasted like healthy vegetables to a six-year-old. Then Matthieu rode his bicycle away, before Sophie could find the five *livres* she was planning to give him.

Chapter XXII

At ten minutes to noon, while Sophie was walking from the bus stop to her parents' house, the sky was robin's-egg blue over Little Italy, on the Left Bank of the Fox River between 84th and 92nd Streets. During the morning, the temperature had gone up to 5° below, Centigrade and the sun was warm enough to soften some of the snow compressed into the street in front of a one-story windowless building. The bottom-half of the walls were sided with Lannon Stone, the long, narrow, cream-colored, rough-hewn stone quarried about 150 kilometers south of Green Bay and popular throughout *Ouisconsin*. Above the stones, the building was painted dark brown. Above the front door was an awning proclaiming the entrance to Luigi's Pizzeria. At one time, the awning was intended to suggest that Luigi's was an eating establishment of refinement and charm, but now it was fading and beginning to fray on one side, suggesting the establishment had become much less refined and charming.

Heading towards Luigi's on *L'Avenue La Follette* was a garish orange and yellow wrecker from Druillette Chevrolet, driven by a very earnest 20-year-old man with black fingernails wearing striped overalls. His name, Robert, was spelled out in white stitching on a blue oval sewed over his heart. He was bemoaning the fact that he had done something, some incomprehensible thing, to cause his girlfriend Brigitte to stop talking to him. He beseeched his passenger, Samuel de Champlain Le Pelleteur, for wisdom and guidance. Le Pelleteur tried to be sympathetic without getting too involved.

The tow truck parked across the street from the restaurant at noon, right on schedule. Le Pelleteur pointed out a black 1939 Cadillac in the parking lot next to the restaurant, surprisingly shiny, not powdered with salt like the other cars in the lot. He asked Robert to go through the plan again. Once assured that Robert knew what to do, the detective left the truck and, while crossing the street, stepped into an ankle-deep pothole filled with bitter cold water the color of used motor oil. The shock shot up his leg like a frozen bullet and was soon replaced by a slightly disgusting, squishy sensation in his shoe.

Inside the restaurant, Le Pelleteur was confronted by a *Maitre d'* in a black tuxedo standing behind a podium. He was the kind of guy who could make you feel he was looking down on you, even if you were 20 centimeters taller than he was. He led Le Pelleteur to the middle of a sea of tables, all empty except for one in the back next to a door marked "*Privé*." At that table sat a man guarding the door, wearing a dark pinstripe suit and reading the newspaper. He looked like he could hold his own in a wrestling match with Robert's tow truck. A few seconds after the *Maitre d'* left, Le Pelleteur moved to the man's table, sat down and announced, "I would like to talk to Bernie *La Bouche*."

The guard lowered his newspaper, slower than the ice melting from Lake Michigan during spring thaw and squinted at Le Pelleteur disapprovingly. "I would like one of the waitresses here to bring me a million *livres* and sit in my lap while I count it, but that ain't going to happen, either."

"Oh, I don't know. The million *livres* might be tough, but as far as the waitress goes, I wouldn't sell myself short if I were a handsome devil like you."

The guard glowered his lack of appreciation of Sam's flattery. "There is no one here by that name," he stated firmly and then returned to his newspaper.

"Well, that's actually kind of a relief. A black 1939 Cadillac is getting towed from the parking lot and I was afraid that it belonged to Bernie." Le Pelleteur leaned back in his chair and chuckled. "Can you imagine what would happen if it *was* Bernie's car? I'd hate to have something like that happen on my watch, especially if Bernie found out that I just sat around reading the paper instead of doing something to stop it." The paper dropped and the guard's face shifted gradually from annoyance to recognition to panic. He then jumped up and quickly stumbled between the tables and out of the dining area.

Le Pelleteur threw open the door to the private room and jumped into the room shouting "Bernie," like he was jumping from behind a chair shouting "Surprise." The room was long and narrow, consisting of a bar along one wall and a large booth at the opposite end, with red leather bench seat with gold buttons in a diamond pattern. Worn, faded red velvet curtains framed the one window between the bar and the booth. *La Bouche* sat in the middle, flanked on each side by two more goons in pinstripes, bigger than the guard. *La Bouche*'s surprise at seeing Le Pelleteur was soon replaced by suspicion and curiosity as Le Pelleteur grabbed a chair and sat down at the table.

"Sammy!" *La Bouche* responded loudly in an uncanny reproduction of Le Pelleteur's voice. They both knew that *La Bouche* hated being called "Bernie" as much as Le Pelleteur hated being called "Sammy." Ever since they met, they had been in an informal series of contests to see who could be the most irritating. Their conversations usually started out reasonably pleasant, like two boxers feeling each other out in the early rounds, but *La Bouche*'s clenched teeth indicated that Le Pelleteur was off to an early led in this bout.

"How's life been treatin' you."

"A lot better since I got out of prison."

"You say that like I had something to do with it."

"Are you suggesting you did not?"

"I would say that your habit of defrauding innocent women and children probably had more to do with it than I did."

La Bouche put his hands on the table, stood up and leaned forward. He switched from his Le Pelleteur voice to James Cagney. "You know damn well I never screwed anyone who couldn't afford it, see? And I never screwed anyone who didn't have it coming, see? I don't know what you're trying to pull here and I just stopped caring, see? Boys, take care of him."

Chapter XXIII

"Let's slow down a minute, here," Sam entreated to Bernie, hoping he could talk him into calling off the muscle that he had just assigned to "take care" of Sam. "You know that I never planted evidence on you and I never beat you up just for fun, unlike a lot of guys in the Bunko Squad. We wound up on different teams, but you know that I always played the game fair. Maybe that doesn't make me your best friend ever, but I think you can spare me two minutes to hear me out, especially when I am here to do you a favor."

La Bouche raised his index finger off the table, freezing his lackeys. He pondered the situation for a couple of seconds, then smiled, sat down and chuckled quietly, in English, in an Irish brogue, "Alright, Sammy, me lad, tell me all about this grand favor you'll be wanting to do for me."

"A few days ago, I made several phone calls to several people regarding a series of art thefts. I have reason to believe that all those calls were in fact answered by one person and I suspect that it was you, because I don't know of anyone else in town who could pull that job off. As you know, I no longer work for the *Sûreté*, so I don't really care who you run your scams on anymore, as long as it isn't me. Since you targeted me this time around, though, I'm inclined to turn you in, but if you answer a few questions truthfully, I will refrain from that. That's the first part of my favor."

"You mean, there's more? Golly!" *La Bouche* gushed in his Shirley Temple voice.

"Yes, there's more. Tell me who hired you for this scam and I'll give you five *livres*."

La Bouche shifted to President Duplessis during Question Period. "Esteemed colleagues, my good and honorable friend here claims to have come before us in order to provide us a *favor*. Let us examine, for a moment, the concept of a *favor*. A favor is usually an act of kindness. Charity. Something done out of the goodness of one's heart for the benefit of a fellow human being. I put it to you in this august chamber that Sammy, our esteemed friend, has not offered us a favor. Rather, he has offered what appears to be a threat."

"At worst, it's a business proposition. If you want to call it a threat, no skin off my nose, but it still seems to me like a pretty good deal for you. Again, not something necessitating 'taking care' of me."

La Bouche leaned back, tilted his head slightly to his right, furrowed his brow and stared into Le Pelleteur's eyes. Le Pelleteur stared back. It seemed like they could stare at each other until the Packers won the Stanley Cup. Finally, *La Bouche* leaned forward and announced in a low, gravelly voice, "Twenty-five *livres*."

"That's a lot of money. I can go up to ten."

"Twenty *livres*."

"Fifteen?"

"Twenty."

"How about seventeen?"

"How about twenty and Jean-Claude here refrains from breaking your kneecaps, today."

The corner of Le Pelleteur's mouth twisted slightly, like a cat getting ready to pounce on a mouse. "Twenty and you give your answers in your normal voice." A sudden hush fell over the room, until *La Bouche* smiled and countered, still in his gravel voice, "I'll take the seventeen."

As he reached into the inner pocket of his suit coat, Le Pelleteur heard the cold, metallic click of a .357 magnum in his right ear. He slowly rolled his eyes and stared at a quietly chuckling *La Bouche*. "Jean-Claude, you can relax a little bit. Sammy, you better not make any sudden moves." Disgusted, Le Pelleteur slowly took his wallet out of the inside pocket of his suit coat with his thumb and index finger. He held the wallet up in front of Jean-Claude for a few seconds, demonstrating that it was not a pistol. He then removed three bills with pictures of Wilfrid Laurier and two with Louis-Joseph Papineau and placed them in the middle of the table. He then looked expectantly at *La Bouche* and asked, "Was it you that I was chatting with a few days ago?"

"Yeah, what of it?" *La Bouche* replied in a Brooklyn accent.

"Did you steal any of the artwork?"

"It wasn't me. You can't pin that rap on me, copper."

"Why did you spend the day pretending to be several art theft victims?"

"I was paid to."

"Who hired you?"

"Beats me, ya screw."

"If that's the best you can do, I want my money back."

La Bouche switched to a Texas drawl. "I heard tell of a newspaper want ad a-lookin' for people who could do voices. I showed up at the XY Building and met a pretty little blond-haired filly who told me about the job. She ponied up fifty *livres* cash and I took it. She never told me her name and I never asked."

"What did this 'little filly' sound like?"

"Like this." Nathalie Juneau's voice floated out from *La Bouche*'s mouth.

Le Pelleteur winced, like he dropped a dumbbell on his foot. Based on the story Nathalie spun for him in her office earlier that week, he believed she might be on the level after all. Looking back at that conversation, he felt like a sap, like someone who did something against his better judgment and was even a little surprised when he got burned by it, like someone who has just touched something with a "wet paint" sign to see if the paint is really wet, like someone who thought a person could be trusted just because they said, "Trust me."

"It was a pleasure doing business with you," Le Pelleteur mumbled distractedly as he stood up to leave. "Oh, by the way, your car was towed from the parking lot. It should be back any minute now. If there's any damage, take it to Druillette Chevrolet and have them put it on my account."

Robert was pulling into the parking lot with *La Bouche*'s Cadillac as Le Pelleteur emerged from the restaurant. He put his dry foot into another puddle as he stomped back to the wrecker.

Chapter XXIV

In Neenah, Sophie followed Matthieu's directions to 957 *Rue de l'Erable*, a forest green geodesic dome with white trim matching the ubiquitous picket fences. She parked four houses past the address, walked back and checked that the name on the mailbox was Wapekeniew. She knocked on the door and a native woman in her late 40s with a spotless apron answered. Sophie introduced herself and immediately had to assure Mrs. Wapekeniew that Matthieu had not gotten himself in trouble again. Relieved, Mrs. Wapekeniew invited Sophie in and offered her coffee. Soon, Sophie learned that her husband had already filed a police report about the stolen pelts, but she agreed to drop the charges when Sophie promised to see that the beavers were returned.

Meanwhile, in downtown Green Bay, Robert was driving his tow truck south on *La Rue Ouisconsin* past the *Journal de Green Bay* Building. The skyscraper overlooked the Fox River and was based on the results of an architectural design contest the paper ran in 1922. In subsequent years in architectural circles, it had become almost unanimous that the "winning" design paled in comparison to several submissions that were rejected and that any of those design ideas, if built, would have become one of the greatest architectural masterpieces of North America. Instead, the *Journal* chose the grey concrete gothic monstrosity it has now, its front facade embedded with stones stolen from the greatest architectural masterpieces of Europe.

Le Pelleteur brooded in the passenger's seat of the tow truck, staring at but paying no attention to the passing office buildings, replaying his conversation with Bernie *le Bouche* in his head. Earlier that week in Nathalie's office, he gave her a chance to come clean, but Bernie made it clear that Nathalie had lied to him, again. It wasn't the first time he'd been lied to. In his Bunko Squad days, he heard more lies in an average week than he did during an average Federal election. So, he thought, Nathalie's lies shouldn't stop the presses, but it felt like a big deal none-theless. It felt like a betrayal.

Le Pelleteur vowed to Nathalie Juneau that he would turn her in to the *Sûreté* or the insurance companies if he caught her in a lie. As he was angrily marching across the Luigi's Pizzeria parking lot, he snarled to himself that turning her in was too good for her. He wanted her impris-oned in some medieval dungeon and he wanted to be the one to shackle her arms to the cell wall. As Robert drove through downtown Green Bay, Le Pelleteur's resolve softened. He still wanted to trust her, or rather, he still wanted her to be someone he could trust. He started to defend her to himself. She might have had some reasonable explanation for her actions, although he couldn't imagine what that explanation could be. During the last six blocks of the trip, Le Pelleteur wondered whether she should be blamed for betraying him – whether it was more his fault for cautiously trusting her in the first place.

Robert dropped Le Pelleteur in front of a four-story brick building near the intersection of *La Rue Ouisconsin* and *L'Avenue La Salle*, a 50-year-old testament to the proposition that fake Roman decor on the front of a building does not make up for the lack of an elevator. The driver thanked the private eye for talking to him about his girlfriend and re-minded him that his car would be ready at the end of the day. As Robert drove away, Le Pelleteur clambered over the small glacier of dirty ice deposited by the snowplows on the curb over the course of the winter and entered the building. He scaled the stairs to the fourth-floor local office of the Mutual of Duluth Insurance Company to the tune of radiators clanging on each landing. The wooden railing was wider than Le Pelleteur's hand with his fingers spread out. Millions of footsteps had worn a pattern into the stone composite stairs.

George-Etienne Shapiro constituted the Green Bay Office of Mutual of Duluth. He was about 20 years older than Le Pelleteur, half a meter shorter and about 20 kilograms heavier. His black hair was beginning to thin. His walrusy moustache was beginning to turn grey. At a little after 2:00, he was finishing a late lunch. Crumbs from his deli sandwich stuck in his mustache, but then again, it always looked like there was some kind of food stuck in it. He sat behind a small desk surrounded by filing cabinets in a strangely shaped five-sided office. A corner of the building had been cut away for the *élevé* tracks that ran centimeters from the window.

"Le Pelleteur, you deadbeat. Let me guess; you haven't put the bite on me for six weeks and you're starting to get the DTs."

"Hello, there, Shapiro. Yes, I am doing very well. Please tell me how things are going for you." Le Pelleteur answered with sarcastic sweetness.

"Oh, shove it, Le Pelleteur. It's been a long week, I got three hours and nineteen minutes to get through before the weekend and I would relish spending that time putting up with your guff as much as I would trying to chew through a brick. I know you're here to argue about your poacher. You know the Company won't pay you unless you save it from paying a claim or actually recover some money. Why dontcha gimme a break?"

"I stopped a poacher. That's going to save your Company from paying a claim."

"No one's made a claim yet, so you can't take credit for stopping a payment."

Le Pelleteur felt a brief urge to pound the crumbs out of Shapiro's moustache with his fist, then remembered why he came there. "All right, we can save this argument for next week. I got something better for you now. I have a client who's been robbing you blind."

"Well, you've been around long enough to know how this works, too. You need more than just an unsupported accusation. You need to give us some evidence that will stand up in court." Le Pelleteur described his dealings with Nathalie and Bernie *La Bouche* for the past week, without naming names. He summarized, "So, someone went through a lot of trouble to arrange for me to talk to a lot of fake buyers and sellers. That tells me there must be something fishy going on."

"Now, let me get this straight." The insurance agent leaned back smugly in his wooden swivel chair and interleaved his short stubby fingers across his mustard-stained brown plaid necktie. "Somebody you won't name here came to you out of the blue and paid you one hundred *livres* to investigate a series of thefts that never took place, then conspired with other unnamed individuals to trick you into thinking that the thefts actually happened?"

"That's about the size of it."

"What the Hell am I supposed to do with a cock-and-bull story like that?" Shapiro inquired, in a strangely deadpan tone, as if he was pointing out a logical flaw in Le Pelleteur's reasoning.

"Where do you get off calling it a cock-and-bull story?" Le Pelleteur raised his voice and began to reconsider punching Shapiro in the chops.

"Don't get so excited, Le Pelleteur. I believe you. In fact, I have a hunch I know who you're talking about. One of our clients is a shipping company and it's been hit too often to be a coincidence. I've already sent a memo to the Head Office recommending an investigation. Besides, you've never lied to me, yet. You're a greedy little pain in the ass, but you're not dishonest. My problem is, I don't think a jury will buy your story after the judge has finished poking holes in it. The first hole is, if you're committing insurance fraud, you usually try to keep it quiet, not pay someone to investigate it."

Le Pelleteur stood motionless for a second, then slowly nodded his head, like a white flag reluctantly admitting defeat. "Fair enough. Maybe the story is a little hard to believe." Le Pelleteur thought silently for a few more seconds and asked, "How about giving me a hand? Could you take a look at my list of stolen artwork, see if anything rings a bell?"

Shapiro reached for the list. He laid the list on his desk, studied it for a minute, then announced, "This one. Bierstadt's *Among the Sierra Nevada Mountains*." He was tapping his cigar butt of an index finger at the list on his desk, almost like some kind of mnemonic device. "Some banker type in the States, New York City, reported this taken in a robbery about a year ago. The police investigated, but never found any robber. We were about to cut a check about three months later, when the shipper reported the same piece missing. We looked into that and found the banker was never robbed. He sold the piece. Even signed a bill of sale."

"Any idea what happened to the painting during those three months?" Le Pelleteur asked, puzzled.

"It changed hands three more times, each time with a bill of sale. We were the insurer for each shipment, so it was pretty easy for us to track that down."

Le Pelleteur thought silently for a few more seconds. Le Pelleteur was not surprised to find that each shipment of the Bierstadt was insured on a case-by-case basis. It was a rare work of art, not some run-of-the-mill piece of merchandise from a mail-order catalogue. It would carry a unique risk of loss and so he could see why Mutual of Duluth would not cover such risks in a general insurance policy. It seemed odd, however, to see the painting shipped so often in a three-month period. He could understand a dealer buying it and immediately reselling it, but this painting changed hands three times in three months.

Le Pelleteur then again asked if he could look at Shapiro's files. Shapiro grunted his acquiescence. Le Pelleteur quickly opened the file drawer marked "J," and found the manila folders labeled as part of the Juneau Company's accounts. He sat down on the floor and analyzed those files over the next three hours, pausing occasionally to discuss the state of the Packers with Shapiro. He was surprised to find that each shipment on his list was bought and sold two or three times before going missing, just like the Bierstadt. It seemed that each piece was sent on its own little odyssey. There were a total 115 insurance policies, one for each leg of the journey that each shipment travelled. Knowing that the last leg of each work's journey was fake, Le Pelleteur figured that at least some of the other shipments were falsified as well. It looked to Le Pelleteur like someone, probably Nathalie, had gone through a lot of effort to manufacture a paper trail for each piece of art. Although he did not have a complete picture of the travels of any particular piece, he noticed that twelve pieces passed through the *Le Studio d'Art Indigène*, at 2257 *La Rue Manuel Lisa* in St. Louis. Le Pelleteur returned the files to their drawer at around a quarter to five. He thanked Shapiro as he left, promising to follow up on one or two things and to get back to him the following week. Shapiro muttered in reply something between a grunt and a moan.

Chapter XXV

Le Pelleteur descended the flights of stairs from Shapiro's office and headed toward the nearest *élevé* stop, over ten blocks away. He walked through an ill-defined neighborhood, between the skyscrapers of the downtown *Boucle* and the tractor and motorcycle factories of the industrial district. This part of town was composed primarily of brick buildings with broken windows: derelict plumbing supply wholesalers and tool and die cutters where, before they went out of business, they made parts for machines used to make other parts for other machines. Between the buildings were vacant lots, former Taschereauvilles, now uninhabited, filled with the remains of their dwellings, discarded scraps of sheet metal and cardboard. A few former residents found work. The rest followed the path taken by fur traders for over 300 years, from the Fox River, to the *Ouisconsin* River and then to the Mississippi, in search of better prospects or, barring that, warmer weather.

None of this mattered to Le Pelleteur at the time. Getting a break in the case left Le Pelleteur in a good mood, or rather, the least bad mood he had been in for three or four months. He had a little hop in his step as he sauntered along sidewalk and planned his trip to the art gallery in St. Louis. He did not notice the dusk slowly enveloping the street. He did not notice anything particularly interesting about the sidewalk, the decaying buildings around him, or the elbow-height snowbank to his left. About four blocks from the *élevé* station, as he was entering the *Boucle* and passing another unremarkable debris-filled vacant lot, he noticed only that the late afternoon cold was starting to penetrate his cheeks. He picked up his pace a little and lit a Du Maurier cigarette, more for the warmth than the nicotine.

A gun shot quickly drew his attention, however.

He felt ice crystals rain down on him before he heard the thunderous crack of a large handgun. His head spun around and his eyes darted to a crater in the snowbank about half a meter behind him. He dove over the snowbank, landing awkwardly on the hood of a blue 1936 Chrysler Airflow import and rolled into the street. He poked his head up as much as he dared and scanned the perimeter of the vacant lot, but could not determine where the shot came from. Another shot echoed through the neighborhood and the snowbank erupted into another shower of ice crystals. A third bullet shattered the front windshield of the Chrysler.

Le Pelleteur ran as fast as he could while crouched down awkwardly beside the row of cars parked along *L'Avenue La Salle*. A few meters past the vacant lot was a gap in the line of parked cars opening up onto an alley. Garbage cans formed an obstacle course along the length of the alley and several thick, white, smooth layers of ice lined the ground. Le Pelleteur went down on his hands and knees and peeked around the rear fender of the car parked next to the alley opening, a 1935 Citroën. He finally saw his would-be assailant, a large man in a black overcoat and a matching homburg hat, about ten car lengths away and closing fast.

Le Pelleteur quickly broke a piece of compacted ice from the bumper of the Citroën, about the size of his hand. He stood up and threw it at the gunman's head, who ducked easily out of the way. In the second it took for the gunman to straighten up and take another shot, Le Pelleteur was already sliding down the alley, using his shoes like skates. He jumped into a doorway, a rectangular hole in a concrete wall barely deep enough to conceal his body, just as his would-be killer entered the alley.

The detective heard a large body slip and fall to the ground, knocking over a garbage can. A few seconds later, he heard another heavy thud, followed by barely audible muffled cursing. He tried the door and found it locked, as he heard another thud and louder cursing, not in French. As time went on, the gunman sounded like a foul-mouthed fish flopping around in the bottom of a canoe. The noise allowed Le Pelleteur to gauge his assailant's progress down the alley, while he came up with a plan.

When the gunman sounded close to Le Pelleteur's doorway, the detective jumped out and grabbed the gunman's right arm with his right hand. Then Le Pelleteur spun to his left, forcing the gunman to point the gun away from him and slamming his back into the gunman's chest. The gunman lost his already unsteady footing and landed flat on his back, Le Pelleteur laying on top of him face up. Le Pelleteur continued to point the assailant's gun hand away from him and pounded his face with his left elbow until he felt he had stopped moving.

Le Pelleteur sat up, turned around and punched the hulking stranger in the face, like a slap shot off a goalie's forehead, just to make sure he was unconscious. He then snatched the gun away and rifled through the gunman's pockets for identification. He had none. The only things he found were a wallet containing six *livres* and a box of bullets. Le Pelleteur put the gun, a Luger, in the inside pocket of his suit coat, stepped over the man on the ground and started to slide his way out of the alley the way he came in.

Suddenly a bright light shone above. In the street at the end of the alley, the streetlight had come on. Night was falling; the sky was slate grey and the last traces of pale yellow were fading from the western sky. Le Pelleteur looked back at the gunman, sprawled out on the ground like a can of spilt paint. A pencil-thin trickle of blood had started to crawl out from beneath his head across the white ice sheet.

"*Batard*," Le Pelleteur announced, like he was simply informing the unconscious body of a fact rather than expressing any anger or frustration. "You tried to kill me, remember? You started this. Why should I care if you freeze to death tonight?" He stood in the alley for several seconds, like he was waiting for an answer. Finally, he came back, took the six *livres* for himself and dragged the man back to the street. Once he was on fairly clear pavement, he rolled the body up onto his shoulders as he learned in the *Sûreté*. This body was muscular, dense, surprisingly heavier than the cheating husband that he had carried across the motel parking lot almost a week earlier. Le Pelleteur carried him over his shoulder the remaining three blocks to the *élevé* stop, asked the attendant to call an ambulance and ran up the stairs to the platform as quickly as he could.

Chapter XXVI

On the *élevé* platform at *La Gare de la Rue Ohieau*, Sam ran to the public telephone and called the operator, who connected him to the police. He reported the shooting on *La Rue Ouisconsin* to a bored desk sergeant who asked him if he was still under fire. "No, I'm not. Sorry to interrupt your busy evening with something as mundane as a shooting in the streets of Green Bay that unfortunately is no longer in progress." The desk sergeant gave no indication he noticed the sarcasm. He told Le Pelleteur to come into the police station to make a statement and hung up.

The detective listened to the dial tone for a few seconds and then hung up the telephone. He was too disgusted to get too angry, but wondered if the situation might pique the sergeant's interest a little more if the bullets were flying past the desk sergeant's head while he was walking down the street. He fished a coin out of his pocket and called Sophie to let her know that he was not coming into the office anymore that evening, finishing the call just as the *élevé* train came into the station. Le Pelleteur took the train to his mechanic's garage and picked up his car just before it closed. He then drove to the police station to give his statement about the shooting, drove to Johnny Blood's for supper and went home. He found a parking spot on the street only a block away from his apartment, next to a one-and-a-half meter rampart of compressed snow, ice and various layers of street grime scraped up by various snowplows. The single streetlight that was not burned out cut a white streak of glare at an angle across the frozen pavement.

By 9:00, he had finished his exercise routine, poured himself a glass of gin, put a Robert Johnson record on the phonograph and pulled down the Murphy bed. Lying on the bed was more comfortable than sitting on any of his chairs. He had started to try to process the events of the afternoon when he heard a knock on the door. He opened it and found Philippe Marleau, Sophie's father and his former partner from his Bunko Squad days, and Guy Mallette, Philippe's partner since he moved to the *Brigade criminelle* and started investigating homicides. Mallette was a large, bulky man wearing a cheap brown suit and a self-satisfied smirk on his face. He was generally a decent cop and generally a decent man, but he was the kind of man who reached conclusions a little too quickly and reconsidered them a little too slowly. Long ago, he concluded he despised Le Pelleteur with a deep, burning loathing that Le Pelleteur never fully comprehended. The detective assumed that part of it was based on Mallette's suspicions that he was on the take when he was on the Bunko Squad and part was jealousy, similar to that a wife might feel for her husband's former girlfriend. Le Pelleteur found him worthy of the same disdain he reserved for other narrow-minded and judgmental acquaintances, such as *Père* O'Shaughnessy. However, unlike O'Shaughnessy, who was too old and weak to defend himself in a fight, Le Pelleteur had no compunction against dropping his gloves with Mallette.

Because Le Pelleteur did not see Marleau every day as he had when they worked together, the effects of age on Marleau were more noticeable, in his eyes more than anything else. At one time, those eyes had seen it all before and knew how to handle it. Now, those eyes had seen it all before and had grown tired of putting up with it.

"Hi, Sam."

"Hi, Phil."

"Mind if we come in for a few minutes?"

Sam saw in his former partner's face that he had bad news. "This isn't a social call, is it?"

"No, Sam, I'm afraid it's not," Marleau offered reluctantly.

"You wouldn't have happened to bring a warrant with you, did you?"

Mallette stepped uncomfortably close to Le Pelleteur's chest. "We can get one if we have to, but it would go a lot easier for you if you co-operated."

"Mallette, this isn't the first time I have had to deal with you and your massive intellectual prowess and I know that I'm going to need to explain everything three times before you start to catch on. So, don't fool yourself. No matter what I do, it is not going to go easy for me."

"We didn't come here for your smart talk," Mallette snarled.

"Too bad. That means I'll have to put up with your stupid talk."

"Very funny. Let's see how funny you are after a night or two in a holding cell."

"Philippe, subtle though he may be, your pet gorilla is making threats. You might want to put him on a tighter leash before he gets him-self into a situation he can't handle." While he spoke to Philippe, Le Pel-leteur stared at Mallette and scowled.

"Sam, this is serious," Philippe intoned. "We need to talk to you about a murder."

"That's a shame," Le Pelleteur replied, turning to Philippe. "Kong and I were just starting to get along. Who was killed?"

"An insurance agent named George-Etienne Shapiro. Ever heard of him?" Mallette inquired rhetorically. "We got an anonymous tip about thirty minutes ago. A man said he heard two shots from Shapiro's office at about 4:45 this afternoon and saw you leave his office just after the shots were fired."

The news left the detective slightly stunned. He had worked with the insurance agent enough to consider him a friend. "I was in his office this afternoon, but when I left, he was just as alive and surly as ever."

"A likely story," Inspector Mallette chimed in.

Le Pelleteur ignored him and spoke to Philippe. "Wait a minute. This anonymous tip came in almost four hours after the fact? Doesn't that strike you a little strange? After all, this guy claimed he saw me in an office building. He shouldn't need four hours to find a telephone."

"Maybe it took him four hours to decide to get involved," Mallette offered.

"Did he speak with an accent? Your anonymous tip could be the same man that tried to kill me this afternoon." Le Pelleteur repeated the statement he gave at the police station earlier that evening. Philippe's jaw dropped, shocked by the attempt on his friend's life. Mallette was not shocked; he simply rejected the story as ridiculous. He picked Le Pelleteur's telephone up and muttered into it for a few seconds.

"I just talked to Gustafsen. He's the Desk Sergeant tonight, but he started at 9:00."

"I gave my statement to Turcotte," Sam explained.

"Gustafsen sent someone to look for him. If he hasn't left the station house yet, he'll call back in a few minutes and tell us if your story checks out or not. In the meantime, how about you stop acting like a *batard* and let us search the place."

Marleau intoned, like a cop letting a speeder go with just a warning, "Sam, if you don't let him search the place, you're going to have to be polite to him while he's waiting for his phone call. Offer him a drink, maybe even talk to him."

Le Pelleteur gave Marleau a small, sarcastic smile in response to his small, sarcastic joke. "OK, you win. Phil, if you want something to drink, help yourself to the ice box. Mallette, if you feel a burning need to search the place, go ahead, but try not to make too much of a mess." Marleau took the three-step journey to the kitchen while Mallette started poking around the living room. When Marleau returned with a bottle of Pepsi, he noticed the burlap sack full of dead beavers tied to the fire escape. Just as Marleau started to ask about the sack, however, Mallette thought he saw Le Pelleteur make some threatening gesture. He slammed the detective onto the kitchen table, holding him down and twisting his arm behind his back. Two seconds later, Le Pelleteur elbowed Mallette in the ribs with his free arm, causing Mallette to loosen his grip and enabling Le Pelleteur to break free and wrestle him down to the floor.

Marleau looked at Le Pelleteur with tired, pleading eyes. "What kind of trouble are you trying to cause now?"

"Your partner attacked me. I defended myself."

"A murder charge isn't bad enough? Do you also want 'Does not play well with others' on your permanent record?"

"Of course, you have to follow your leads, even baloney from idiot anonymous informants. But that does not mean that I have to put up with getting pushed around by this animal."

The telephone ring interrupted them. Mallette shouldered Le Pelleteur out of his way and walked across the room to pick up the phone. He said "uh-huh" a few times, hung up and turned to his partner. "Well, Le Pelleteur was at the Station when he said he was and he gave the same story he gave us. He also handed in a Luger that he said this alleged assailant used to shoot up the town this afternoon. Turcotte also said he walked the gat down to the coroner after his shift and the coroner told Turcotte that the insurance man's gunshot wounds were consistent with a Luger. So, this jackass," Mallette jerked his head in Le Pelleteur's direction, "could be telling the truth, or he could have plugged Shapiro and then come into the Station with a load of hooey to cover his tracks."

"You can't be serious!" exclaimed Sam.

Detective Marleau sighed. "I don't like it either, but if we don't take you in for further questioning now it looks like we are giving you special favors."

"That's right. We can't play favorites," Mallette crowed.

"I'll tell you what. I'll come along quietly if that one over there," Sam proposed, pointing at Mallette, "can make some effort not to piss me off until we get to the station house and the official interrogation starts."

Philippe asked Detective Mallette if he could behave himself and Mallette promised he would. Le Pelleteur called Sophie at her apartment to ask her to get in touch with his lawyer, told Philippe his daughter said hello and was led away.

Chapter XXVII

While Le Pelleteur was spending the afternoon perusing insurance records in George-Etienne Shapiro's office, Sophie was driving from Neenah back to Green Bay. By ten minutes to six, Sophie had returned her parents' car and had taken the bus back to the office, where she sat at her desk under the gentle buzz of the bright florescent lights, surrounded by her philodendron forest and the University's morbid, blood-stained religious art. The sun had set and the window to Sophie's back revealed nothing but inky blackness. She had just finished the next-to-last chapter of her textbook and was debating whether to try to finish reviewing the book before she went home. She had read almost as much of *Electro-magnetic Fields* as she could stand for one day. Alternatively, enduring the bitter cold night *en route* to a lonely supper in an empty apartment was less than enticing. She recently purchased the French translation of a new Charlie Chan novel from a mail-order house in Martinique, but unfortunately, her shipment was at least three days away. The closest thing to entertainment for her that evening would be re-reading one of the many old Inspector Maigret detective novels she kept in her apartment, or listening to the mindless melodrama of *Un Homme et son Peche* on the radio.

The telephone rang. It was Sam checking in from the *élevé* platform to tell Sophie he wasn't coming back to the office that evening. Living vicariously through Sam's daily adventures was one of the biggest perks of the job for Sophie. His decision not to come back to the office eliminated the last reason for Sophie to stay any longer. She quickly told her boss she found out who the beaver pelts belonged to, hung up the telephone, put her coat on and went home.

Sophie's apartment was not much bigger than Sam's, but it seemed more nicely furnished. Most of her furniture was hand-me-downs from her parents or her older brothers, but she found a way to make it look like it all fit together. She ate dinner and was about one-third of the way through *Maigret on the Riviera* when she received Sam's call from his apartment.

Sophie immediately found her telephone book and looked up the number for Sam's lawyer and former law school classmate, Stephane Henderson and called to tell him about Sam's emergency. "Emergencies are for those who pay their legal bills on time," the attorney replied condescendingly, as if he thought almost everything he said needed to be explained slowly. "Advise *Monsieur* Le Pelleteur that I will be available to represent him upon such time that I am adequately compensated for the representation I have provided in the past." Sophie explained that she would pay his bill if he would give her a ride to Sam's office, so she could find Sam's business checkbook.

Stephane Henderson spent his life believing himself cursed by his great-great-great grandfather's name. Josiah Henderson was among the hordes of Americans that flooded into East Louisiana, the region between the Appalachian Mountains and the Mississippi River, in the 1790s and early 1800s. After twenty years of trying to fight that flood, in 1812, France gave up and sold the part of that territory south of the *Rivière Ohieau* to the United States, as part of the treaty in which the United States agreed to enter the North American theater of the Napoleonic Wars on France's side. In addition, France designated the Wabash River Valley as a separate colony north of the *Ohieau* and tried to encourage American settlers to migrate there. As a result, by 1940, the Region of *Indianie Sud-Ouest* had established English as its official language and adopted local laws based on English Common Law and there were small communities scattered throughout the area that would become southern Québec where the majority of residents continued to speak English. However, Josiah's second son married into a *Québécois* family and all of his descendants, including Stephane, now spoke French as their first language. Many, including Stephane, could not speak English at all. Nevertheless, Stephane Henderson was convinced his Anglophone name condemned him to a second-class existence in *La République Québécoise* and limited his clientele to people like Le Pelleteur who demanded his services in the middle of the night and yet always paid their bills late.

It was 10:30 by the time Sophie and the attorney arrived at the 28th District Police Station. While Henderson was working to extricate Sam from his interrogation, Sophie tried to cool her heels in the Station's public waiting room, a grey cavernous space decorated with uncomfortable wooden chairs and a bulletin board with "wanted" posters. The room was empty, except for Sophie, another woman her age, clearly worried and a man in his 50s, clearly frustrated. The slight hum of the fluorescent lights might have been comfortably familiar, even relaxing, in Sam's outer office, but this hum gave her a headache. She spent the time alternating between pretending to enjoy talking with the Desk Sergeant, who claimed to remember meeting her when she was 11 and visiting her father, pacing the floor nervously and watching the thin red second hand crawl painfully slowly around the clock hanging on the wall opposite the bulletin board.

Chapter XXVIII

The interrogation ended about 12:30, which felt to Sophie like long enough for half her hair to turn grey. Henderson kept Le Pelleteur from getting arrested, but he was still a suspect in the Shapiro murder. They walked together into the waiting room, Le Pelleteur thanking his attorney profusely and Henderson telling his client to go to Hell. Sophie ran up and threw her arms around Sam like he'd just finished doing hard time. After he escaped her octopus-like grip, he tried again to thank his attorney for his help. Instead, he watched him walk out of the building muttering something about ungrateful clients who have him running all over town in the middle of the night. Sam then realized that Henderson was not going to give them a ride home. He walked to the payphone on the wall and called for a taxi.

After a few minutes, Sophie and Sam put their coats on and went into the frigid night to wait for their cab. While they walked gingerly through the icy police station parking lot, Sam lit a Du Maurier cigarette and Sophie asked incredulously why he had been taken into custody. Sam recounted the events of the previous 12 hours while they were huddled in a small radius around a lamp post, beyond which everything was black and murky, as their toes went numb.

The Checker cab showed up 20 minutes later. Sam held Sophie's hand as she struggled to maintain some dignity stumbling over one of the snowbanks lining every street in the city. Once in the cab, Sophie asked about the interrogation. "Just what you would expect," Le Pelleteur said off-handedly. "They asked me where I was this afternoon. I told them I was busy getting shot at. They asked me again and I told them again and again, over and over. Your father was the 'Good Cop.' They kept that up until they got tired and let me go. So, they didn't arrest me, but they told me not to leave the jurisdiction."

"So, what's our next move?"

"Leave the jurisdiction."

Sophie sat silently, composing her thoughts and choosing her words carefully. Then she made a fist and thumped her boss in the chest. "What the Hell's wrong with you?" she shouted. "If you try to skip town, you're going to get caught and you'll look even more guilty."

For a second, the detective felt anger pushing on his brain. He closed his eyes, inhaled deeply though his nose and let the air out though his mouth. When he had relaxed a little, he responded, "I appreciate your concern. However, if you will indulge me, I would like to make two observations. First, Green Bay's Finest has decided not to follow us."

"Perhaps they assume you have three grams of common sense and you know how stupid it would be to skip town."

Sam let Sophie's remark slide. "Second, let's review our progress on this case to date. Our client, who you think would be on our side, has been jerking us around since she sashayed into the office. I've been grilled for the past three hours on a bum rap. And for the main attraction this week, I spent the afternoon dodging bullets. Try it sometime. You'll find that it gets old pretty fast. The only fairly decent break that's come our way is finding an address in St. Louis where we might be able to figure out what the Hell is going on. I am not going to take our only decent break and just throw it away. In addition, George-Etienne Shapiro paid for that small stroke of fortune with his life. If nothing else, we owe him."

"I can make a pretty good guess what the Hell is going on right now, without going 800 kilometers out of our way. Want a hint? It involves your sashaying client."

"I concede it seems likely that Nathalie is involved in the insurance scam, but that doesn't mean she knows anything about Shapiro's murder. Moreover, let me reiterate that one highlight of my day involved playing hide and seek with a particularly heavy gunsel shortly after *Monsieur* Shapiro met his very unfortunate demise and my gunsel was carrying the same caliber pistol as the pistol that caused that demise. This strongly suggests to me that there may be more going on here than a simple insurance scam. In summary and returning to my original point, I don't know what the Hell that is and I am very interested in figuring it out."

Sophie considered Sam's argument carefully, then replied, "I still think you're nuts."

"He's right," a voice announced. It seemed to emanate from someplace in the upper stratosphere through the roof of the taxi, until Sam and Sophie realized it was the cabbie, someone who seemed to melt into the background previously. "If you're facing a bum rap, you're facing it on our own. I've been driving a hack for seventeen years and I've seen a lot of life through this windshield. If you're waiting for anything that looks like justice, you're going to wait a long time. The big cheeses make the law and they make sure it's slanted in their direction. They're not about to go out of their way to do any favors for you or me. The law is a velvet door and they won't let you through the door unless you can show them you belong. And if you can't make it through the door, you're better off skipping town."

The cabbie rambled on, describing his life as a series of skirmishes against the forces of wealth and privilege, the forces that control the "velvet door" that separates themselves from the cabbie and the rest of humanity. He drove through the downtown area on *La Rue Michigan*, lined with upscale clothing boutiques catering to sophisticated clientele, bustling during business hours but isolated at 1:00 on a Saturday morning. The streetlights illuminated only the towering snowbanks lining the street and bottom three floors of the skyscrapers, their windows dark like the blank stares of corpses. The light formed a tunnel of existence through an otherwise black void. To the cabbie recounting his long, lonely, one-man battle, the city at night made his isolation more palpable.

While the cabbie continued his soliloquy, Sophie leaned and whispered in Sam's ear, "You realize this guy has gone off the deep end, don't you? Do you really want to take advice from him?"

"I don't care. I'm going to St. Louis. Can you be ready to go in an hour?"

"You want me to come with you?" Sophie asked, surprised.

"You've been bugging me for years to assign you field work. Your Neenah excursion went well enough to earn you another assignment. Pack for at least a week. Bring some dark clothes and don't forget your passport."

Chapter XXIX

At 3:00 in the morning, Sophie waited at the foot of the dark wooden stairs in the small lobby of her apartment building, holding a small suitcase next to a row of mailboxes that always reminded her of the automat in downtown Green Bay. She stood on a floor of small white hexagonal tiles, almost completely covered by a floor mat that had been perpetually waterlogged with cloudy grey snowmelt since mid-October. She had been staring out of a narrow lead glass window for ten minutes. The road was lifeless. No movement was visible in the dark, except for the lake effect snow just starting to fall, flakes like big white feathers floating down in the cone illuminated by the streetlight in front of her building.

In spite of the stillness, Sophie struggled to rein in her excitement. When she was a little girl, she dreamed of joining the *Sûreté* and being like her father, the way the other kids dreamed of becoming a fairy princess, or a *voyageur*, or the Packers' star goalie. Every Sunday, she read the French translation of Dick Tracy in the *Journal de Green Bay* comics, convinced that her father's modesty was the only impediment keeping his adventures from their rightful place of honor beside Detective Tracy's exploits. Later, she watched her three older brothers with pride and envy as they signed up with the *Sûreté*, knowing that there would never be room for her to join them in her lifetime. She took the job as Le Pelleteur's secretary hoping but not daring to believe that she would get an opportunity to do detective work someday. So, this trip, working with a detective on a case, was the fulfillment of a wish she had given up on.

Not only was she going to work on a case, but she was going to St. Louis. The Missouri Territory, also known as French Missouri or French North America, included most of the Great Plains area between the Mississippi River and the Rocky Mountains and north of the Republic of Texas. In the 1800s, pioneers in wagon trains would pay the Natives to escort them to Oregon, but the Territory had been officially off limits and largely unknown to outsiders since 1861, with the exception of St. Louis and a few other river port cities, such as St. Paul, Dubuque and Cape Girardeau, and Denver during ski season. Because the Missouri Territory's borders were closed, St. Louis provided a small point of access to a foreign world. As a result, while some neighborhoods were tourist traps, others were exotic and mysterious.

One of the neighborhoods that Sophie had always imagined as exotic was *Vieux St. Louis*, the neighborhood within the original fortification walls of the city, built in 1765, that looked like a 18th Century French provincial village, but felt like Sophie's image of Paris, with the streets lined with sidewalk cafés teeming with young, beautiful people dining casually on wine and baguettes. Sophie also hoped that she would have a chance to visit Mid-town St. Louis, which provided a plethora of opportunities for entertainment, ranging from fine dining establishments and nightclubs catering to the upper classes and lobbyists, to neighborhood family restaurants, to taverns attracting French Foreign Legionnaires on leave from one of the prairie outposts, or oil workers, mostly Natives in their 20s, who work on the rigs in the Oklahoma area for months at a time, then come to the Big City in cowboy hats and blue jeans looking to blow off steam and to blow their paychecks on women and booze.

While Sophie waited as patiently as she could, Le Pelleteur was driving towards her apartment building. He was not as excited as Sophie by the prospects of a trip to St. Louis. Officially, France looked at its colonial empire as a great and noble "Civilizing Mission," aimed at bringing the benefits of French culture and values to the unenlightened souls of the North American Plains, as well as the West African and Southeast Asian jungles. As a practical matter, the "Civilizing Mission" boiled down to extracting maximum profits from the area without more than a minimal investment. In most of French Missouri, the meager infrastructure they had facilitated providing forced labor for the oil industry. For every native working in the oil fields voluntarily, three were working off tax debts. On the other hand, there were some city services provided in St. Louis to help promote tourism. However, the throngs of people attracted to the city also attracted throngs of pickpockets and the underfunded *Gendarmerie* of St. Louis was not nearly sufficient to address the problem.

Moreover, it just so happened that Le Pelleteur was taking Sophie to St. Louis at a time when there was more than rampant thievery to worry about. He had read rumors in the newspaper that Nazi Germany was planning to invade France soon and French North America was already becoming politically unstable. According to the rumors, while the Governor General and the French Foreign Legion detachment in St. Louis were officially loyal to France, there were handfuls of German supporters in some outposts and in some native communities. It was impossible to guess how many there were, or when or if they were planning to revolt.

Finally, Sophie saw Sam's car pulling up in front of her building. She burst out the door and ran down the cement steps like a kid on Christmas morning, only briefly delayed by the barricade of dirty ice on the edge of the sidewalk. She tossed her suitcase in the back seat next to a burlap sack and hopped in front next to Sam, thanking him effusively for taking her on the trip. As they drove through town, it stopped snowing, but Sophie's ebullience showed no sign of letting up. If it could have been wired into the engine, it would have provided enough energy to get them to St. Louis and halfway back. They had 11 hours to go and watching Sophie bounce off the ceiling for ten minutes had already worn him out. "You might want to pace yourself," he advised his secretary as he lit a Du Maurier cigarette. "At this rate, you're going to explode before we get fifty kilometers out of town."

"You sure got up on the wrong side of the bed, didn't you?" she asked playfully, refusing to let Le Pelleteur's grumpiness dampen her spirits. "By the way, what's in the sack?"

The car began to fill up with blue cigarette smoke, until Le Pelleteur cracked his window and the smoke was sucked out as if by vacuum cleaner. "Beavers. You said that you figured out who owns them. Since Neenah is on the way, I thought we could drop them off."

When they reached Neenah, Sophie provided directions to the Wapekeniew house. Thirty minutes later, they had left the sack of beavers on the porch and were heading south on Highway Q41, following Lake Winnebago until it meets the Upper Fox River. To their left, the moon painted a soft white streak across the pale grey lake ice. As Sam drove, Sophie thought about what he had recounted to her during the taxi from the police station: meeting with Bernie *La Bouche*, finding the gallery address in George-Etienne Shapiro's files, the gunfight in the alley and Sam's arrest for Shapiro's murder.

"There are a few things I still don't understand," Sophie announced. "Why are you taking me along? Not that I'm complaining, but I have asked to do more than take your messages before and you've usually put the kibosh on it."

"Right now, all I have is the address of an art gallery. I don't know what I'm going to find when I get there and so I am bringing you along in case I need your help to deal with it." Le Pelleteur was also concerned that the unidentified gunman might come after Sophie if he left her in Green Bay alone. He did not see any reason to share that with her, however.

"I guess that makes sense. Next question: why did we leave so early? The last time you got out of bed before 9:00, the sheets were probably on fire."

"Getting into St. Louis shouldn't be a problem if we can do it before anyone in Green Bay notices that we're gone and declares me a fugitive from justice."

"It's going to take us hours to get to St. Louis. It will take the police five minutes to call the St. Louis border station and tell them to watch for you. How could we possibly get to St. Louis before they make that call?"

"The police didn't follow me after I left the station and no one is tailing us now." Sophie turned around and confirmed that the highway behind them was vacant. "When they decide to check up on me, it will take a little while for them to realize that I have left town. Then, it will take more time to issue an arrest warrant and more time for the *Sûreté* Headquarters to notify all the Divisions to look out for me. So, there is a chance that we can make it across the border before the paperwork is complete."

"Why don't we fly to St. Louis? We would get there a lot faster that way."

"Plane tickets don't exactly grow on trees, nor does the money needed to buy those tickets. Besides, once the police notice me missing, one of the first things they'll do is check the airport and then they'll know where we went. This way, when they notice me missing, it will take some work to track us down."

Sophie thought about Sam's explanation and conceded, "Well, I guess that might work. But I have just one more question. When you were facing the mysterious stranger in the dark and lonely alley…"

"'Mysterious stranger?' You have been reading too many of those detective novels of yours."

Sophie ignored him. "He had just tried to kill you and he'll probably try again if he got the chance. In fact, I have to think that part of the reason we're on the lam is to get away from him. So, when you knew that this guy was bad news and that leaving him to fend for himself would be perfectly justifiable self-defense, why did you go through all the effort of saving him?"

Le Pelleteur had been wondering the same thing in the back of his mind ever since he saw the stranger out cold in the alley, when he wanted to walk away, but found that his feet had turned into a sticky, gelatinous substance similar to guilt that held him in place until he decided to help his assailant. Ever since he was strongly encouraged to leave the *Sûreté* as a punishment for his idealism, he tried to cultivate a complete lack of concern for those around him. However, in spite of his efforts, he was not as cavalier about the needs of other people as he wanted to believe. Even though he didn't want to, he gave a damn. Even though he didn't want to, he believed that there was such a thing as the right thing to do. Finally, even though he didn't want to, he believed that the Universe would be in some way a slightly better place if he gave a damn and did the right thing, even though his personal experience showed that doing so would just leave him vulnerable to those who didn't.

Sam didn't explain any of this to Sophie, and couldn't have articulated most of it. Instead, he offered, "It seemed like a good idea at the time."

Chapter XXX

Sam and Sophie spent the day Saturday trading off driving toward St. Louis and sleeping in the back seat of the car. The trip was largely uneventful, although Sophie jumped whenever she saw a *Sûreté* Highway Patrol cruiser. At 4:30 PM, they had just driven through Cahokia and were about 15 minutes away from St. Louis. Sam pulled over to the side of the highway.

"What's wrong?" Sophie asked.

"Nothing. I'm going to hide in the trunk and let you drive into St. Louis."

Sophie looked at Sam like he had grown another head and the heads were proclaiming in unison the most utterly ridiculous thing she had ever heard. "As I recall, at some point during this twelve or thirteen hours, you assured me that leaving Green Bay in the middle of the night would enable us to get into St. Louis without any trouble. I have to tell you, proposing to hide in the trunk makes me wonder about the reliability of your assessment."

"I said that getting into St. Louis shouldn't be a problem if we can do it before anyone notices we're gone. I didn't 'assure' you that we would get here before anyone notices we're missing. I didn't 'assure' you of anything. Hiding in the trunk just seems like a reasonable precaution."

"I also seem to remember having a conversation last night, trying to explain to you just how stupid coming here would be and you decided to take the advice of a cabbie with a persecution complex over mine." Sophie based her diagnosis on a Psychology 101 textbook that she reviewed in 1937. "If your plan makes going through a border crossing hiding in a car trunk seem like a 'reasonable precaution,' that should be a point against you and your cabbie friend and a sign that we should head back home before it's too late."

"Look, I never said that this was a good idea. I said I wanted some answers in this case; answers to, in my opinion, very valid questions, like, 'why did I spend yesterday afternoon dodging bullets?' and 'why is George-Etienne Shapiro dead?' So, I'm going into St. Louis whether it's a good idea or not. I invited you to come along on this little excursion because I thought your help would be nice, but also because you have been bugging me to do more non-secretarial work since the first day you were in the office. If you want to back out, just say so. I'll take you to the Cahokia station and put you on a train back home right now."

Sophie thought deeply. She suddenly felt sheepish, like a dike made of sugar that would dissolve as soon as it's needed. On a more selfish level, or what she what she believed was selfish, she also realized that Sam was giving her an opportunity to do the kind of field work she always dreamed of. If she didn't take advantage of this opportunity, the Great Beaver Pelt Caper she worked on the previous day could be her last case.

"I don't want to leave you short-handed," Sophie explained. "I just think it would be a bad idea for you to hide. Sometimes, border guards make random searches and if they find you in the trunk, I could be arrested for bringing you into the Missouri Territory for immoral purposes."

Sam laughed, thinking that the chances that Sophie might be accused of being a white slaver were pretty slim. However, he agreed with her that, if the border patrol found him in the trunk, it would be obvious they were doing something they shouldn't. He agreed to drive through the border station himself and hoped that the *Sûreté du Québec* has not sent out the alert to the French Foreign Legion stationed in the Missouri Territory.

Sam and Sophie had their debate at a point in the highway where their view of the City was blocked by a small ridge running along the east bank of the Mississippi River. Cresting that hill dazzled Sophie, like seeing the Emerald City in *The Wizard of Oz* for the first time. The bright lights of her home city's skyline immediately paled by comparison in her mind, like a 25-Watt bulb sputtering in a cheap lamp. The fortress of Old St. Louis was three stories tall, imposing even though it was overshadowed by skyscrapers to the south. The fortress had been coated with multiple layers of glistening black tar over the years to protect against the spring floods, transforming it into a stunning, sophisticated older sister of a fairy tale castle. In the foreground, between the fortress and the River, a stubble of grass was barely visible above the surface of the snow. Sophie had never seen grass in February in her life. St. Louis was five degrees Centigrade warmer than Green Bay. For Sophie, unlike the residents of St. Louis, it felt like springtime and she could hear the sidewalk cafés calling to her.

They took the *Rue Chouteau* Bridge across the Mississippi River and stopped at the Missouri border crossing station. They sat while the border guard gave Le Pelleteur an interminably long dirty look, the kind that would make you think the guard had just stepped in something disgusting. They sat motionless for what seemed like hours, until Sophie was convinced the guard was allowing time for an angry crowd of patrol officers with billy clubs to gather. However, he just asked why they were coming to St. Louis. Sam said they were sightseeing and the guard let them pass.

To get to the closest gate to the old part of town, within the walls, they had to drive through the business district, past the skyscrapers that thrilled Sophie when she saw them from the Québec side of the River.

Next came the theater district, bustling like Broadway in New York City. This was where the latest plays from Paris made their North American debuts. It was getting dark enough for the marquis lights to start flashing, which Sophie found even more stunning. Next, they entered *St. Louis de l'Ouest*, a residential area inhabited primarily by Plains Indians. Although most families lived in ranch houses, there were a few old-timers still living in teepees and a few more living in pick-up trucks and campers parked in otherwise empty lots. The trucks were fitted with tractor wheels six feet in diameter, which were less likely to get stuck during a buffalo hunt. The teepees and campers were nothing like the geodesic domes favored by the Algonquin Tribe members who lived near Green Bay.

St. Louis de l'Ouest also had a downtown area with grocery and hardware stores, restaurants, dry cleaners and other small businesses. Sam pulled into a small, local diner owned by a Pawnee family. The dinner rush was wrapping up; there were only three customers remaining. The only waitress, a Native woman in her 70s, had a brown buckskin-colored polyester uniform. The cook behind the counter wore a greasy apron and smoked a cigarette while she tended her grill. She looked like she could have been the waitress's mother. Le Pelleteur and Sophie sat down in a red metal flake upholstered booth near a window overlooking the street and each ordered buffalo burgers and corn on the cob. They had no Pepsi, or for that matter, any carbonated beverages. They settled for an indifferent but adequate 1939 cabernet sauvignon.

After they ate, they asked the waitress for directions. From the diner, they went to Oldtown, drove through the old town square past the Governor General's Mansion and found *La Rue Manuel Lisa*. Twenty blocks farther and they finally reached the object of their quest, the art gallery that Le Pelleteur discovered in George-Etienne Shapiro's office. This was the part of the street where most of the mid-level bureaucrats lived 50 years before. Now it was a row of rundown Second Empire houses, mansard roofs topped with rusting iron *fleures des lis* and peeling paint exposing red brick. Retail outlets occupied the street level. In addition to the art gallery, there were small clothing boutiques, souvenir shops and a sidewalk *bistro* or two, all with merchandise selections with delusions of tastefulness. Fortunately, *L'Hotel Napoleon III* was across the street and two doors down from the gallery. The hotel seemed a little out of place, with its flashing neon arrow three times bigger than any other commercial sign on the street.

They stepped into a small, dim, grey lobby, not much bigger than a walk-in closet. Behind a window on the opposite wall, the desk clerk, a man in his 20s who never completely lost his baby fat, sat in a brightly lit booth. From a small ledge about waist level to the ceiling were iron bars that made the booth look like a miniature prison cell. The clerk was reading a comic book and ignoring everything else around him. He was the kind of guy who always assumed that he was smarter than all the hotel guests, because he could and on occasion would deign to give them directions to local restaurants. There was an enclosed staircase to the left. Le Pelleteur tapped the bell on the ledge, which seemed to startle and annoy the desk clerk, but not enough to divert his attention from his comic book.

After several seconds of inaction, Le Pelleteur started to become frustrated. He spoke very slowly and clearly, "We would like a room, please."

The desk clerk peered over his comic book, then dropped the magazine to his lap to reveal a smirk, like he just got a dirty joke he heard five minutes earlier. "I'll bet you would." The words oozed from the clerk's mouth.

"The room will be for the lady."

"Hey, we get all kinds around here, Pops, especially on Saturday nights. We're not prudish around here. If you get a kick out of Little Miss Muffet here, it makes no never-mind to me."

Like a bolt of lightning, Sam's arm shot between the bars of the booth. He grabbed the lapel of the desk clerk's ill-fitting suit and yanked back until the clerk's face was pressed against the bars. Le Pelleteur stared into his eyes, like two power drills boring through his brain and into the back of his skull. In his peripheral vision, he noticed Sophie, horrified at his behavior. He immediately became embarrassed and released the clerk, allowing him to collapse back into his chair. "The room will be for the lady," Le Pelleteur emphasized "the lady," making the words sound like a threat.

"There's one on the fourth floor. Room 4C. Thirty-nine francs a day. No luggage, pay in advance." The clerk recited the words like repetition had imprinted them into his brain, as he returned his attention to his comic book. This also annoyed Le Pelleteur, because it would become obvious to the clerk if he moved his head that Sophie had luggage.

The detective took a deep breath and tried to relax. "Can we see the room first?"

At that question, the clerk looked up, amazed and somewhat revolted by the prospect of expending any physical effort. "What the Hell for?"

Le Pelleteur growled, "We would like to see the view."

"This ain't the Chateau Laurier, Pops. If you're lookin' for a view, you're in the wrong place."

The effort Le Pelleteur needed to keep his temper under control made his hands tremble. "Excuse me, but if it would not disturb you too much, or cause too much of an interruption to the clearly important work you are doing," Sam nodded towards the clerk's comic book, "my colleague, your customer, would nevertheless like to see the view, now."

The desk clerk emerged from the booth, with all the charm and grace of a teenager asked to take out the garbage. He walked obliviously past Sophie and Sam's luggage. Sam took a deep breath, resolved not to lose his temper in front of Sophie again and grabbed the two suitcases. They followed the desk clerk while he slogged up four flights of stairs. Finally, the clerk unlocked Room 4C with his pass key, threw the door open and stepped aside so the hotel guests could see the room. It was barely big enough for the shabby bed and dresser it contained. Le Pelleteur remembered seeing jail cells in his *Sûreté* days with more charm.

Sam walked to the window, looked down at a small courtyard and inquired, "Do you have anything on the other side of the building?"

"The view here is much better."

"Thank you so much for your advice. We would still like to see what you have on the other side of the building."

The clerk shook his head, finding it hard to believe that anyone would discount his expert opinion and opened the door to Room 4B across the hall. It was equal to 4C in both size and shabbiness. "You won't like this room. Everyone complains about the hotel sign. It blinks and shines into this room at night."

Sam looked out the window and found a perfect view of the art gallery across the street. "We'll take it."

The clerk's jaw dropped in shock for several seconds, before he recovered and announced, "Thirty-nine francs a day. No luggage, pay in advance." Sophie thought she heard the clerk call them idiots under his breath. Sam briefly considered pointing out that Sophie had luggage by hitting the clerk on the side of his head with one of her suitcases. He resisted the impulse, however, still trying with significant effort to avoid losing his temper again.

"Do you have a weekly rate?"

"A hundred and sixty-nine francs. That's also pay in advance."

"Seven *livres* should cover it." Sam said, opening his wallet.

"The hotel's exchange rate is twenty francs to the *livre*."

Le Pelleteur knew that the exchange rate should be a little over 25 Missouri francs to the *livre*. He also knew he was not the first man from Québec to get cheated in St. Louis over the currency exchange. He pulled two *livres* out of his wallet and told the desk clerk, "We'll try one day to start with."

Sophie and Sam trailed the desk clerk back to his booth to get the room key. Then, they went to bed early, Sophie in the room and Sam in the car, so they could be ready for the stakeout the following morning.

Chapter XXXI

The next day was a Sunday. At 6:00 in the morning, Sophie diligently assumed at her post next to her hotel room window, closely watching the *Le Studio d'Art Indigène*. Three hours later, she observed a man who appeared to be the gallery owner unlocking the front door and took careful notes. The man was European, had grey hair and was barely 170 centimeters tall. He wore thick round spectacles and a bowler hat, which in her opinion mirrored his well-rounded mid-section. He also wore a grey-and-white houndstooth overcoat, hanging down to his ankles. Sophie thought most people in Green Bay would find it too warm for a coat that heavy. The owner carried a walking stick and he walked carefully, like his knees were made of glass and any sudden movement would make them shatter.

Le Pelleteur showed up for his shift a couple hours later, after spending the morning at one of the multitude of sidewalk cafés in St. Louis, the *Café Napoleon*, two blocks away from the hotel. He hoped that a croissant and four cups of coffee would give him enough strength to hold his eyes open for the rest of the day. While Sophie left to find lunch, Sam took over the watch and lit a cigarette. He occasionally witnessed one or two customers, none of whom particularly noteworthy, wander into the shop and wander back out ten minutes later. Between customer sightings, his mind wandered to Nathalie Juneau, in spite of his efforts to steer it in some other direction. Sophie had pegged her as bad news the minute she laid eyes on her and he had found nothing during the course of his investigation to suggest that Sophie might have been wrong. In fact, this Juneau dame hadn't been straight with him once during this job. One would imagine, Samuel de Champlain Le Pelleteur told himself, that this body of evidence would at least slightly tarnish Nathalie Juneau's luster for him. And yet, he found that he could not purge from his mind the vision of her elegantly crafted gams crossed alluringly in his office on the day she hired him.

During the rest of the day, while Sophie felt her enthusiasm for the stakeout wane, she and Sam observed about 10 or 12 customers between them, none particularly interesting. The gallery owner locked the door and left promptly at 6:00 PM and nothing at all happened from that time to when he came back the next morning. Monday was even slower. There were only four customers by mid-afternoon, when Sophie announced in a sarcastic monotone while staring through the window, "Wow. I knew your life was filled with adventure and danger, but I didn't fully comprehend what non-stop, heart-pounding excitement felt like until I lived it myself."

"If I didn't know better, I would think that you are less than ecstatic over your first stakeout."

"Well, so far, it isn't quite as stimulating as *Electromagnetic Fields: Theory and Practice*, but it wouldn't be so bad if it didn't feel like such a colossal waste of time."

"So, after a full day-and-a-half of detective work, you feel qualified to offer opinions on what is or is not a good use of our time?" Le Pelleteur paused a couple of seconds for dramatic effect. "Well, you could be right. This could be a colossal waste of time, but we can't do much of anything else until nightfall, so we might as well keep watching until then."

Sophie perked up. "What are we doing tonight?"

"We are going to break into the place, see if we can find something useful."

"Why did we have to sit around for two days? Why didn't we just break in when we got here?"

If he had been working alone, Sam probably would have broken into the gallery on the first night. However, as well as trying to shield her from his occasional bouts of quick temper, Sam also wanted to shield Sophie from unnecessary risks, such as getting caught breaking and entering. Therefore, he did not want to give up on the stakeout until neither of them could stand it any longer. Rather than offer that explanation, however, he replied, "I like to have some idea of what I'm getting into before I break into a place."

"We could have posed as customers and walk in and case the joint."

"If we did that, you would have missed out on all the fun of your first stakeout."

At 10:00 that night, Sophie and Sam approached the back door of the art gallery carrying flashlights. He wore a black sweatshirt and slacks. She wore the navy blue cocktail dress she bought for her brother's wedding the previous year, not realizing what Sam had in mind when he recommended bringing dark clothes before they left Green Bay.

Sam wrapped a handkerchief around his hand and was about to break the window in the alley door, when Sophie stopped him.

"Wait!"

"What's the matter?" Sam asked, puzzled.

"If we break in, he'll know we were here."

"So what? We'll take one or two paintings and he'll think he was robbed. He won't know anyone searched through his files."

"But if we pick the lock, he won't know that anyone has been here."

"That takes too long and it's not as easy as your detective novels make it look."

"I can do it."

"Since when?" Sam asked, incredulous.

"Shortly after you hired me, I went to the University library and found a book on the history of lock making. After reading that, I was eventually able to figure it out. I knew there would be a time when you would need me to be able do this." She did this during her senior year, when she was answering his phone for him after school. One fall day, after reading about a break-in in one of her detective books that Sam dismissed so readily, she called her parents and said she was going to study in the University library that night. She read the lock book she found in four hours. Then she went home, waited for her parents to fall asleep and started to practice on the back door. She figured out how to pick that lock in half an hour. Since moving away from home, she had been practicing regularly on her apartment door lock.

"Go ahead. Give it your best shot," Sam invited. Sophie unlocked the alley door in less than two minutes.

They found a hallway that led to the gallery, past a windowless four-meter by four-meter office, four dingy walls surrounding a small wooden desk and a filing cabinet. It looked like the nerve-center of a very small, sad, lonely universe. By 1:00, they had thoroughly searched the filing cabinet, the rest of the office and the counter area in the gallery. They failed to turn up anything interesting, other than confirmation that all the artwork listed as stolen by the Juneau Shipping Company passed through that gallery. They moved on to the storage room in the basement and found only a small step stool and some paintings covered with sheets and leaning against a wall. They came back upstairs, turned their flashlights off and sat on the floor resting against the front of the counter, frustrated, in the dark.

A streetlight outside the plate glass front window illuminated the gallery showroom in front of Sam and Sophie. Art and craftwork of various Plains Indian Tribes were on display, such as a Kiowa blanket, a Mandan cradle board and several paintings of buffalo hunts. One painting stood out—the Virgin Mary depicted as a Blackfoot girl in her late teens. Le Pelleteur figured that it was probably painted by a Jesuit. Starting in the early 1700s, the Jesuits operated missions scattered throughout French Missouri, waging a tenacious but largely unsuccessful campaign to save Native souls, until the Great Drought forced the last of them to shut down in the 1930s. The Blackfoot Mary reminded Le Pelleteur a little bit of a gypsy, or more accurately, a younger version of a 50-year-old woman posing as a gypsy that Le Pelleteur arrested during his first year on the Bunko Squad.

An idea hit Le Pelleteur, like a bucket of cold water in the middle of the night. He snapped his head towards Sophie. "What did you say about electromagnetic fields?"

"I didn't say anything."

"Yes you did, about eight or nine hours ago."

She furrowed her brow for a moment. "I said that your stakeout was slightly less exciting than the textbook on electromagnetic fields that I was reviewing before we left Green Bay. So what?"

"Electromagnetic fields are radio waves, aren't they?"

"That's the most common practical application."

"Could you build a transmitter?"

Sophie paused briefly. "I could probably figure it out if I had enough time and the right materials."

"Once, I arrested a woman posing as a fortune teller. She had a radio transmitter and receiver hidden in her room. While she pretended to read a crystal ball, she would give a signal. Her partner had a radio set three houses away and he would pretend to be a long-lost relative speaking from beyond the grave. We could do that here. Once you build the transmitter, we can hide it someplace in here and maybe figure out what's going on."

Chapter XXXII

Sam spent most of the next day watching the art gallery from the hotel room, while Sophie took the car to the historic Grand Marketplace to collect the parts she needed for her radio transmitter. The Grand Marketplace was like a Middle Eastern bazaar occupying 15 city blocks, most of the area between *Vieux St. Louis* and Midtown. As she parked the car and walked towards the bazaar, Sophie estimated that a building a third as large would still dwarf the largest warehouses in Green Bay's port district. Inside, as Sophie looked up, the vaulted ceiling seemed to stretch out as far as the Gulf of Mexico. The maze-like aisles between the booths were only slightly narrower than those in the stacks of the *Université de Green Bay* library. Instead of the silence of the library, however, it sounded to Sophie like she was in a zoo, except that the screeching, roaring animals were replaced by shouting vendors hawking their wares.

You could buy almost anything there, if you could afford it, including appliances and furniture, tariff-free French wine and all kinds of clothing, from *haute couture* from Paris to the latest styles of women's shoes and purses in buffalo leather. Part of the maze was devoted to jewelry, ranging from white diamonds to men's and women's watches to variously colored plastic Bakelite bracelets. The food section included stalls hawking dried salmon from the Oregon coast, shrimp from New Orleans, as well as herbs and spices, some of which were purported to have medicinal or magical properties, claims that Sophie found hilarious. Also available were salted and sugar-coated acorns from the native regions of *Ouisconsin*, pine nuts from the western regions of French Missouri and locally prepared pemmican sold as snacks. The market had other, more mundane sections, such as housewares, where they offered dishes and cutlery, in addition to sponges, mops and other cleaning supplies and a hardware section, where, among other things, one could find radio components.

When Sophie arrived at 9:30, it was already packed with people, like millions of ants swarming through an unfathomably oversized anthill, or an *élevé* train car at rush hour. Sophie was thrilled to be part of the teeming throngs of bargain-hunters squaring off against the carnival-like hucksters, flogging their merchandise in French, English and Sioux. Half the time, she couldn't tell if the customers were negotiating prices or arguing over a matter of family honor. A heavy-set man in a business suit was clutching a ten-year-old boy by the wrist, scolding him for trying to steal his wallet. Old women miraculously navigated their tea carts through the pandemonium, bringing coffee and frybread to stall operators for a mid-morning snack.

By 11:15, she had purchased almost everything she needed: some tools, 20 meters of rope, a 100-meter spool of copper wire and a cheap Philco table radio that she planned to disassemble for vacuum tubes and other parts. She sat at a table on the sidewalk in front of *Le Café du Jardin*, on a side street four blocks away from the market, staring at her coffee and paying no attention to a recording of Django Reinhardt's jazz guitar. Although she spent the drive from Green Bay dreaming of visiting a sidewalk café and imagining how Gertrude Stein or Henri Matisse might have felt in 1920s Paris, nothing like that crossed her mind at that moment. She was too preoccupied with trying to think of someplace where she might find the last item on her shopping list – a microphone.

Sophie at first assumed the café was playing a phonograph record for its patrons, but realized it was playing the radio when the station announced its call sign. That gave Sophie an idea. She walked into the café and asked to borrow the telephone book. Thirty minutes later, she was pulling into the parking lot of the local radio station studio, on the west side of town just within the city limits. At the far end of the lot was a short cement path leading to what looked like a small farmhouse in the French countryside, with a 50-meter antenna tower extending skyward from the back yard and the call letters of the radio station, FSTL, on a small sign over the front door. Next to the walkway was a flag pole flying France's *Tricolor* flag.

Sophie walked into the lobby and asked the receptionist at a small desk just inside the door if she could talk to an engineer. The receptionist made some unintelligible squawking noises over the loudspeaker and invited Sophie to sit on a slightly worn couch in a waiting area to her right. A few ancient magazines thrown on a coffee table was someone's idea of making visitors feel comfortable.

Five minutes later, a *Métis* man in his mid-20s, in a short-sleeved white-collared shirt and a narrow black tie, half a dozen pencils in his shirt pocket, marched quickly into the lobby, like he had just been interrupted in the middle of performing open heart surgery. Radio listeners would often come to the studio asking to talk to the one of the characters in their favorite programs. As the youngest person on the staff, in addition to his engineering work, he was called upon to point out to those listeners that the people they hear on the radio are recordings of actors and actresses made someplace else, usually in Paris. As a result, he was a little annoyed when he asked, "Can I help you?"

Sophie did not notice his unusually quick step or his unusually annoyed voice. Instead, she focused on the way he floated into the lobby the way Adonis might descend from Mt. Olympus and the way his voice sounded like sirens singing. She forgot to breathe for a few seconds, captivated by the deep brown eyes behind his horn-rimmed glasses, until she realized that he had spoken to her. She explained that she was trying to build a ham radio transmitter and was looking for some advice. He was pleasantly surprised and introduced himself as Charles Gautier. He was about to take his lunch break and so invited Sophie to join him. Charles led Sophie to the break room in the back of the building. Sophie sat at a grey speckled circular Formica table that seemed to take up most of the room. The only decorations on the dingy grey walls were a darker grey punch clock and a calendar depicting a naked woman holding a case of capacitors in front of her strategically. Sophie felt her cheeks grow pink, like she was leaning over an oven and guessed that the receptionist seldom ventured into this room. When Charles noticed Sophie's reaction, he took Miss Capacitor off the wall and put her face-down on top of the refrigerator.

Charles opened the refrigerator and took out a brown paper bag containing a Virginia ham and French Beaufort cheese sandwich and a bottle of better-than-average 1937 chardonnay from the Ozark foothills to the south of St. Louis. He offered her half his sandwich and asked her to grab two wine glasses from the cabinet behind her. As he sat down and poured the wine, he explained that he had only half an hour for lunch and started to give his abbreviated version of Radio Engineering 101, but Sophie immediately asked a question that belied an understanding of radio physics just as deep as his. They ended up spending twenty minutes, discussing the more arcane complexities of radio theory and practice, completely fascinated with the conversation and each other.

When she noticed that his lunch break was almost over, Sophie decided that she had better get to the point. "That was great. Thank you very much. However, what I really need help with is the microphone. Do you know where I might be able to get one?"

"I know of one or two mail order catalogues that should give you everything you need."

"I was hoping that I could find something today. I promised my cousin in Green Bay that I would try to finish my rig in time for me to talk to her tonight."

The engineer thought for a second and then asked Sophie to follow him to an equipment storage room and gave her a microphone. It looked like a pill big enough to choke the Trojan Horse and swiveled in a fork-shaped stand. "This should get you up and running tonight, but I need it back before anyone notices it missing, or I could get in trouble." Sophie promised to return it in two or three days.

Chapter XXXIII

After her lunch with Charles, Sophie returned to the hotel. She spent part of the afternoon with Sam going over their plans for that night. She also disassembled the radio she had bought and removed the microphone from its desk stand. Finally, Sophie packed all her parts and tools into one of her suitcases so that they would be easier to carry.

A little after midnight, they drove Sam's car into the alley behind the art gallery. Sophie picked the lock to the alley door again and then got to work installing the transmitter, while Sam helped where he could. When they left at 1:30, there was a radio transmitter made up of a coil of copper wire, three vacuum tubes and an intricate rectilinear web of wires running half the length of one of the ceiling joists in the basement. It blended in with the building's plumbing and electrical wiring, if you didn't look too closely. They had removed the microphone from its desk stand and mounted it to the underside of the counter on the main floor and had drilled a hole in the floor under the counter so that they could wire the microphone to the transmitter.

Next, they needed to make an antenna. They ran the copper wire from the alley to the transmitter through a basement window. Then, Sophie gave Sam a diagram she drew just before they left their hotel room and Sam climbed up the side of the building using the rope that Sophie bought earlier that day. Sophie tied the spool of copper wire to the rope so that Sam could haul it up to the roof. Finally, Sam fashioned a T-type monopole antenna following Sophie's diagram, by stringing a length of copper wire to the *fleurs de lis* border lining the top of the mansard roof along the front of the building and connecting the wire from the basement transmitter to the center point of that wire.

The morning after they installed their transmitter in the art gallery, Sophie was stationed at the window in the hotel room across the street, her grogginess from lack of sleep more than offset by her anticipation of a break in the case. Sam sat on the bed, back against the wall, sorely missing the coffee that Sophie would have made if they were back in the office. Sophie flipped the switch on the radio receiver as soon as she saw the gallery owner unlock the door. It crackled to life and immediately revealed that the little man who owned the gallery liked to hum when he was alone, primarily American Big Band songs from Benny Goodman and Tommy Dorsey. During a routine sale of a painting, they found that the owner's French had a Parisian nasal quality, but he had been in St. Louis long enough to give his accent some of the rhythms, cadences and pronunciations of many Sioux languages. As the morning wore on, they learned nothing further, other than the owner's name, Auguste Dumont.

Their big break came early afternoon, when they heard the telephone ring. They listened to *Monsieur* Dumont's half of a conversation in German for about two minutes. Sam understood none of it. Sophie thought she caught "10:00" and "Rick's place." Le Pelleteur ran down the stairs to the desk clerk. "Excuse me. A friend of mine from back home said that Rick's was a good place to find a little fun. You ever hear of it?"

The clerk put down his comic book and smiled, happy that Sam asked him to demonstrate his mental prowess rather than expend any physical effort. "*Le Café Français du Richard.* Sooner or later, everybody goes to Rick's." He drew a map to the nightclub and proudly presented it to Le Pelleteur.

That night, Sophie and Sam got dressed up as much as they could. Sam wore the grey suit that he wore to the office four days previously.

Sophie put on her navy blue cocktail dress. They drove in Sam's car, following the desk clerk's map, to a large, one-story building on the corner of a block otherwise occupied by small non-descript bars, arriving at 9:30.

The *Maitre d'* led Sam and Sophie into a cavernous theater-like space. They had to wait a few seconds for their eyes to adjust to the dimness. A huge chandelier hung from the ceiling like a stalactite formation, adding to the cavern effect. A long aisle stretched out in front of them. The aisle inclined slightly downward towards the polished wooden dance floor that seemed half a kilometer away. The stage beyond the dance floor hosted a 20-piece big band that, from where Sam and Sophie were standing, could have been made up of six-year-olds, or midgets. Small tables formed wide terraced semicircles around the dance floor in front of the stage, each with a pink tablecloth and a little table lamp with a red fringed shade. Sam thought it looked like someone tried to set up a Paris sidewalk bistro in the seats behind one of the goals at the Packers' City Stadium. Maroon velvet curtains covered the walls to each side. Sophie thought the sequins on the curtains twinkled like little stars. Sam was reminded more of the worn-out dress of a prostitute that had been walking the street since her flapper days.

They sat at a table near the back of the room, while the *Maitre d'* squinted at them, like they were worms in an apple he had just bitten. Sam scanned the audience for Auguste Dumont, without success. He was surprised to see that the place was so full on a Wednesday night, until he noticed that all the cocktail napkins had little red hearts printed along their edges and he realized it was Valentine's Day. Meanwhile, Sophie gazed around the room with eyes like sponges soaking in all the glitter. The patrons generally wore finely tailored tuxedos and elegantly sequined evening gowns. Sam looked a little out of place in his rumpled business suit, but Sophie did not notice as she half-expected Fred Astaire and Ginger Rogers to dance across the floor any minute.

While they waited for someone to take their drink orders, a young, shapely Native woman, satin gown the color of moonlight with a slit going up above her knee, was draped over a solitary black grand piano in the middle of the stage. She sang *La Vie En Rose* in Lakota, with an Oglala accent. About two tables away, Sophie noticed someone sitting by himself, barely touching the drink in front of him. He was younger than she was and looked like a boy in a new suit waiting for his high school graduation picture, or, more likely, a young bureaucrat seven thousand kilometers away from home on his first job. She watched him mouth the words to the song in French while the woman on stage sang the Lakota version. Sophie could almost smell his homesickness wafting through the room, like the smell of old honey might have if it could go bad.

The next act started with a single timpani establishing a steady beat: BOOM, boom, boom, boom, BOOM, boom, boom, boom. The beat gradually evolved into a more complex, hot jazz rhythm. Then the rest of the band joined in with *Drum Boogie* and twenty dancing girls, wearing nothing but large white feathers and strings of pearls, ran onto the stage kicking in unison.

Near the end of the number, Sam observed the gallery owner by himself, in a white suit and a black bow tie, being led to a table three rows in front of them. Sam noticed details that were not apparent from the hotel room, such as the dark brown curly hair. Dumont was older than Sam, but he seemed too young for the furrows in his forehead. Sam saw his hands tremble. He interpreted that as fear until he saw the psychotic gleam in the gallery owner's slightly bulging eyes. Sam recognized that from his time as a Bunko Squad detective as the half-starved expression of eager anticipation that dope fiends wear on their way to the opium dens in Green Bay's Chinatown. Sam did not know what the addiction was, but he was certain there was one.

After a few minutes, Sam and Sophie moved to his table and sat down uninvited, Sam on the owner's left and Sophie on his right. They both crowded in close to him, in part for intimidation and part because the table was rather small. "Excuse me. Do I know either of you?" The gallery owner inquired, somewhat affronted.

"No, you don't know us," Sam responded. "But I think you'll find that I'm a heck of a guy and my partner here is one swell gal. How about I buy the next round so we can all get acquainted?"

Dumont turned and shot a look at Sophie like she just offered him an arsenic sandwich. She smiled and wiggled her fingers at him. He turned back to Sam, intending to sound polite but firm but instead sounded more like a schoolboy begging for pity from a bully. "Unfortunately, I don't have time for a drink. I have an appointment in a few minutes that I need to keep. Perhaps some other time."

Sam concluded that the addiction at issue was not alcohol and changed tactics. "Well, we don't want to keep you, then. We have just a few questions for you. Tell us what we want to know and we we'll get out of your way."

The little man looked at his watch impatiently. It was five minutes to ten. "If you won't leave me alone until I talk to you, come with me to the casino. If you explain what this is all about, I will consider telling you what I can there." Sam nodded his head happily, asked Sophie to stay put and followed the gallery owner as he left the table. Sophie thought for a second, then jumped up and followed them, struggling to keep up.

Chapter XXXIV

The art dealer ran down the steps and floated along the edge of the dance floor with short, mincing steps, like a roach on black-and-white checkered kitchen linoleum. Sam and Sophie were surprised at how quickly he skittered. The threesome slipped through a small door in the opposite wall near the edge of the velvet curtain, into a dark alley illuminated only by a single bulb in a light fixture mounted above the door. Sam and Sophie pursued him down a flight of cement stairs in the alley, past a bouncer and into a small foyer area. The walls were white stucco and a large potted fern sat in the corner. A wide arched passageway led to the casino tables and throngs of people. To the right of the foyer entrance, there was a coat check counter and a barred window that looked like the teller area of a bank.

The young blond woman behind the bars greeted *Monsieur* Dumont by name and gave him a stack of chips. Dumont dove into the crowd and started to swim towards the roulette tables. Sam bought 300 Missouri francs in chips and followed, with Sophie close behind. It was impossible to go anywhere without squeezing around somebody, like navigating through a can of sardines. However, the crowd was surprisingly quiet, practically refined. The polite conversations were nothing more than a slight background murmur, easily overpowered by the sharp sounds of roulette balls clacking in their wheels, the muffled sounds of dice bouncing along their felt craps tables, the boogie woogie music on the upright piano in the corner next to the bar and the occasional throaty but sophisticated laughter of a woman in a tiara and a white sequined gown, smoking a cigarette in a holder almost as long as a hockey stick. The dim lighting came from overhead lights above each gaming table that reminded Sam of the fixtures overhanging billiard tables in most Green Bay pool halls.

The croupier also greeted Dumont by name as he sat down at a roulette table and placed a small stack of chips on red. Sam, close behind, sat beside him and placed a 50-Franc chip next to Dumont's chips, while Sophie was still working her way through the crowd. Dumont watched the ball circle the roulette wheel like it was hypnotizing him.

Sophie arrived just in time to see Dumont and Sam win. While Dumont heaved a sigh of relief, like he had just removed a painful thorn from his foot, Sam gave Sophie a look like he just realized how unlikely it was that Sophie would stay in the nightclub as she was asked. He slipped a few chips into Sophie's hand and told her to blend in. Sophie sat down beside them and put a chip on Number 28, in what she thought was a nonchalant manner. Dumont placed another small stack of chips on red and Sam bet on black. While Dumont stared at the spinning roulette wheel, Le Pelleteur fought for his attention. "*Monsieur* Dumont, I think you're here because of a telephone call you received this afternoon. I would like to know who you were talking to and what you talked about."

Dumont continued to stare at the spinning roulette wheel, so enthralled by it that he never thought to ask how Sam knew about the call or why he wanted to talk about it. "Two or three times a month, I get a call like that. Don't know who it is. Never said his name. He tells me to watch for a package from some address. The package includes some artwork and a letter spelling out two or three addresses and a telephone number for a shipping company. I call the shipper and ask them to fill out the paperwork for sending the package from one address to the second address and from the second to the third. Then, after I close for the day, I take the package to the German Consulate and give it to a guy who meets me at the front gate. I get the shipping invoices in the mail about a week later and I take those down to the Consulate, as well. For this, I get 2500 francs in chips at this casino." This time, Dumont lost and all of his attention became consumed by the roulette wheel. Le Pelleteur realized that he heard everything that Dumont was going to tell him. He turned to talk to Sophie, letting Dumont focus on his compulsion.

As Le Pelleteur turned, he briefly glimpsed a tall, muscular, blond-haired, blue-eyed man with a bruised, swollen face playing blackjack on the other side of the room. It was the foreign gunman who had followed him from George-Etienne Shapiro's office. Their eyes met and Le Pelleteur's stomach muscles tightened. He was in danger and Sophie would be as well unless he did something quickly. He pasted a dopey, drunken smile onto his face and instructed Sophie, "Turn your back to me in a huff." She paused and looked confused. "Now!" he demanded.

She still didn't understand, but knew that Sam must have had a good reason for his request, so she spun around theatrically, crossed her arms and scowled. He leaned over and whispered in her ear from behind, "Look annoyed. I want everyone in this room to think that I am making inappropriate advances towards you. In a minute, I am going to grab your behind. I want you to slap me hard enough to knock a tooth loose and send it flying at least twenty meters. Then, walk away, march out of this casino, back to the hotel, find the car and drive." At that point, Sam slipped his car keys into her purse. "Don't stop until you get back to Green Bay. Ready?"

Without waiting for a reply, Sam placed his hand gently on Sophie's lower back. She jumped, pivoted, hit Sam with more of a right cross than a slap in the face and stormed out of the suddenly quiet casino. The punch carried more force than he expected, causing him to stumble backwards a couple of steps. As she left, he yelled out, "Aw, come on, Sister! I was just lookin' for a little bit of fun. It would probably do you good to relax a little bit." Then, to no one in particular, he shrugged. "Oh, well, you win some, you lose some." As people returned their attention to their gambling, Le Pelleteur looked at the gunman to see his reaction to the performance and sat down at the roulette table.

Soon, the gunman sat down beside the detective and suggested, casually but menacingly, in French with a heavy German accent, "We have a need to talk, I think."

Chapter XXXV

Le Pelleteur's right hand squeezed reflexively into a fist. It squeezed so hard that his bicep bulged until his suit coat became restrictive. Veins popped up along his forearm like grey-blue oak roots under his sleeve. He formed a plan in two seconds—he would wrap his left hand around the throat of the stranger who tried to shoot him down in Green Bay a week earlier, while he pounded his face repeatedly with his right.

Two seconds after that, he realized that he needed to give Sophie as much time as he could to get out of town. That meant he needed to stall and that required a little more finesse than a punch in the eye. He smiled at the stranger, which took more effort than he anticipated, and said as pleasantly as he could, "If you have something to say, by all means, spit it out."

"A little privacy might be more appropriate," the stranger replied.

"I hate to leave now. I'm on a lucky streak."

"I can ask more persuasively."

"Somehow I don't find that surprising. How about the bar?" Le Pelleteur pointed to the bar area on the opposite side of the room. "I'll tell ya what. Since I've won a few francs tonight, I'll buy the first round."

On the way across the floor, the detective pretended to trip and fall into a man at a craps table. He apologized profusely and loudly enough to attract offended stares from everyone at the table. He eventually stumbled to the bar, his erstwhile assassin following a few seconds behind, trying to avoid being seen too closely with him.

As they mounted two high-backed black leather chairs at the bar, Le Pelleteur tossed a chip on the bar. The bartender offered the assassin a Tiger Bock beer, then asked Le Pelleteur for his order. Le Pelleteur asked for gin, turned to the stranger and observed casually, "The bartender seems to be a friend of yours. My guess is that you've been here before."

"I have found this place convenient for meeting a variety of colleagues in the past," the German explained. After a few moments of silence, he enquired, "That woman who left earlier. She is a friend of yours, perhaps?"

"Never seen her before tonight. Not so much a friend as the most recent example of my inability to make a good first impression. Even so, don't get me wrong. I'm sure you're charming in your own special way, but if I thought I stood a chance with her, I would be chasing after her right now instead of sitting here with you."

"You are funny, you must think."

"I'm guessing you disagree."

"I agree that, at good impressions, you are not good. You did not make a good first impression with all the people here, I think."

"But I did make an impression." The gunman thought for a moment and then nodded. They implicitly agreed that Le Pelleteur had made enough of a scene that it would be difficult to remove him from the room quietly in the near future if he did not go of his own accord.

"Speaking of first impressions," Le Pelleteur interjected, "your first impression on me was not exactly stellar. With all the attempted murder going on, I don't think we were properly introduced."

"I am Johan Schmidt." Le Pelleteur recognized the name as a Germanicized version of "John Smith," and grumbled to himself that the assassin might as well have introduced himself as "anonymous." "Speaking of the last time we met," Schmidt continued, "we have unfinished business."

"I don't mind leaving it unfinished."

"That is very kind of you, but I am afraid I must insist?"

"Why?"

"Do not play the dummy with me, *Monsieur* Le Pelleteur. It insults us both."

"I had no intention of insulting you, Johan. I apologize if I've hurt your delicate little feelings." Schmidt found Le Pelleteur's comment mildly annoying, but tried to hide his reaction. "You said we have unfinished business. OK, let's talk business for a few minutes. Unless I miss my guess, you're in the business of smuggling Western art and Native artifacts to Germany and it looks like business is booming. I'll bet you have an operation like a corporate octopus, with men like tentacles stretching across North America, breaking into mansions, taking high-end landscapes and sculptures and forcing people at gunpoint to sign receipts so it looks like you paid for it. You probably have more men scouring French Missouri for blankets and moccasins that belonged to somebody's great grandparents and have been in their families for generations. I don't know if you even bother with forcing them to sign a receipt. Maybe you steal it and get away before anyone notices it missing. Maybe you just take it at gunpoint and murder its owners. It probably doesn't matter too much, at least not to you.

"Next, you ship the art and the artifacts to that little man over there drooling on the roulette wheel," Le Pelleteur nodded in Auguste Dumont's direction, "and he works with a shipping company in Green Bay to create a fake paper trail to cover your tracks. One of the more interesting aspects of your little business enterprise is the considerable effort that you've devoted to keeping it under the table. I wonder why. You can't be afraid of the city police departments or local tribal authorities.

They can't touch you once you're outside their jurisdictions. My guess is that you're steering clear of the national law enforcement types, like the FBI, Texas Rangers and the Royal Oregonian Mounted Police. They would shut you down in a heartbeat if they found you harassing their most prominent citizens out of their priceless masterpieces. And let's not forget the French colonial government, who are the only ones who could get in your way in Missouri. And they would if they ever found you trafficking in native artifacts, turning a profit on their turf and not giving them their cut."

"Very insightful." Schmidt replied. "Perhaps your words are meant to be disconcerting to me, but it has nothing to do with the unfinished business between us, that we started in the alley in Green Bay and will be finished tonight." Schmidt's icy blue eyes met Le Pelleteur's menacingly.

"Do you mean you're going to thank me for saving your life and dragging your amazingly heavy ass out of that alley?" Le Pelleteur glared back into Schmidt's eyes.

"For breaking my nose, should I also thank you? Your jokes again, they grow tedious."

"OK, let's be serious. Just between you and me, Johan, you might want to leave the business from the alley unfinished. If you play your cards right, you and I could come to an agreement that would be good for both of us."

"What deal can you make?" inquired Schmidt softly.

"You may not have realized it, but I've become an important part of your operation. As I'm sure you know, I didn't come to your little soiree uninvited. The shipping company came to me, not the other way around. I figure I was hired because you assumed that, if I dug around long enough, I would find some excuse to pin the alleged art thefts on somebody and divert attention away from your favorite art gallery and mine.

However, if you finish what you started in that Green Bay alley, eventually my absence will be noticed and there will be an investigation. The investigation could easily lead to St. Louis and then it is just a matter of time before they start poking around *Monsieur* Dumont's gallery. That will lead to this casino and then you. Also, we should remember our mutual friend, George-Etienne Shapiro. Right now, I'm the one in the frame for his misfortunes. It stands to reason that you arranged for that with an anonymous telephone call, shortly after I took pity on you and decided not to let you freeze to death next to a pile of garbage. If I'm not around to take the fall, you never know what could happen next. You could end up on the hook for Shapiro before too long. The way I see it, all of that gives me some bargaining power here. If I'm going to continue playing my part, I want to be adequately compensated. Part of my end of the deal is I walk out of here upright, but that's just the start."

"You have, as they say, the colorful imagination. It is all very amusing. I am our little talk enjoying. But I still think some kind of joke you make. We all have a fate. The Fatherland is fated to rule the world. Herr Shapiro met his fate. Your fate you will meet soon, either tonight, with my bullet in your forehead, or in the near future in the electric chair. To suggest that your fate you might have any control over is foolish."

"Free will and determinism. Fascinating. Let's think about this for a minute. Am I fated to end up in the Chair? I'm not even fated to set foot in *Québécois* jurisdiction again. Maybe I would enjoy life right here in St. Louis. Maybe I could travel the world. Maybe you and I could move to the Fatherland and start a sausage stand together. Wouldn't that be fun?" Le Pelleteur inquired rhetorically, slapping Schmidt playfully on the shoulder. "The point is, the longer I stay out of Québec, the longer the Shapiro case is open. And every day that case is open is a day that the cops might trip over something that leads them to you. Now, maybe that doesn't bother you. Maybe you're just like me and you can just walk away from Québec as well. But my guess is that your smuggling ring is just one of several little scams you're running across North America. I'm also guessing that abandoning Québec would leave some business associates holding the bag for some of those scams. They might frown on that and might react strongly. Also, unlike the *Sûreté du Québec*, my guess is that your business associates would not have any problem crossing national borders, tracking you down and expressing their displeasure to you personally. Now, is anything in my little story 'fated?' I don't think so. I do think it's possible, though, and as long as it's possible, eliminating me forces you to run a risk you don't have to."

"A colleague of mine advises that sometimes you have to roll the dice, even when the odds are with the House. In this case, I think, my odds are not so bad."

"Well, Johan, I'm sorry to hear that. I think you've figured the odds wrong and I have to admit that I assumed you were smarter than that. But you have to do what you think best." With that, Le Pelleteur lit a cigarette and stared into Schmidt's eyes again, daring him to do his worst. Schmidt stared back, perhaps just as Montcalm and Wolfe stared each other down across the Plains of Abraham almost 200 years before.

Over the years, Schmidt had learned that there are several ways to intimidate, several ways to generate fear in an adversary. The method Schmidt preferred was to project an air of mild insanity; to show that, while he understood the boundaries imposed by civilization, he had no qualms ignoring them. It was rare for him to face someone who seemed crazier and more reckless than he was and he found that unnerving. Schmidt hid it well, in part because he had spent years developing a good poker face and in part because the bruises Le Pelleteur gave him helped to camouflage his facial expression. He looked away and laughed. "Truly a comedian you are, *Monsieur* Le Pelleteur. Perhaps on the stage of this night club your act you would like to try? What is your price for giving up your theoretical sausage stand and going to your execution?"

"I'm not planning to be executed. I got friends in the Green Bay Bureau of the *Sûreté du Québec* and it wouldn't take much grease to get the murder rap knocked down to manslaughter." Until this time, except for the occasional staring battle with Le Pelleteur, Schmidt had been casually scanning the room while talking to Le Pelleteur. Now, he looked at Le Pelleteur out of the corner of his eye for a few seconds. Le Pelleteur took this to mean that Schmidt had finally started to take him seriously. "Just to show you that I'm a nice guy," Le Pelleteur continued, "and so you don't hurt your head trying to convert currencies, let's make this simple. I take the rap for Shapiro's murder and you get to keep your art theft ring and insurance fraud going, in exchange for an even million Deutschmarks." Le Pelleteur calculated that to be about 111,000 *livres*. "I would need at least a quarter of that up front. That should give me enough to pay off Green Bay's Finest."

"You overestimate my generosity. I could just call the police and turn you in, no?"

"You could, but there would be nothing stopping me from calling every insurance company in North America and telling them about your fun and games. The reward would let me bribe enough people to keep me out of the electric chair, but there wouldn't be much left over. More importantly for you, your days as Patron of the Arts would be over. So, it seems to me that some kind of deal would be in both of our best interests."

The German contemplated the proposal while staring into his beer. "You will receive 500,000 marks, 100,000 in a week and the rest upon the completion of your sentence."

"How about we split the difference: 750,000 marks total, 200,000 in a week?"

Schmidt paused to consider whether to continue negotiating, or to simply pretend to accept the offer and kill Le Pelleteur on his way back to his hotel. Suddenly, "There he is!" came booming across the room. Schmidt, Le Pelleteur and everyone else in the casino dropped what they were doing. The only sound was a little ball rolling around a roulette wheel, making a gentle whir interrupted by loud wooden clacking. The crowd held its breath and stared apprehensively at the doorway, where Sophie appeared with two St. Louis beat cops and the nightclub *Maitre d'*, pointing out her boss. The cops were Osage, both about 190 centimeters tall. They wore black uniforms with two yellow stripes along the seams of their trousers. The jackets were double-breasted, with two rows of brass buttons and a silver badge in front. Their shaven heads carried pillbox caps with feathered hat bands, a custom that evolved from the feathered headdresses their ancestors wore in the 19th Century.

"The ugly one at the bar. He's the one who attacked me," Sophie proclaimed.

Chapter XXXVI

A collective sigh of relief signalled the resumption of the games of chance. A small gap in the crowd opened in front of the cops and closed quickly behind, like a begrudging Red Sea parting for Moses against its better judgment. Sophie followed in their wake, complaining loudly that it was becoming impossible for a girl to go out after dark without being attacked by a dirty old man. Sam couldn't help smiling at the spectacle Sophie caused. He turned to the bar for a moment to finish his drink and to put a more serious look on his face, then hopped off his bar stool and stood at attention with his hands up.

Sam thought Sophie's performance was excellent in the role of a very proper and easily offended woman, although at times he was afraid that she was laying it on a bit thick. She circled the cops as they took Le Pelleteur into custody, trying to get their attention so she could bark orders at them. The cops, not feeling in need of Sophie's instruction, occasionally mumbled, "*Oui, Mademoiselle*," but largely ignored her. She looked like a border collie puppy herding two rams twice her size, except that the rams were not being herded so much as begrudgingly humoring her. The two patrolmen grabbed Le Pelleteur by the arms and led him out of the casino. Schmidt, impressed, admitted to himself that Le Pelleteur won this round, but vowed that this would make killing him at their next meeting more pleasurable.

The patrol officers marched Le Pelleteur through the alley and onto the sidewalk, where they quickly found a police telephone mounted on a utility pole near the corner. Sophie followed the trio, continuing to complain loudly that Sam was a dirty old man. A paddy wagon soon appeared, a 1937 Renault panel van, siren blaring. Sam was forced into the back with the two patrolmen, while Sophie was invited to sit in the front with the driver.

Sophie settled into the front seat of that van like it was a throne and she had just been crowned Queen of the Private Eye Secretaries. She didn't know exactly why Sam had sent her away, but it stood to reason that he had been in some kind of danger. Not only did she get him out of that danger, she provided him with a police escort. She felt a little bad about getting him arrested, but she did not think that Sam would be in any real trouble from now on. After all, he was arrested for getting fresh, not for something serious like murder as he was a week earlier. Besides, he was a cop himself for eight years and knew how to work the system. Finally, if Sam was locked up for too long and things started to get sticky for him, she could just drop the charges.

Le Pelleteur, handcuffed, rattled around on an unpadded bench in the dimly lit back of the paddy wagon. Although he was impressed with Sophie's quick thinking and resourcefulness, he was not as optimistic as she was regarding his immediate future in the custody of the St. Louis constabulary. All he knew about St. Louis criminal procedure was that it was nothing like procedure in Québec. The Ministry of Overseas Affairs, not the Ministry of Justice, administered the legal system in French North America. As a result, there were no investigating magistrates as there were in Green Bay. In theory, French citizens, including Natives who elected to adopt French citizenship, were subject to French law. Non-citizen Natives were subject to the *Code Indigènes*, which theoretically took the form of edicts issued by the Governor General in St. Louis to roughly ten to twelve Lieutenant Governors throughout French North America, who in turn issued the edicts to *Commandants de Cercles*, who issued them to the tribal chiefs. As a practical matter, however, the interpretation and enforcement of the edicts were left to the discretion of the *Commandants*. As a result, instead of the Napoleonic Code or some other reasonably consistent body of law administered by a centralized colonial authority, there was simple brutality, the level of which varied from region to region depending on the personality of the *Commandants*. The only law enforced consistently was the tax law, which usually took the form of a few weeks of forced labor every year building roads or working in an Oklahoma oil field. St. Louis, together with New Orleans and Dakar, Senegal, however, were officially considered part of France rather than colonies. They each had a representative in the French Parliament in Paris. Le Pelleteur assumed that citizens of St. Louis were subject to the Napoleonic Code, but he was not a citizen of either St. Louis or the French Empire and he could not remember anything from law school covering the St. Louis law applicable to non-citizens of European descent.

Chapter XXXVII

Sam and Sophie were taken to the Headquarters of the St. Louis *Gendarmerie*, a run-down brick building in the new part of the city, surprisingly reminiscent of the 28th District station house in Green Bay. Sam went through a process he saw from a different perspective a hundred times: fingerprints, mug shot, holding cell, sit and wait. Meanwhile, Sophie was asked to wait in the outer office of the police station, a place she found frustratingly similar to the waiting room where she spent two hours watching the clock a week earlier.

After an hour lying on a jail mattress only slightly less comfortable than a porcupine, about 12:30, a corporal led Sam to the office of someone named Lieutenant Tunapi. Another went to the waiting room and asked Sophie to join them. Lieutenant Tunapi was in charge during the Graveyard Shift, from midnight to 8:00 in the morning. He was a barrel-chested Native American man in his mid-50s, with a salt-and-pepper crew cut. His size made his bookshelf-lined office and gray metal desk seem small by comparison. He wore a white shirt unbuttoned at the collar, a shoulder holster and a loosened necktie with Otoe designs. A brown suit coat on a hanger and a matching fedora hung on a stand next to the flag pole flying the French *Tricolor*. Sam recognized the type from his days on Green Bay's police force. He was nearing the end of his career. He had enough knowledge and experience, but not the connections, to be the Chief of Police. He was put in charge of the night shift because somebody needed to be in charge and everyone else qualified for the job had enough clout to get a better shift. Lieutenant Tunapi's eyes were tired, the kind of tired that comes from getting the short end of the stick so often it's not worth the effort to get surprised anymore.

The Lieutenant invited Sam and Sophie to sit down in the well-worn wooden chairs facing his desk. "So, you are Samuel de Champlain Le Pelleteur, of Green Bay, Québec," Tunapi said in his interrogation voice, reading from a folder on his desk.

"Yes," Le Pelleteur replied, unsure of whether it was a question or a statement.

"And you are Sophie Marleau, also of Green Bay?" Tunapi looked up briefly at Sophie.

"Yes," she replied.

"And you both were at Rick's Place earlier this evening and *Monsieur* Le Pelleteur was a little too forward."

"He made improper advances towards me." She tried to project solemn gravity to cover up her nervous laughter.

"And you slapped him."

"Yes."

"You know, it seems to me you gave *Monsieur* Le Pelleteur what he deserved when you slapped him. That slap and a fine for disturbing the peace should be punishment enough. An assault charge means a trial, which would happen about three months from now at the earliest. That means that you'll need to come back to St. Louis at that time so you can testify. You could save yourself some inconvenience and save us a lot of paperwork if you just drop the assault charge."

Sophie anticipated dropping her charges at some point, but not for a day or two, hoping that that would be enough time for Sam's trouble, whatever it was, to die down. After thinking fast, she felt a wave of inspiration wash over her, as if the spirit of Katherine Hepburn or Fifi D'Orsay descended from a movie screen and took control of her. She jumped to her feet, knocking her chair over for dramatic effect. "You men are all alike. You have no respect for women and you think mistreating them is some kind of joke. I'll bet every policeman in St. Louis gropes a woman three times a week while making his rounds and then comes back to the station to brag about it. I should've known better than to ask you for help."

Tunapi leaned back in his chair. "Well, what a surprise," he announced, sarcastically. "Another *Québécoise* Holy Roller Bible Thumper who lives in mortal fear that someone, somewhere, might be enjoying himself instead of measuring up to your lofty standards. Of course, women deserve respect, but you can show them respect and still have a little fun with them now and then. I got another bit of news for you. The real world extends a long way beyond what *Père* Jean-Baptiste sees from his pulpit and out here, most of us are normal human beings, not a bunch of saints waiting for the Pope's permission to live our lives. Out here, every once in a while, a man steps out of line. Then a woman slaps him and they're even. That should be the end of it."

"I hate to disagree, Lieutenant," Sam interjected, "but you can't let me go. I'm wanted for murder in Green Bay." During Sophie's tirade and Lieutenant Tunapi's lecture, Sam had time to think about his options and he decided that he liked his chances back with the Green Bay Police significantly more than he did on the streets of St. Louis with Johan Schmidt on the loose. So, he exaggerated and said he was wanted instead of explaining that he had been simply brought in for questioning.

Tunapi sat back in his wooden swivel chair, his jaw agape. Disturbing the peace fines were fairly minor, 200 francs, roughly equivalent to eight *livres*. Most people, even innocent ones, gladly paid the fines to avoid spending any more time than necessary in the police station. In fact, the cash Tunapi skimmed from those fines made up more than a third of his monthly income. He was less than thrilled with the prospect of giving up his share of the fine he expected Le Pelleteur to pay in exchange for the bother of feeding and housing a prisoner pending an extradition hearing. He explained to Le Pelleteur like if he was talking to a six-year-old. "I have news for you, too. I'm trying to get you off the hook with just a fine. Why would you turn around and try to turn this into an international incident?" He shifted his attention from Sam to the ceiling. "Why do all the screwballs come out after midnight? Does the Nut Hatch declare shore leave every night during my shift?" Then he announced to Le Pelleteur, "I don't know what you're trying to pull, but it smells like trouble, the kind I need like a two-for-one coupon for root canals. I ought to throw the both of you out on the street while I still have the chance."

"Well, Lieutenant, let's stop for a minute and think about our choices here. Either I'm on the level and I'm a cold-blooded killer wanted in Green Bay, or I'm some kind of screwball. Either way, you can't put me on the street and trust me to behave myself. You strike me as someone with a wealth of wisdom gleaned from years of experience. A man like you can imagine what kind of bureaucratic nightmare would hit whose fan when the press hears that you let me walk, just to terrorize loyal citizens of the French Empire.

"On the other hand, maybe you have a point. Holding me until I am extradited to Québec is inconvenient for you, or perhaps worse. If I am some kind of screwball, maybe I like starting fires in jail cells. Who knows what I'm capable of? Maybe I can cause enough damage to put you over budget and that could bring more attention from Paris than you're used to.

"Fortunately for you, there is a third option. I pay the disturbing the peace fine and you shove me into a squad car and dump me with the border guards at Cahokia."

Lieutenant Tunapi pondered Le Pelleteur's speech, trying to figure out if he had some kind of angle. After a few moments, Sophie realized what Sam was trying to do and followed his lead. "If this beast is sent back to Green Bay, then I'll drop the charges here."

"Now you drop the charges? After all those demands for respect?" he asked, incredulously. Then his voice shifted to a low growl. "If you were a murder suspect," pointing a finger at Le Pelleteur, "you would be trying to get further away from Green Bay, not get shipped back. Clearly, there's more going on here than a dirty old man and a woman with vitamin-enriched *Québécois* morality, but I'm happy to let the Québec border guards straighten it out. If you two know what's good for you, you're going to stay out of this town until I retire. If I catch you here before then, I swear I will figure out what just happened here and I will make you pay for it one way or another."

Chapter XXXVIII

As he dialed the candlestick telephone on his desk, Lieutenant Tunapi informed Sophie that she was free to go, sounding like he was reading an official Government edict. He offered to have a patrol car give her a ride back to her hotel. She asked to be driven to Sam's car instead. She stared out from the back seat of the squad car at the small bistros, teeming with sophisticated nightlife at 1:00 in the morning and showing no sign of letting up. The driver took a small measure of pride in pointing out where some locally well-known Lakota jazz trios perform. Although in other circumstances she would have been reminded of a few of the more exotic locales in her detective novels and her skin would have tingled at the thought, she was so distracted that the scene barely registered.

She was still a little stunned by the sight of two St. Louis *Gendarmerie* officers escorting Sam away from Lieutenant Tunapi's office. Sam wasn't merely her boss. She had known him more than half her life. When he was still her father's partner in the *Sûreté* and she was a little girl, he would come to visit her parents for dinner two or three times a month. He always found time to play one or two games of Pichenotte, that uniquely *Québécois* combination of pocket billiards and table hockey, with her in the basement before her bedtime. When she was nine, she thought she was going to marry him someday. She had long since outgrown that childhood infatuation. She was certain of that. However, he was still her oldest and best friend. Although getting straight A's throughout grade school and high school was very rewarding, it did not make her popular among her classmates. After graduation, while she found most of what she read in the textbooks she proofread to be fascinating and that working for a "private eye" provided a vicarious thrill neither job contributed anything to her social life. Thus, Sam was not only her oldest and best friend, but one of the few friends she had. So, it was particularly unsettling to watch two muscular policemen forcibly removing him from the room.

And, possibly, from her life. This felt very different from the situation she faced the previous week, when she had heard that her father had taken him in for questioning. Then, she was confident that her father would be fair to Sam. She was also cautiously optimistic that, once she delivered Sam's lawyer to the station house, *Monsieur* Henderson would make it clear sooner or later that it was all a big misunderstanding and that Sam would then be released, hopefully without too much damage. Now, however, Sam was in a new country and dealing with an unknown legal system. Even though everything in Lieutenant Tunapi's office appeared to go according to some kind of plan that Sam cooked up on the fly, she had no guarantee that Sam would successfully negotiate his way from the Border Patrol of Québec back to her father's jurisdiction.

For that matter, she asked herself, how could she know whether everything had gone according to plan? The last time they talked to each other was in the Casino, when he told her to make a scene and then head back to Green Bay. At the time, she thought she was being helpful, getting the police to escort him out of the building before he was murdered in the back alley. However, for all she knew, he had an entirely different plan he didn't have time to tell her about. Maybe, if she had left him alone, he would be on his way back home right now, in the bar car of a northbound train, savoring a glass of gin, perusing the sports section of the Cahokia newspaper and cursing the Packers for their latest loss. Instead, she imagined Sam stuck in a holding cell at the border crossing

Then, Sophie briefly let her imagination take over, picturing a half-starved Sam in ragged clothes and a half-meter long beard, shackled to an oar in the bowels of one of Louis XIV's Mediterranean slave galleys.

Sophie's driver stopped next to Sam's 1927 Chevrolet and opened Sophie's door for her. The officer embarrassed Sophie by kissing her hand, adding to the embarrassment caused by her short but gruesome reverie. As she watched the policeman drive into the night, she promised herself not to let herself drift away from reality like that again. In fact, when she stopped being melodramatic and started to think logically, the answer was clear. Sam was in legal trouble, so she needed to find him a lawyer. She would call *Monsieur* Henderson in the morning. With any luck, he would be in a better mood than he was the last time she called him.

Chapter XXXIX

While Lieutenant Tunapi was making arrangements to have Sophie escorted back to Sam's car, Sam suddenly felt two uniformed policemen grab his arms and lift him out of his chair. They handcuffed Le Pelleteur and practically dragged him from Tunapi's office through the station and out to an idling police car. Then, Sam was driven across town. During the trip, the detective tipped off the patrolmen that Auguste Dumont was trafficking in stolen goods and gave an address. The cops promised to look into it, but Le Pelleteur doubted whether they would bother.

Le Pelleteur was driven to the border crossing at the *Rue Chouteau* Bridge, from St. Louis to the North Side of Cahokia, in the Region of *Illinois*. There, a Missouri border guard ordered the detective out of the car and grabbed his upper arm like it insulted his mother. Le Pelleteur was led past the border crossing station, which looked like a toll booth, to a narrow cement footpath. It was separated by a thin handrail from a three-lane highway on one side, with the occasional car flying past even at this time of night, making Le Pelleteur's tie flap around like a trout in a canoe. On the other side of the walkway was a 30-meter fall into the roiling Mississippi-Missouri confluence. In the 2:00 AM darkness, it looked like a maelstrom of ink.

During the ride in the police car, and now as he started to trek more than one-and-a-half kilometers across the bridge while a border guard strangled his bicep, Le Pelleteur wondered about Sophie, like a mother sparrow watching her baby bird fly away towards the horizon. He took her to St. Louis thinking that she would be safer there. Instead, he practically introduces her to the Nazi assassin he thought he had left behind in Green Bay. She might be OK, he hoped, if she headed for Green Bay immediately after they left the St. Louis police station like he told her to. If she stayed in town to try to mount another heroic rescue, Le Pelleteur thought it would be just a matter of time before Johan Schmidt tracked her down.

Half-way across the bridge, Le Pelleteur decided to try to stop worrying about Sophie's situation until he could do something about it and to start worrying about his own situation. He began to notice a Québec border guard approaching from the opposite shore. As they approached each other, Le Pelleteur saw that he seemed young, in his early 20s. His blue uniform did not fit right; it was a little too big. The guard was scowling, perhaps in reaction to the wind, or perhaps in a misplaced effort to develop some form of *gravitas*.

When they met, Le Pelleteur was handed off and escorted the rest of the way across the bridge. As they walked, Le Pelleteur shouted above the wind howling around them. "I don't know what you've heard about me. My guess is that someone has said something about an outstanding murder charge. I can explain."

"Shut up."

"I was framed!"

"Shut up!"

Sam tried a different tactic. "I have been out of town for a little while. How are the Blues doing these days?" he asked, referring to the Cahokia hockey team.

"When I want to chitchat with a bum like you, I'll let you know. In the meantime, shut up!"

It took almost 15 minutes to walk across the bridge. Sam was marched past another toll booth, to a red brick building that looked a one-story ranch house. Grey metal letters spelling "*Bureau d'immigra-*

tion du Québec" were mounted next to the door. He was deposited in a room that could have been a reconstruction of the interrogation room from his Bunko Squad days, decorated only with a beat-up wooden table and a few beat-up wooden chairs. The guard handcuffed the detective to his chair, bade him *adieu* by telling him to shut up and left him alone in the room.

Chapter XL

"How incredibly, colossally stupid," Sophie silently repeated to an empty coffee cup and a half-eaten croissant at a small table in front of a sidewalk café three doors down from the hotel. If no good deed goes unpunished, Sophie told herself, her good deed was waiting until 9:00 AM, normal business hours, to call Stephane Henderson. Her punishment was hearing from the attorney's secretary that he will be in court all day and unreachable, defending someone accused of forming a labor union.

Immediately after the telephone call, she checked out of the hotel, walked to the café and spent 20 minutes cursing her breakfast, ignoring the pleasant spring morning and refusing to bask in the sun as it gently warmed the street. Between curses, she weighed her options. She could just leave town, like Sam asked her to do the night before, but she refused to do that without making certain he didn't need her help. She did not like the idea of waiting until the end of the day and calling Henderson again. If Sam needed help, he would need it sooner than that.

She could cross the border into Cahokia and pick a lawyer out of the Yellow Pages in a phone booth. She dug her wallet out of her purse and found three *livres* and 54 Missouri francs. That was barely enough to buy gas to get her back home. Any decent lawyer would charge at least another 20 *livres*. She could hope that the lawyer she picked at random would take pity on a complete stranger and provide some reasonably reliable legal advice on credit. The probability of that event seemed so remote as to be laughable. Unfortunately, Sophie did not have any good ideas for raising money quickly, either. She could ask one of her brothers to wire her money from Green Bay, but they were all at work and she would not be able to reach them before the end of the day. She could go back to the casino and try to win some money, but that seemed almost as unlikely as finding a lawyer with pity. She did not know anyone in St. Louis well enough to ask to borrow money, with the possible exception of Charles Gautier, the engineer at the radio station.

"Damn!" she announced, barely audibly, like someone halfway to her driveway when she realized that she left her car keys in the house, and glared at the art gallery across the street. Until that moment, she had forgotten that the microphone she borrowed from that engineer was still hidden in that gallery. Barring some future flash of brilliance on her part, borrowing money from Charles was the least bad option she had, but she couldn't ask him for the money unless she could return his microphone.

She briefly considered breaking into the gallery that night to retrieve the microphone, but rejected that idea because she wanted to get help to Sam sooner than that if she could. So, she asked herself, was there any way she could get the microphone back sooner, in broad daylight? She quickly developed a plan. It seemed reasonable, provided Auguste Dumont did not remember her from the previous night. She told herself it was dark in the night club. Besides, even if he did notice her, she was dressed differently, so she thought there was a good chance he would not even recognize her.

She took ten francs out of her purse and put it on her table, using the coffee cup as a paper weight. Sophie then stood up, brushed her hair back, took a deep breath and marched across the street, into the gallery and up to the front counter. She looked *Monsieur* Dumont in the eye, smiled and said forcefully, "Excuse me. I seem to have lost my microphone. I think I was here a couple of days ago and I wonder if I might have left it here by mistake."

"A microphone?"

"Yes a microphone. About yea long." Sophie held out her hands like she was describing a fish that got away. "It was grey. Kind of oblong-shaped."

"No, I haven't seen anything like that."

"Would you mind being a dear and checking in back, just in case another clerk found it?"

"I am sure there is nothing like that in back, either."

"I would feel so much better if you could take two minutes and check."

As Sophie had hoped, she looked only vaguely familiar to him and so he assumed that he must have seen her in the gallery a few days before. Still, Sophie's story sounded so ridiculous that he could not believe that she was on the level. While Dumont squinted at her, trying to figure her angle, Sophie stared back with the widest, most innocent-looking eyes she could muster. Eventually, he muttered a mildly frustrated grunt, locked the cash register and went into the back room. He tried to hide behind the door jamb to watch her. Sophie waited patiently for a few seconds, pretending not to notice him spying on her, then yelled, "Do you think my microphone might be someplace out here?"

"No, probably not," Dumont replied, sheepish at being noticed.

"Then would you mind checking to make sure it isn't back there behind a box or something?"

The gallery owner tried to think of a snappy comeback, until the moment passed. He silently admitted defeat in his short skirmish of wits and started looking in the back room for a microphone he knew was not there. As soon as she saw he was not looking, Sophie crawled under the front counter to where the microphone was hidden and yanked it hard enough to break the wires it was connected to. She went back to where she had been standing and exclaimed, "Oh, I found it! All this time it was in my purse under my lipstick. Sorry for putting you through all that trouble." The gallery owner immediately emerged from the back room with a baffled look on his face to see Sophie leave the gallery carrying the 30-centimeter microphone.

Chapter XLI

Le Pelleteur watched the border guard leave the Spartan interrogation room, grinding his teeth, thinking, "If that snot-nosed kid tells me to shut up one more time, I'll shut him up with a knuckle sandwich." After a few minutes, it dawned on him that punching the Guard might not be the most strategic move he could make. He also realized that things were going fairly well for him that night. After all, he thought, he successfully avoided getting killed by a Nazi spy. Admittedly, this was a positive development. He noted that Sophie should get the credit for that; she came up with the plan for getting him out of the casino. He habitually thought of her as the precocious little girl that he met when his former partner first invited him to dinner twelve years earlier, or occasionally the amazingly clever high school junior that he hired as his secretary in 1935. He had never seen her think on her feet like she did in the casino before then. He decided that, if he ever gets home, he should reconsider his conclusion that anything but the most routine of detective work is too dangerous for her.

At that point, his eyelids grew leaden. His watch said twenty-to-three. He rested his head on his unhandcuffed arm on the table. What felt like five minutes later, Le Pelleteur was startled awake with a firm nudge to his elbow. He bolted up in his chair and found a man offering him a white ceramic mug full of coffee. "I am Special Agent Hebert."

Le Pelleteur rubbed his face and blinked a few times. He glanced at his watch again and saw that it was ten after eight. He swallowed a mouthful of hot black elixir of life, or perhaps, elixir of not-quite-so-much-like-death. "*Merci beaucoup*. I am Samuel de Champlain Le Pelleteur," he mumbled, sizing up his new host while trying to clear the fog in his head. He appeared to be in his early 50s, clearly senior to the snot-nosed kid he'd dealt with earlier. A short, round man with the last wisps of grey hair and a bushy mustache of the same color, he looked like Santa Claus without the full beard or the jolliness. His uniform jacket was unbuttoned and his shirt was not tucked in, making him look about as good as Le Pelleteur felt. Yet, while Special Agent Hebert lacked in sartorial polish, he made up for it by making a surprisingly good cup of coffee. (Le Pelleteur assumed that he made the coffee because he did not see anyone on the premises other than Snot-Nose when he was brought in.) Le Pelleteur guessed that he had spent his life building a sloppy, disorganized exterior as camouflage for a tough investigator who didn't miss much. Like Santa, he knew who was naughty or nice, but the naughty ones got something much worse than a lump of coal.

"Well, I have to say that your interrogation room accommodations fall a little short of four-star," Le Pelleteur complained. "How did you sleep last night? Well, I hope."

The Special Agent chuckled quietly. "My evening was fairly routine, until a rather unpleasant phone call woke me up in the middle of the night. It took me fifteen minutes to get back to sleep. As it happens, the St. Louis *Gendarmerie* left a surprise on our doorstep last night."

"Is this surprise something I might know about?" Le Pelleteur inquired sarcastically.

"I had hoped that you might have some passing familiarity with it. When the *Gendarmerie* passed you along to us, they said you claimed you were wanted for murder in Green Bay. Is that true?"

"I don't know. Neither the *Gendarmerie* nor your charming young associate confided in me about what either of you told each other."

"Are you wanted for murder in Green Bay?"

"Yes," the detective lied.

"You see, this is where your surprise becomes unpleasant. After my colleague called me last night, he called the Green Bay Bureau of the *Sûreté*. They told him you're not wanted for murder in Green Bay, or for anything else. So, right now, you look like someone trying to get into the country under false pretenses. You're a spy, or you did something in French North America so heinous that posing as a murder suspect in Green Bay is a step up for you. Either way, I think the best thing to do is to march you across the bridge back to St. Louis right now."

The last thing Le Pelleteur wanted was to be sent back to St. Louis. "You can't deport me. I have a Québec passport."

"I don't see how that helps your case. If your passport was valid and you could just glide over the border like a good forward crossing the blue line, why was the police involved? Again, the passport could be fake and you could be a spy. Or, the St. Louis *Gendarmes* that delivered you are fake and you are running away from some truly horrible sin in Missouri. Or, maybe both."

Le Pelleteur thought for a second. "I think I might be able to explain the confusion. I am a suspect in a murder investigation in Green Bay. I told the *Gendarmes* that I was wanted because I assumed an arrest warrant would have been issued in that investigation by now. There must have been some delay in the paperwork, which would prevent me from turning up on the Green Bay Bureau *Sûreté* desk clerk's official Wanted List. If you could call again and ask for the detective in charge of the Shapiro investigation, Philippe Marleau, he'll tell you I'm a suspect and corroborate my story."

Special Agent Hebert looked Sam in the eye, looking for his angle. Le Pelleteur responded, "If I'm handing you a line, you can send me back to St. Louis after the call. Keeping me here another five minutes is not going to make any difference to you. However, if I'm on the level, you have a murder suspect in your custody. If you send me back to St. Louis and the press hears about it, they're going to say that you let me get away, that you let me 'escape justice.' That can't be good for you. Something like that could trigger an internal investigation, maybe even Parliamentary hearings." Le Pelleteur paused for dramatic effect, then inquired, "Forgive me for asking a personal question, but I am curious. How long do you have to go before you get your pension?"

Special Agent Hebert chuckled again. "You've spent some time in law enforcement; enough to understand the bureaucracy. I hope this story of yours pans out, for your sake."

Chapter XLII

While Sam was waiting in the interrogation room, Sophie was pulling into the radio station parking lot. After she parked the car, Sophie walked past six or seven cars in the parking lot and into the lobby and asked to see Charles. The receptionist explained that he would not be available until 11:10, after the next news report. Sophie looked at her wrist watch, which said 10:45, and decided to wait on a slightly worn leather couch.

When he appeared from the studios, he almost ran across the small lobby and positioned himself on the couch next to Sophie, close, but not too close. He said "Hello," with the same excited nervousness that he remembered when he tried to talk to Chantal Couillard in Grade 7.

"Hi," Sophie responded. After a short but slightly awkward pause, she proclaimed, "I have your microphone."

"Oh, great. Thanks. How did it work?"

"It was terrific. I can't thank you enough for letting me use it."

"I have my lunch break in an hour. I would be interested in hearing about your rig."

Sophie thought about the offer, about how wonderful half a ham and cheese sandwich and a glass of wine would taste if she could eat it while staring into his eyes and reluctantly said, "Sorry, but I can't today. I have a friend who needs my help this afternoon."

"What kind of help? Maybe I could help, too, if it can wait until after work."

She looked into his eyes again. She knew that there would never be a better time to ask for money than that moment. Yet, she couldn't do it. She suddenly felt like she was using him and it suddenly felt wrong. "Thanks, but my friend can't wait. Besides, I don't want to inconvenience you. Perhaps we could have lunch together some other time." She handed over the microphone and left. He watched her walk to her car, wondering what he did wrong, before reluctantly going back to work.

Sophie walked past about half a dozen cars in the parking lot on her way to the 1927 Chevrolet, one of which was an unremarkable late-model wine-red Ford coupe. Unbeknownst to her, this coupe was occupied by Johan Schmidt and his associate, Gerhard Wilmer. The previous night, as the St. Louis *Gendarmerie* was removing Sam from the Casino, Schmidt signalled across the room to Wilmer, one of his most trusted goons, who immediately started to follow Sam. He then leaned back against the bar and watched Sam struggle, but not too much, against the forces of law and order that had ensnared him.

"Do you know what I think?" he innocently asked the bartender. That simple question generated the kind of fear that strangled the bartender's brain. He knew there were at least 8000 ways to answer and none of them were what Schmidt wanted to hear. It was also common knowledge among casino employees that the penalty for failing to live up to Schmidt's expectations could range from mild condescension to a quiet rendezvous involving tire irons in the back alley. Fortunately for the bartender, it was a rhetorical question and Schmidt paid no attention to the bartender while his voice box was crippled by terror.

Schmidt thought there was something fishy about Samuel de Champlain Le Pelleteur. He could not be certain this annoying man had planned to have a police escort away from the casino, but it seemed suspiciously convenient. There was also the matter of Auguste Dumont. Schmidt studied the art dealer as he remained enraptured by the roulette table and oblivious to the rest of the world. Yet, if Schmidt remembered correctly, Le Pelleteur and Dumont were talking to each other when he initially noticed Le Pelleteur. That was probably the first time Dumont ever spoke to anyone while playing roulette. Le Pelleteur's connection with Dumont was not clear, but he appeared to be more deeply involved in Schmidt's business than Schmidt preferred.

Wilmer returned to the casino to report that he lost the detective when he was taken into the police station. After the obligatory pistol whipping, Schmidt decided that they should pay a visit to Dumont's gallery in the morning. They arrived just in time to observe Sophie leave the gallery carrying a microphone. Schmidt immediately recognized her as the woman who slapped Le Pelleteur the night before and they immediately started to follow her.

Chapter XLIII

Sophie sat for a moment in the parking lot and stared back at the farmhouse-style radio studio. She was tempted for a long time to run back in to tell Charles that she changed her mind about lunch. Then she sighed and drove away, telling herself that it was just lunch and even if it was something more, it would never have worked out anyway. She decided to take her lead from almost every detective novel she had read in her life. In particular, she remembered her first detective novel, *Monsieur Lecoq*, which had originally belonged to her grandmother, who gave it to her as a gift for her ninth birthday. Lecoq was a young but brilliant police officer who had just joined the French *Sûreté* and was stationed in Paris in the 1860s, sarcastically nicknamed "*Monsieur*" by his supervisor who dismissed the clues he gleaned from a crime scene as ridiculous speculation. He never allowed anything to get in the way of following those clues, even when the suspect turned out to be a wealthy French nobleman with nearly unlimited resources that he could devote to covering his tracks and even when his supervisor became increasingly dismissive of his theory. Like *Monsieur* Lecoq, she wouldn't let anything get in her way, not even a cute radio engineer.

Sophie resigned herself to her failure to find legal help for Sam and stared into the radio station parking lot trying to develop another plan. She eventually had an idea. She did not particularly like it, but could not come up with any better alternatives. She heaved a sigh, put the Chevrolet into gear and started to drive back into town. She drove through a residential neighborhood on the western edge of the city, where the roofs of the older houses, built in the late 1880s and inspired by the teepees popular among many house buyers at that time, looked like turrets on miniature castles. She proceeded to creep through the lunchtime traffic jams of the art deco canyons of downtown St. Louis and the 17th Century provincial charm of the *Le Vieux St. Louis*, to the line-up of cars waiting to cross the *Rue Chouteau* Bridge to *La République Québécoise*. She hoped some other brainstorm would strike her before she finished inching across the bridge, but by the time she reached the row of toll booth-like gates on the *Illinois* Region side of the Missouri River, she had no other options and she had run out of time.

To the right of the border crossing gates was a one-story red brick house with a sign reading "*Bureau d'immigration du Québec.*" Sophie pulled up to the house, parked the car, took a deep breath, walked up to the door and knocked. A bald, heavy-set man in a blue uniform and a grey moustache answered.

Before he could say anything, Sophie performed her best impersonation of a lawyer. "I have reason to believe that you are holding a Samuel de Champlain Le Pelleteur. I am his attorney and I demand to see my client at once."

"You're an attorney?" He asked, smiling the way Sophie's mother might smile at a kitten wrestling with a ball of yarn.

"Yes, I am," she said defiantly, as if defiance might convince him to take her seriously.

"And you demand to see your client?"

"Immediately."

"Well, ordinarily, I would be happy to let you see him. In fact, I would let you see him even if you were simply a friend of his and not clearly a very important attorney demanding to see your client for official legal purposes. The problem is that he is not here. Agents from *Sûreté* headquarters took him away this morning."

Her defiance melted into concern. "You mean from Montréal? Not from the Green Bay Bureau?"

The old man nodded. This news was worse than Sophie had feared. If the Feds have gotten involved, then it must be because Sam fled the jurisdiction. She thought back to the cab ride from the 28th District station house and wanted to hit Sam again. He had at least two things in his favor on the murder charge: he didn't do it and she knew her father wouldn't railroad him. Now, he can't argue that he didn't try to run out of the country and there is no way of knowing whether the agents or the Investigating Magistrate handling his case now are going to give him a fair shake.

"Do you know where he was taken?" By this time, Sophie was too shaken to keep up her attorney bravado.

"If I had to hazard a guess, I would say they are on a train to Montréal right now, but there's a chance they took him to their field office here in Cahokia. Sorry I can't tell you anything more, honey." He sounded disappointed, like he was telling his granddaughter that the circus had just left town.

Chapter XLIV

Three hours before Sophie arrived at the border station, Le Pelleteur was jolted awake a second time. Again, he felt like he had been asleep for five minutes, but his watch claimed that it was 10:00. Special Agent Hebert was offering him another white ceramic mug of coffee. The detective raised the cup slightly and muttered, "To your health." He sipped the coffee, rubbed his face and asked if Special Agent Hebert had called Green Bay.

"Detective Marleau returned my call twenty minutes ago."

"I take it that he confirmed my testimony?"

"Well, not exactly."

That woke Le Pelleteur up quickly. "What did he say, exactly?"

"He confirmed he was originally investigating the Shapiro case at one time, but the *Sûreté Nationale du Québec* later took over. He referred me to Montréal and after a few phones calls, I found out that someone from the Feds' Office here in Cahokia is coming to take you in for questioning."

A few moments later, Snot-nose burst into the room, followed closely by two average-looking men of average height, in black trench coats and matching fedoras. One wore glasses with heavy, black frames. Snot-nose unlocked Le Pelleteur's handcuffs, then stood Le Pelleteur up and spun him around to face him, so that one of the men in black behind him could put a different pair of cuffs on him. For a few seconds, Le Pelleteur growled at Snot-nose, quietly, deep in his throat, like a German shepherd whose hair is just starting to stand up at the back of his neck.

One of the men in black tossed Le Pelleteur's coat over the shoulders of his wrinkled suit, while the other squashed his fedora onto his head. Then, each grabbed an arm and dragged Le Pelleteur out of the building like they had to rush to get him to the curb before the garbage truck came. They threw him into the back seat of a grey 1938 Oldsmobile sedan, got into the front seat and drove away.

Le Pelleteur was bounced around in the back seat, unable to keep his balance with his hands cuffed behind his back. He tried to engage the backs of their heads in conversation, but they remained stone-silent. The car was parked in a lot next to the Vigilant Building, an office building in downtown Cahokia that seemed to blend in with the other office buildings in downtown Cahokia. Cahokia at that time was in the midst of a unique architectural movement: Indian Deco. Like buildings going up in New York, Montréal and Green Bay in the 1930s, Cahokia's business district was filled with 50-story buildings that scallop to a point someplace in the upper stratosphere. However, instead of gargoyles or other decorative features found on skyscrapers in other cities, the Vigilant Building was festooned with chieftain faces and concrete headdresses descending ten stories.

The two men marched Le Pelleteur across the lobby, which was two stories tall. The red marble decorative pillars matched the leather couches. The ceiling was arched into a semicircle and tiled with a diamond pattern, bright red inside sunlight yellow inside brilliant kelly green, each color with stepped borders. If Le Pelleteur had looked up at the ceiling, he would have found it breathtaking. It looked like a medieval European cathedral dedicated to a native spirit.

In the elevator, the man in the glasses offered, "We apologize if we were a little abrupt. We needed to match our behavior to the story we gave to the Ministry of Immigration and Border Patrol." Meanwhile, the other man unlocked the handcuffs.

"What was the story you gave?" Le Pelleteur inquired.

"We told them that you were wanted for murder by the *Sûreté Nationale du Québec*."

"If this is a 'story,' can I assume that I'm not wanted for murder?"

Both men just stared into space. Le Pelleteur then asked, "Are you with the *Sûreté* or not? What's going on here?"

Glasses, continuing to stare at the elevator door, replied, "That information is on a 'need to know' basis." Le Pelleteur realized that questioning the two men further would be a waste of time, but he surprised himself by finding their silence more intriguing than infuriating. He spent the rest of the elevator ride, to the 23rd floor, studying the pair, like some random facial tic might interrupt their stony silence and give Le Pelleteur some insight into their secrets.

When the elevators opened, the two men strode purposefully, like they were used to being pressed for time. Le Pelleteur followed them closely to the end of the hallway to a door marked "Janitor." One of them unlocked the door to reveal a small office, empty except for a filing cabinet and a telephone on the floor in the far corner. They invited the detective in and then Glasses picked up the telephone and dialed while the other re-locked the door.

"The package has been delivered." Glasses announced into the telephone handset. After two or three "uh-huhs," he handed the phone to Le Pelleteur and said, "It's for you." Confused, Le Pelleteur took the phone and inquired, "Hello?"

"So, when is Green Bay going to get rid of those bums and put a real hockey team on the ice?" Eventually, Le Pelleteur gathered his wits enough to stammer incredulously, "Uncle Edouard?"

Chapter XLV

"Yes, it's me," Uncle Edouard bellowed to Le Pelleteur in reply. He developed his habit of shouting on the telephone before World War I, when long distance calls tended to be more static-laden. "Are you still following that pee wee hockey team in Green Bay?"

"That's very funny, but I don't see the Montréal *Québécois* doing anything to brag about."

"My team is doing better than yours."

"Well, I hate to change the subject," Sam interjected, with two dozen questions on subjects he considered much more important than hockey small talk, "but as long as I have you on the line, I was wondering if you could help me figure something out. I'm in a small office with a 'Janitor' sign on the door, with two men in black suits who refuse to tell me who they are or what I'm doing here. You were talking to one of them on the phone just before I got on the line and from what I could see, it looks like you know a lot more about what's going on than I do. I was hoping you could fill me in."

Edouard thought for a moment. "Filling you in is more complicated than you might think. I guess I should start at the beginning. You know how I have been telling you for twenty years that I work as an accountant for the *Commission de la communication du Québec*? Well, that's a little white lie that I tell people so that I don't have to tell them what I really do for a living. I work in the *Sûreté*'s *Bureau de la Securite Exterieure*."

"Well, I kind of guessed already that your two friends here, Patty and Laverne, were spies as soon as they refused to tell me their names."

"Just to be clear, I'm not really a spy. I used to be, but I don't do much field work anymore. I am more of a supervisor. Field agents report to me and I put the pieces together into a bigger picture and report that up to the next level on the bureaucratic ladder. Sometimes I do a little recruiting work."

"Just out of curiosity, how long have Patty and Laverne here been spying on me?"

"Since last night, when you became embroiled in the French North American system of justice. We have been watching your friend Johan for two months. When the St. Louis *Gendarmes* took you away, you weren't too hard to miss."

"If you were watching Johan, why did you let him murder someone and why didn't you say something to the police when I was arrested?"

Edouard was caught by surprise. "Who did he kill?"

"George-Etienne Shapiro, an insurance agent in Green Bay, about a week ago."

"We knew he was in Green Bay, but we lost track of him for a few days. I would be interested in hearing what you know about his movements."

Le Pelleteur recounted his showdown with Schmidt in the alley. He also summarized his conversation with Schmidt in the casino, in which Schmidt admitted that he killed Shapiro. Finally, the detective explained his theory, that Shapiro was murdered to cover up an insurance fraud operation that was somehow tied to a scheme to smuggle Indian art to Germany.

"Well, that's clever." Uncle Edouard sounded like he begrudgingly admired Schmidt. "We've heard that both Hitler and Herman Goering onsider themselves big art aficionados. There are stories of them loot-ng all over Nazi-occupied Eastern Europe. It looks like they have ex-anded into North America and they used the insurance fraud as a over."

"And murder. Don't forget that Schmidt murdered someone to over this up. What about him?"

"He has diplomatic immunity. The best we could do is send him ome and we don't want to do that until we figure out who he's working or."

"What makes you think he's working for someone else?"

"Johan is more of the middle-management type. He's never been he kind of guy who could be the brains of an operation."

Le Pelleteur furrowed his brow, like he just realized that he must ave missed something important earlier in the conversation. "If the 3SE is watching Schmidt, then you must think he's a spy, but this scam ust doesn't add up as some kind of secret intelligence operation. A ninute ago, you said the Nazis usually start looting as soon as they in-ade a new country. I thought I heard not too long ago that they are lanning to invade France right now. So, why are they going through all his trouble to sneak art out of the Missouri Territory now when they ould just loot it after they conquer France? Have the Germans given up n invading France? Did Hitler want an Indian blanket so much he ouldn't wait for the invasion?"

Edouard contemplated briefly. "I wish I could tell you. I'm more han a little curious myself. However, Hitler doesn't confide in me nearly s much as I might like. One thing I can tell you, though, is that giving p on invading a country doesn't sound like the Hitler we have come to now and despise. I think we can rule that out." Uncle Edouard paused. Sam heard the quiet gurgle of his uncle's pipe over the telephone. "And nother thing—sneaking the art out doesn't sound like the Nazis' style.

When they decide to do something, they're not generally the shy or self conscious type. Instead, they have all the finesse and subtlety of a Panz er Division. So, my guess is that neither Hitler nor Goering is making the line changes in this game. More likely, they're sitting up in th bleachers watching instead of standing behind the bench."

Sam heard more gurgling. "One possibility," Edouard continued "is that your pal Johan is working for someone trying to curry favor with the Nazi brass. Maybe someone is looking ahead, betting that France i going to fall and angling for a job running French North America afte Germany takes over."

The quiet gurgling sound came over the phone again. Le Pelleteur looked at Patty and Laverne, as if seeing their faces might provide som indication of what his uncle was thinking. Eventually, Uncle Edouard' voice returned. "You said that I knew what was going on around here Actually, I wouldn't mind knowing a little more and I think you coul help me out on that. How would you like to find Schmidt's boss?"

Chapter XLVI

Le Pelleteur suddenly realized where the conversation was going. His uncle was about to ask him to "do his part." That phrase immediately reminded him of a little lake about 150 kilometers northwest of Montréal in early summer 25 years earlier, in 1915. The summer sun was slowly gliding downward in the western sky. Its bottom half was hidden by the pines now silhouetted on the other side of the lake. A gently wafting trail of orange-yellow sparkles danced across the lake as the water shifted slowly from sapphire to midnight blue. The ten-year-old Sam had spent the day fishing with his favorite uncle. They had feasted on campfire-broiled perch and Pepsi in bottles cooled by the last vestiges of the spring run-off. They had just finished washing the dishes. Now they were sitting in silence by the side of the lake, mesmerized by the grandeur. It was as if the lake usually performed this miracle in seclusion, but decided to make an exception and share it with Sam and his uncle this time.

"I'm going to miss this next year."

"Why?"

"What?" Uncle Edouard inquired, realizing too late that he was speaking out loud, or that anyone was listening to him.

"Why can't we do this next year?"

Edouard looked at Sam, then back at the lake. For those few seconds, Sam was not sure if he saw embarrassment, pity, or pained awkwardness in his uncle's eyes. Uncle Edouard drew on his pipe. He had started to smoke that pipe in college six years earlier, which was as long as Sam could remember. The tobacco briefly glowed orange as dusk was falling and made a quiet, gurgling sound.

"I don't know if you read the newspapers, but there's a war going on." Sam was aware of World War I, perhaps slightly more aware than the average ten-year-old at the time. At the time, he and his family lived in Montréal, because his father was the Chief of Staff of the Member of Parliament for the Green Bay-North district. Sam told his uncle what he learned from his father, that the War was something happening someplace else, far away and it was important that we not get involved.

"Well," Uncle Edouard replied, "a lot of people agree with your father, but there is another way to look at it. The way I see it, this is a war against a country that can sink a cruise ship with hundreds of innocent women and children as passengers without blinking. Much more than any other war in history, this is a war of barbarity against civilization and decency. I don't want to let the Barbarians win knowing that I could have done my part but decided not to."

Thousands of men elsewhere in North America were feeling the same need to do their part. The Dominion of Oregon entered the War shortly after it started in 1914. Texas was starting to send troops to France during Edouard and Sam's camping trip. The *Lusitania* had been sunk about two months previously and eighty-two of the people who died on the *Lusitania* were Texans. The United States was neutral at the beginning of the War, but joined later in 1917. Edouard grew up hearing stories of his relatives' heroic exploits through history, going back to the Plains of Abraham and he felt a moral obligation to follow in their footsteps. Uncle Edouard's reaction to the War was unusual in Québec, however. Most *Québécois*, including Sam's father, figured that neither France nor Britain ever did them any favors and did not feel any particular need to travel thousands of kilometers away to die in a cold muddy lonely trench.

Sam never forgot that conversation with his uncle on that summer evening. He carried it with him through his teen years, like a carpenter keeps a tape measure attached to his tool belt. During a time in his life when he was hormonally predisposed to disapprove of everything his father did, he relied on the conversation to prove to himself that his father didn't measure up. His father eventually ran for office himself, following a tradition set by more than one of his ancestors. From Sam's perspective, his father's conception of doing his part seemed confined to fancy fundraising parties, an imperfect if not anemic reflection of Uncle Edouard's understanding of the phrase. It was his desire to emulate his uncle and "do his part" that eventually led him to police work. "Doing his part," of course, was a major contributing factor in his unceremonious departure from the Bunko Squad, which in turn led to the steady if not monotonous downward trend his life has taken ever since. Ultimately he was convinced that "doing one's part" is the universe's way of bending you over so it could more easily kick you in the ass.

Samuel de Champlain Le Pelleteur had spent the previous five years steadfastly avoiding anything suggesting public service, or getting involved, or giving a damn, or anything else that smacks of "doing his part." He had no intention of allowing anyone to subvert his carefully cultivated philosophy of self-centeredness—not even his favorite uncle, who took him camping every summer when he was growing up.

"Well, I really would like to help," Le Pelleteur lied, "but I've already told you everything I know about this case. All my leads on this case are dead ends and I don't think I'm going to turn up anything else."

"It would be nice if you could try. You have been in Green Bay a lot longer than any of our agents. You know your way around town. You have connections with locals that my people don't have. If anyone can figure this out, it's you."

"Even if I had any leads, I couldn't help. Times are tight and I can't afford to pass up paying clients to devote all my time to your case."

"If we have to hire you to get you to serve your country, we can do that."

As Le Pelleteur tried to think of another excuse, Uncle Edouard interjected, "OK, let's step back and review the situation here. Do you remember what you were doing about an hour ago? You were locked in a room, waiting to find out if you were going to be shipped off to stand trial for murder in Green Bay, or given back to St. Louis, where for all you know you could have ended up on a Mississippi river barge headed towards Devil's Island. So, if I can't persuade you to do this any other way, how about this: you owe me right now and I'm not going to let you weasel out of it with some kind of half-assed whiny excuse."

Chapter XLVII

Upon learning that she had missed Sam, Sophie asked the border guard if she could borrow the telephone and a phone book. He invited her in and led her to his office. She sat at his desk and looked up the number for the Cahokia branch of the *Sûreté du Québec*. An overworked, slightly impatient voice explained that there was no record of a Samuel de Champlain Le Pelleteur being held in custody, but the paperwork probably had not been completed if he was picked up as recently as that morning. She then tore a page from a note pad on the desk, copied the address of the Cahokia station house out of the phone book and asked the border guard for directions. He drew a map for her. Sophie then ran back to the car and drove as fast as the early afternoon downtown traffic would allow.

While she drove, she decided not to pretend to be Sam's lawyer again. She clearly didn't fool the border guard into thinking she was an attorney, so it made sense to try something else. By the time she arrived at the station house, a blocky-looking brick structure at the edge of town, she had developed a new plan. She stomped through a lobby that looked much like the lobby in the station house where her father works: brick walls, painted industrial gray, with a heavy film of boredom mixed with hopelessness.

She glanced at the name plate on the desk sergeant's desk, then looked the man in the eye and announced, "Sophie Marleau, *Journal de Green Bay*. A little bird told me that you're holding Samuel de Champlain Le Pelleteur, a desperate criminal, wanted for murder up in the

City by the Bay. Sergeant Tremblay, you need to let me talk to him. My readers need to know what he has to say."

Sergeant Tremblay was in his late 40s, with graying hair and a physique reflecting too many years spent behind a desk. He was the kind of guy who saw people come in off the street fifty times a day to tell him what he needed to do and found what little joy he had in life showing them they were wrong. He picked up a clipboard from his desk, looking at Sophie like he was doing her a bigger favor than she deserved.

"Sorry, ma'am," Sergeant Tremblay said, clearly not sorry at all, "we are not holding anyone by that name at this time."

"By what name?" Sophie inquired.

"The name you just said," Sergeant Tremblay explained in a tone intended to sound authoritative, but failed to hide his confusion.

"And what name was that?"

Sergeant Tremblay wrinkled his brow, more confused. Sophie offered, "Could it have been 'Simon de Champaign Le Pollinor?'"

"Of course."

"No, it was not." Sophie sounded like she was talking to a misbehaving puppy. "You were not paying attention and you didn't even bother to look at your little list before you decided the man I asked for isn't here. You know, Officer Tremblay, if I can't get the story I came for maybe I'll write a story about the shocking and gross incompetence of the *Sûreté's* Bureau in Cahokia."

"The name is '*Sergeant* Tremblay'," he replied, his smugness sounding more than a little defensive.

"How long do you think you will *stay* '*Sergeant* Tremblay' after write my story?"

He was taken aback, like he had never heard a threat before then that he couldn't brush off like the white flakes on his black uniform. He picked up his clipboard again and asked, "What was that name again?"

Sophie pronounced slowly and clearly, "Samuel de Champlain Le Pelleteur."

Sergeant Tremblay studied the list of names on his clipboard carefully and then chuckled, like he just told a joke no one else got. "As I informed you before, there is no 'Le Pelleteur' here."

"You wouldn't mind if I took a look for myself, would you?" He held up the clipboard for Sophie to see. "No," she explained. "I meant taking a look at your holding cells. After all, if he is here and his paperwork has been misplaced, it wouldn't be the first time something like that happened, would it?" She remembered her father telling stories about lost paperwork on detainees when she was growing up and guessed that Green Bay was not the only police department where things like that happened.

The Desk Sergeant sighed, like considering Sophie's request might cause him to pull a muscle, then picked up the telephone and called for a guard to escort Sophie through the holding cells in the basement. However, after she was given the full tour and heard more than one prisoner make improper advances, she verified that Sam was not there.

Sophie emerged from the *Sûreté* station house frustrated, assuming that Sam was being taken to Montréal accompanied by a police escort. She was out of options and she could not come up with another plan while she racked her brains walking the three blocks back to the car. Sophie climbed behind the steering wheel and tried one more time to come up with a brilliant idea. After five minutes, she gave up. There was nothing more she could do there. Perhaps her father or Stephane Henderson could do something. Despondent, she started the long drive back to Green Bay.

Chapter XLVIII

Meanwhile, as Sophie was arguing with the Sergeant Tremblay in Cahokia, Samuel de Champlain le Pelleteur was rocketing across *Illinois* at 125 kilometers per hour in a red and orange striped blur called the *Chief Pontiac Limited*, also known as the 12:15 to Green Bay. Ninety minutes into the trip, he was almost a third of the way home and finishing a late lunch of poutine and gin in the dining car, sitting alone, his elbow resting on the table, his feet crossed on the chair next to him. He was somewhat disappointed at the unavailability of Green Bay style poutine with the blobs of cheese on a railroad that claimed to provide all the finest amenities. A thin string of bluish white smoke rose vertically from his cigarette, then broke into wispy curls about a meter above his head. Having drained his glass, he used it as an ashtray. The ashes made short hisses when they touched the remnants of his ice cubes, almost inaudible above the drone of the streamlined train's electric turbine engines.

Earlier, while he was eating, Le Pelleteur read the morning edition of the *Journal de Green Bay*, Thursday, February 15, 1940, and discovered that the Packers had started a winning streak the day after he left town. The newspaper said that they were playing better than they had in years. This seemed logical to Le Pelleteur. Regardless of any ephemeral glimpses of reasonably good fortune that life might bestow on him from time to time, he remained convinced that, not only was he was destined for bad luck, but that he generated a field of bad luck that among other things generated static on all radios in a 20-block radius, added half a meter of snow to any blizzard he endured and doomed to failure any hockey team he supported. By leaving town, he lifted his bad luck field from Green Bay and allowed the Packers a brief flowering of success.

Now, the pages of the newspaper were scattered over the dirty dishes on the table as Le Pelleteur stared out the window at the slate-grey blur of the paper-thin ice on the *Illinois* River. He was trying to think again about his new case, the one his uncle buffaloed him into taking, the one with the Central Government of *La République Québécoise* as his client, the one he doubted would come to any good.

One bright spot, however, was that that Uncle Edouard's associates, who would always be known to Le Pelleteur as Patty and Laverne, paid for his train ticket. Another was that the detective did not anticipate requiring extensive thought at that point to solve the case. He knew that Nathalie Juneau was responsible for the insurance fraud. Bernie *La Bouche* had fingered her and he had no incentive to lie. It made sense to Le Pelleteur that she would also be the mastermind behind funneling the stolen art to the Nazis. He marked her as the prime candidate for the brains behind Johan Schmidt's brawn.

He spent the rest of the trip stewing, until the train pulled into *La Gare de L'Avenue Montmagny*, 20 minutes late, at 7:00 PM. He found a phone booth at the station and called Sophie at the office for a ride, but got no answer. He tried her apartment and got no answer there, either. At that point, he almost panicked, just before realizing that she must still be on the road. His Chevrolet sedan was no diesel train. If she slept in and got a late start from St. Louis, he figured that she might not get home until 9:00 or 10:00. He resumed stewing while he marched two blocks to the nearest *élevé* stop and went home.

Chapter XLIX

While Sam's train was racing along Lake Michigan about an hour way from the Green Bay station, Sophie was chugging along at 65 ilometers per hour, heading north on Highway Q66, referred to locally s Pontiac Trail, about two hours past Cahokia, through acres of farm-and. She was heading towards Joliet, then on to Racine and eventually ome. To her left, the sun was setting and the sky was turning pink and range, like an Easter egg. The fields were an endless expanse of pastel olors, as the snow covering the rich soil reflected the sunset. To her ight, a cloudless sky the color of the flag of *La République Québécoise* vas receding into a deep cobalt. The two-lane road stretched out ahead f her, like a line bisecting a plane in the geometry book she reviewed ne previous summer. Except for the driver of a car barely perceptible on ne horizon in her rear view mirror, she felt like the only human being vithin a thousand kilometers.

As she drove, a hundred emotions were spinning in her head, like rains of sand in a dust devil. First, she worried about Sam and she felt uilty for failing to get Sam out of jail, even though she didn't know vhat else she could have done. She was also proud of her work in St. ouis and felt she was now qualified to call herself a real detective. Vhen she remembered Charles Gautier's eyes, she regretted not accept-ng his lunch invitation earlier that day. But most of all, Charles' eyes nade her feel excited and nervous, weak in the knees and butterflies in ne stomach, as she started to plan another trip back to St. Louis as soon s she could save up the train fare.

She suddenly realized her mind was wandering. She imagined he father kindly but firmly lecturing her, as he did when he taught her t drive five years before. She regained her focus and saw that the scen around her had not changed, except that the car in her rear view mirro had grown from a dot on the horizon to a wine-red 1938 Ford convertible coupe about a kilometer away. A loud "ping" announced that th driver's side mirror had leapt off the car. Sophie was intrigued as sh watched it skip along the road ahead of the car, then vault into the ai spinning end over end, into the ditch on the opposite side of the road.

She was startled by a loud crack, like lake ice telling you tha you've ventured too far from shore. Suddenly, tiny fissures crinkled ou from a small hole in the middle of the windshield. She checked her rea view mirror again. Tiny fissures in the rear windshield, like those in th front, obscured most of the view, but she could still see the red Ford. Th car was now close enough to see that the top had been taken down and man was standing next to the driver aiming a rifle at her.

She ducked her head down so that she could barely see the roa over the dashboard. A quick giggle popped out, which surprised her, because she had always considered herself much more logical than giggl in the past. Sophie then floored the gas pedal and started to swerve bac and forth across the road, figuring that would make her a harder targe She inched her head up slightly and looked around and adjusted the rea view mirror so she could see her attackers while crouching. The swerving seemed to help. Three or four shots hit the trunk of her Chevrol during the next five minutes, but none threatened to hit her and severa others missed altogether. But the red Ford coupe crept closer and close like a lion gaining on a wildebeest. Sophie suddenly remembered tha Sam kept a handgun in the glove compartment and felt stupid for nc thinking of it earlier. She quickly learned that it wasn't easy to aim a something behind her and keep the car on the road. She put three bull holes in the back seat and shot out one of the passenger's side windows before she gave up and dropped the gun on the seat beside her.

When the Ford had pulled to within 100 meters, Sophie heard a metallic "gulp" from the rear of her Chevrolet and saw in her mirror that she was now leaving a trail of gasoline on the pavement behind her. Sophie winced, like she stubbed her toe, and said to herself, "Well, I guess it's time for me to come up with some kind of a plan." She glanced again at her gasoline trail. While she saw it as a source of obvious concern, it also seemed like a trail of flammable liquid on the road should be something she could use to her advantage.

She checked again in Sam's glove compartment and found a half-full fifth of gin and one of his silver cigarette lighters. She considered igniting the lighter and throwing it out the window behind her, but then had a better idea. She grabbed one of the blankets from the back seat and ripped a strip of material away with one hand and her teeth. She then took her foot off the accelerator for a few seconds, pulled over to the left side of the road and slammed on the brakes. As the other car flew past and the rifleman hit the passenger's door twice, Sophie shifted into reverse, made a three-point turn and sped away southbound as quickly as her in-line six engine could go.

As Sophie hoped, because the other car was going much faster than she was, it took much longer for it to stop and turn around. Keeping one hand on the steering wheel, she pulled the cork out of the gin bottle with her teeth and spit it into the passenger's seat and stuffed the blanket swatch part way into the bottle with her free hand. After that, she cranked down her window and crossed the center line to drive next to the gasoline trail she had left driving northbound. She lit her crude Molotov cocktail and threw it down onto the pavement.

For several excruciating seconds, the puddle of gin dribbled across the pavement, while the rag smoldered nearby. Sophie stared at a slender curl of smoke in her rear view mirror, until the gin finally reached the rag and erupted into flame. The burning alcohol immediately ignited the northbound and southbound gasoline trails, like intertwined rocket-powered fire snakes, their brightness intensified by the gathering dusk, racing in both directions away from Sophie's gin bomb. The driver of the Ford instinctively tried to dodge what looked like two Biblical pillars of fire swerving back and forth and charging towards him like two forwards racing through the neutral zone. He wedged the car into the ditch on the side of the road, too tightly to be extracted without a tow truck and threw the rifleman five meters ahead of the car.

Sophie heaved a sigh of relief when she saw her pursuers' coupe in the ditch behind her, but quickly returned her attention to her gas tank, which was still a bomb on wheels with a lit fuse. She thought about pulling off onto a dirt road and kicking the dirt onto the gas trail so that the flames would not reach the remaining fuel in her tank. The problem with that was that there were no dirt roads in sight. Besides, once she stopped the car, she assumed that the rest of the gasoline would drain out and she would be on foot from then on. Before she let that happen, she wanted to get further away from the men who were shooting at her just a few minutes earlier.

Her only other option was to continue south, staying ahead of the streak of neon orange cutting through the growing darkness until she ran out of fuel. Sophie crushed the gas pedal to the floor for 30 tense minutes, until the engine sputtered and died. Then she shifted into neutral and let the car coast for another five minutes, when it finally crawled to a stop. She looked back to see a tiny orange dot, fading like a spent match just after it was thrown into an ashtray. There was no sign of the red coupe. She settled back into her seat and sat for a moment with her eyes closed. She felt like she had just lived through a chapter from one of her detective novels. The blood-thirsty killers in the red coupe had given her more excitement over the past hour than she expected to have for the rest of her life and she needed a moment to catch her breath.

Eventually, when her heart no longer felt like a tin can spinning around in a tornado, Sophie tried to decide what to do next. The only sign of civilization she had encountered since leaving Cahokia was a little town she drove through earlier that evening, before the shootout. She hadn't seen the town again during her escape, so she concluded it must be further south. She started at the car's roof liner trying to remember when she came through the town. Then she estimated how much ground she covered since that time, both before and after she was forced to turn around. The town probably wouldn't be too far away if she kept going south. She also vaguely remembered seeing a gas station in that town. Sophie decided to walk there and try to get help. However, she quickly realized that she had no idea if that gas station had a tow truck. If not, she was afraid that she might have to walk back to the car and push it into town. She decided to start pushing right away and save herself a trip.

Chapter L

A little under four hours and a little over five kilometers later, Sophie and her car straggled into the gas station in a town whose apparent claim to fame was that it happened to be the point at which a gravel road intersected the highway. She hopped up into the car to apply the parking brake, then climbed out and sat down on the running board to catch her breath. In the pale light, Sophie saw a single gas pump in front of a big cubic building with one overhead garage door and a little room tacked onto the side for an office area. It was white with red block letters reading "Morrisonville Garage." The paint was flaking away, almost molting like a snake, revealing grey concrete. The rest of the town was composed of a church, a tavern and what appeared to be a post office.

The only sources of illumination in this bustling metropolis other than the stars were a single streetlight and a sign that read "Pabst Blue Ribbon" in the middle of the silhouette of a fairly non-descript one-story building across the gravel road. There was no visible sign of life anywhere in the town, other than the "Pabst" sign. Sophie walked across the road towards the church and found that the heavy wooden door was locked. She pounded on the door, with no effect. She tried the tavern next, hoping that the lit beer sign meant that someone was still around. However, the tavern door was locked as well. A sign in the window listed the hours as noon to midnight, Monday to Saturday. She was five minutes late. She tried the other building, with no better luck.

She wandered back to the center of the intersection and looked at everything around her, hoping for some kind of inspiration, or at least a hint for what to do next. Suddenly she noticed a patch of blacknes slightly darker than the blackness surrounding it, in the distance next t the gravel road. It was in the shape of a house shaded by, in Sophie's estimation, the only deciduous tree in a 200-kilometer radius.

Sophie was not thrilled by the prospect of still more walking. Eve though she was wearing sensible shoes, her feet were swollen and throbbing. After pushing Sam's sedan all night, her shoulder and back muscle felt like the car had run her over and then backed up and run her ove again. But the mysterious gunmen made the alternative, sleeping in th car and hoping that someone who could help her shows up in the morning, seem like a worse idea. Although Sophie didn't focus on the gunme while she was pushing the car and although she felt safe for the moment she didn't know how long she would stay safe if the gunmen found way to get their car out of the ditch.

She sighed and started the long trek down the gravel road. The uneven stones constantly threatened to twist her ankles. Eventually, sh could see that the shadowy house-shaped object was a white farmhouse two stories, with a front porch running the width of the house. An oa tree towered over the house in the front yard and a black, rust-pitte Ford Model A pick-up truck was parked in the driveway.

At quarter after 1:00 AM, as she stumbled into the driveway, Sophie was immediately greeted by an old hound dog, howling, "Woo wo woo woo." Five seconds later, the porch light came on and a shotgu blast echoed into the night. She dove behind the truck, then peeked up t see a middle-aged man in a blue plaid bathrobe holding a shotgun an standing in the front doorway. He was short and muscular. He wore hi salt-and-pepper hair in a crew cut, which made him look like a steel bristled Fuller brush.

"Who's out there trespassing on my land!" the man bellowed i English, a language Sophie had not spoken since her freshman year o high school and barely understood. Although she was blessed with a near photographic memory and remembered almost everything she learned in every other class she took, English was her Achilles' heel.

"Bob, what's going on?" The shooter's wife appeared at the door in a yellow floral print robe.

"Go back to bed, Alice, I'll take care of this."

"That's nice, dear, but what's going on?"

"There's a prowler out there, someplace. I said I'll take care of it."

"You sure Digger wasn't barking at a squirrel again?"

"I'm sure. There's someone out there."

"Have you seen him?"

"No."

"Then how do you know?"

"I heard him running around out there someplace."

"I don't know how you could hear anything with that dog barking and all the noise you made with that damn rifle of yours."

"It's a shotgun and I tell you, there's someone out there!"

Bob peered out into the night looking for his prowler. Alice stared at Bob, as if she might see through his skull if she concentrated and finally understand how his brain works. After a few moments, Alice inquired, "How do you know it's a prowler?"

"What?" Bob asked, incredulously.

"He could just be someone with car trouble who wants to borrow the telephone."

"That's ridiculous!" he snarled. "If he was someone with car trouble, why is he lurking out there?" A gentle breeze rustled some of the oak leaves. Bob turned and fired. The explosion filled the countryside, together with the sound of sheet metal being shredded. As the echo slowly dissipated, Bob and Alice heard their mailbox rolling down the gravel road and coming to a stop.

When the ringing in her ears stopped, Alice suggested, "Maybe he's afraid you'll shoot him."

Bob gave Alice a look that told her that he thought her tone was more than a little sarcastic and that he did not find it helpful at that particular moment. He then explained, struggling to remain calm, "I wouldn't shoot him if he wasn't sneaking around."

"Maybe he doesn't realize that because of the way you keep shooting your gun."

"Alice, you just don't understand these things. Clearly, he's a prowler. If he wasn't a prowler, he wouldn't sneak around like this. He would just stand up, show himself and say what he wants."

"If he was in a car accident, maybe he can't stand up. Maybe he's hurt and lying in our yard right now and needs our help."

All this time, Sophie was cowering beside the truck, trying to estimate her chances of surviving any attempt to talk to these people. Although she picked up only a tenth of Bob and Alice's conversation, she understood "help." While they continued to bicker, she decided to try her luck.

"Help!" Sophie shouted, but not loudly enough to distract Alice and Bob from their petty argument. Suddenly, from the deepest pit of her memory, a phrase floated up into her conscious mind, the one phrase her English teacher, *Madame* Bergevin, used more than any other and she screamed: "Quiet, class. Now settle down."

Alice fell silent, more confused than anything else. Bob's jaw dropped. Then, he muttered under his breath, "What the Hell is that supposed to mean?"

Now that Sophie had their attention, she poked her hands up over the side of the truck to show she was unarmed. When they weren't shot off, she stood up and explained, "I am having the need of the help of you, if it pleases you."

"It's just a girl!" Alice exclaimed. "Bob, I told you whoever was out here might need our help. Put that thing down!" Alice demanded, pointing at the shotgun. Then she clutched her robe close to her chest and came down the porch steps and around the truck to talk to Sophie. It looked like she was running on tiptoe. When Alice asked Sophie what she needed, in accented but fluent French, it was the best sound that Sophie had heard all day.

Chapter LI

While Sophie was dodging bullets in *Illinois*, Le Pelleteur carefully ended his seething anger at Nathalie Juneau. He continued to stoke his anger through the night, like a camper building a campfire until it is big enough to burn the forest down. He paused only to call Sophie's apartment occasionally to see if she was home yet, until she called him at :30 AM. She said that she was all right, but stuck in what sounded like some two-bit burg in the middle of nowhere in the *Illinois* Region, although she described it more kindly. He offered to wire her some money to get the car fixed and she suggested waiting until morning to see what the repair bill would be.

Early the next morning, he took the *élevé* towards the XY Building. As he rode the elevator to the 17th floor, he remembered the last time he visited Nathalie Juneau. It was only a week earlier, but it felt like a lifetime. Before he entered the outer office, he took a breath and tried to calm down a little. He then strolled in and sat on the edge of Claire's desk.

"Hi, Gorgeous. Is your boss anyplace around here?"

"She's in her office. I can let her know you're here, dear." Claire replied.

"Thanks, but that won't be necessary. Anyone else in there?" He asked, bobbing his head towards Juneau's office door. Claire shook her head, slightly confused by the smile growing on Le Pelleteur's face, like a leopard closing in on a baby gazelle.

He walked over to Nathalie's office door and kicked it open. The door knob crashed into the wall and left cracks in the plaster. He grabbed her coffee cup and launched it against the wall, like a hockey puck breaking through the back of the net. A brown starburst covered half the wall, followed by a short rain shower of hot coffee and ceramic gran ules. Then he leaned over her desk with his nose five centimeters from hers: "Now that I have your attention, give me a reason why I shouldn't deck you right here and now."

"Do you have a screw loose? What is wrong with you?"

Le Pelleteur trembled for a moment while his face turned plum then he took a deep breath and snarled, "Let me explain this to you very slowly and simply: I am upset with you. You lied to me. You have been lying to me since the day you slithered into my office. I usually don' need much more provocation than that to pummel a guy until I have splattered his blood against a wall. But on top of that, you had a friend of mine killed and you tried to have me killed, too. Now, don't think that this little escapade hasn't been a barrel of laughs, because it hasn't, but am expending a considerable amount of mental strength clutching to my last slender thread of rationality. That will break at any second and so you don't have much time to convince me not to break you along with it."

Nathalie Juneau's exasperation melted into confusion and horro and she stammered something incoherent. Le Pelleteur couldn't tell if h had pushed her too far or if she was simply stalling for time to craft an other lie. That infuriated him further, but he concentrated and eventually found a way to swallow hard and push his fury down into the pit of hi stomach. He took a deep breath and sat in the chair in front of her desk.

"All right, let's hear your side of the story," he suggested when he had regained some of his composure. "Tell me why he had to die. Did you really think that he might pose some kind of threat to you? Or di you get a kick out of it? Or was it just a simple business transaction? How many pieces of Nazi silver did you get for handing someone over to them?" In the back of Le Pelleteur's mind, he was surprised that he made a Biblical reference and thought that perhaps the monks on campus were having a bad influence on him.

At that point, Le Pelleteur's tirade had overwhelmed Nathalie, so that she was unable to do anything other than blurt out "Oh my God!" turn away and erupt into tears. Samuel de Champlain Le Pelleteur felt his stomach dry up into dust and blow away. He sat down on the couch in her office and looked out the window so that he would not have to watch her sob. He sat there for what seemed like an hour, ashamed that he had made her cry, but still too angry to apologize. Eventually, she sat at her desk, dried her eyes and asked who died.

"His name was George-Etienne Shapiro and he was an agent for one of the insurance companies you defrauded." Nathalie shot him a dirty look with her bloodshot eyes. "Look," Le Pelleteur replied, "I am willing to consider for the sake of argument that I stepped a little out of line when I accused you of murder, but I know you're mixed up somehow in all of this. I think it's time you start coming clean."

Chapter LII

After Alice found Sophie in her gravel driveway, she shouted to Bob to call the police. Bob muttered something about trespassing on his land while he dialed the telephone. Meanwhile, Alice put her arm around Sophie and walked her into the house. They went to the kitchen, where Sophie told Alice about her previous six hours while Alice made some coffee. Sophie repeated her story for the *Arrondissement* Sheriff when he showed up. The Sheriff drove Sophie to the gas station so she could show him the bullet holes in Sam's Chevrolet. Then they went up Highway Q66 so he could see where the red Ford coupe went into the ditch. The car was still there. The Sheriff got out of his car to examine the Ford, but found no sign of the gunmen. Finally, they went to the station house, where Sophie asked to borrow the telephone. After she called Sam, the Sheriff offered to let Sophie spend the night in an empty jail cell. While Sophie slept, the Sheriff called the Highway Patrol division of the *Sûreté du Québec* and filed a report on the gunmen chasing Sophie the night before.

The next morning, the Sheriff told Sophie that the gunmen had not been found yet and gave her a ride to the gas station. By 8:15, while Sam was on the *élevé* heading towards Nathalie Juneau's office, Sophie was sitting on the running board of Sam's Chevrolet, waiting for someone who worked at the gas station to show up. She sauntered over to the office and checked the sign in the window, again. It still claimed the place was supposed to open at 8:00.

Sophie meandered back to the car. Five minutes later, a white wrecker with red lettering on the door matching the "Morrisonville Garage" painted on the building came down the gravel road, followed by a cloud of dust. The tow truck made Sophie laugh; she didn't have to spend the previous night pushing the car across *Illinois* after all. The wrecker pulled into the gas station parking lot and a tall man with dark hair emerged, walked to the office door, unlocked it and went inside. He was the kind of guy that spent most of his life in an almost impenetrable fog of blissful ignorance. Only on rare occasions, during his finest moments, would the fog dissipate into a hazy mist, so that the outer edge of an idea most would consider a basic tenet of common sense briefly becomes barely perceptible to him, although nevertheless beyond his grasp.

Sophie stood up and followed him into his office. She found him sitting at a desk reading the comics in the local newspaper.

"Excuse me, but I was wondering if you could help me," Sophie inquired in French.

"What?" The mechanic asked quizzically in English.

Sophie thought for a moment and explained, "The carriage of me has the need of reparations." To Sophie, the mechanic looked like he was in his mid-40s. Sophie observed the name "Bill" embroidered on the man's overalls over his left chest. As they walked towards the car, Bill asked if she could start the car. She said no, but before she could explain further, he demanded the keys. She then watched him try and fail to start the car and then open the hood and start inspecting the engine.

Sophie gave him a few minutes and then walked up beside him and stared at the engine. "Is it that you have discovered something?"

"This is going to be tough. I don't see why she won't start."

"During the time you think of that, is it that you can regard another something?"

Bill reviewed Sophie's request in his head and eventually said, "Sure, why not?" Sophie led him to the back of the car, kneeled down and pointed out the bullet hole in the gas tank. Bill mulled things over and proclaimed, like he was telling Sophie something she didn't know, "You got a hole in your gas tank. There's your problem right there!" Sophie decided that, even if she could be sarcastic in a second language, it would be too subtle to make an impression.

"What is the price to do the reparations?" Sophie inquired as neutrally as she could.

Bill shifted into his official-sounding voice and pointed out how hard it will be to find a gas tank for a car this old, because they aren't making parts for them anymore, and explained that he will need to cut off the old tank and weld the new one on. Then he scratched the back of his head while he mumbled some numbers, seemingly at random. Finally, he confidently proclaimed, "250 to 300 *livres*, plus about three weeks to find the part."

Sophie studied Bill to see if he was serious. Even though he appeared to be, she couldn't believe it. If she had 250 to 300 *livres*, she could buy a new car. An idea suddenly struck her. She marched around the car, reached under the passenger's seat and found the cork from the gin bottle that she had taken from the glove compartment the night before. She then crawled under the rear of the car, pushed the cork into the hole and kicked it several times to make sure it was tight. After that, Sophie motioned to Bill to help her push the car to the gas pump. While Bill filled the tank, Sophie checked to make sure that the cork was not leaking. She paid Bill for the gasoline and drove away, reaching Green Bay late that evening.

Chapter LIII

"I didn't kill anybody," Nathalie Juneau insisted.

"In my book, sister, 'coming clean' usually involves a little more in the way of detail."

"OK. I faked some shipping orders, but I wasn't involved in anyone's murder and I wasn't working for any Nazis."

"How about explaining how it all worked?"

"About a year and a half ago, I got a letter in the mail with a twenty-*livre* bill. The writer didn't have anything to ship, but he wanted me to fill out two fake invoices, one for shipping something from St. Louis to someplace else and the other from there to a third address. He asked me to send the invoices to the St. Louis address. I couldn't see any harm in that at the time. Ever since, about twice a month, I've gotten a phone call asking for two or three more fake invoices. I send them off to St. Louis and I get mailed twenty *livres* in the mail for each invoice about a week later."

"You couldn't see any harm?" Le Pelleteur asked incredulously. "Some complete stranger comes to you and asks you to do something obviously dishonest and it never occurs to you that this could be part of something illegal, or at least lead to some kind of trouble?"

"What are you, some kind of Boy Scout? Of course, I knew it was dishonest. I assumed the guy was documenting phony expenses to embezzle funds from the company he worked for. I didn't think he was some kind of gangster shooting bank guards or doing anything to hurt anyone physically and as long as it wasn't my company getting embezzled, it wasn't any of my business."

Le Pelleteur was not sure what he thought of Nathalie's story. Her cavalier attitude toward embezzlement left a stale taste in his mouth, but he also knew that times were tough and that she wouldn't be the first who bent her scruples for a little egg money. Also, embezzlement was theft from a company's shareholders, who tended to be wealthy investors who could afford it. Looking at it that way, while he didn't agree with her, he could understand why she might think that there wouldn't be any harm in what she did. He decided not to grill her any further on this question. Pushing her for some kind of admission of guilt would probably result in more "Boy Scout" accusations rather than giving him the answers he really wanted.

"Did you send the invoices to the same address every time?" he asked, trying to steer the conversation back on track.

"Yes."

"Do you remember what the address is?"

Nathalie extracted a yellow piece of paper from the bottom drawer of her desk and read an address that he recognized as Auguste Dumont's gallery. He asked her to describe the voice on the phone and she said it was an old man with a St. Louis accent. Le Pelleteur thought it must have been Dumont's voice.

"So, why did you drag me into your little racket? It seems to me like that was quite a bit of time and expense to cover something up if it wasn't any of your business."

"I found out later it wasn't embezzlement at all. The day before I came to your office, I got a phone call from someone who told me she had been impersonating me and using the fake invoices to submit phony insurance claims. She said the insurance companies were beginning to catch on and threatened to implicate me as an accomplice in her scam unless I do what she said. If she did that, not only would I be forced to resign my position here at this company, but the scandal would ruin me in Society. Then, she gave me this elaborate plot about hiring a detective to investigate the 'thefts.' The idea was that an investigation would help to convince people that the shipments and the thefts actually happened. She also gave me the number of some kind of voice actor and told me to hire him to play all the different buyers and sellers. Finally, she said she would convince the telephone operator in the building to route all your calls to the voice actor."

The seething anger that he felt for every lie that she'd thrown at him ever since she hired him started to cool. "Let's say for the sake of argument that I believe you. Who called you?"

"I don't know."

"You said 'she'? 'Unless you do what *she* said?'"

"Yes."

"Can you describe her voice?"

"She was an old woman and she seemed very impatient – kind of crabby."

"Old and crabby? Good." Le Pelleteur replied, thinking that "old and crabby" was not helpful at all, but hoping that some encouragement would improve her memory. Then he asked, "Was there anything else? Did she have an accent? Did she use any unique or unusual phrases?"

"No, that's it."

Le Pelleteur studied her for a moment. When he came into her office that morning, he was certain that she was the one running the scam. Now, he was wondering whether she might finally be telling the truth, which would mean that her hands were less dirty than many in Green Bay. He was tempted to go so far as to consider her a victim, deceived into participating in a scheme much less benign than she realized at first. Le Pelleteur found himself feeling increasingly sheepish about storming into her office ready to accuse her of George-Etienne Shapiro's murder. He also started to notice, again, how much she reminded him of his former fiancée. He grew increasingly sympathetic towards her, in spite of his better judgement, like a small snowball starting to roll down a mountain.

He was suddenly jolted back to reality, like someone picked up that snowball and threw it in his face. He stared at her for a moment and then he chuckled quietly at her. It was the kind of a laugh that suggested there wasn't really anything to laugh at. "You're good," Le Pelleteur complemented. "You almost suckered me again. I'm amazed how easy I fall for the bull you dish out. You're the only one around here who filed any phony insurance claims. Nobody else could file those claims behind your back, because the insurer would not pay them without doing some checking first and so would immediately tip you off. I also don't believe that this started out with you handing out a few fake shipping invoices to some charitable stranger. If that were the case, then Cloutier and your brother would not have heard about any art thefts until you told them you hired me. When I talked to them, they didn't say anything to suggest that they had heard of the art thefts only recently. I'm willing to give you the benefit of the doubt and believe that someone else approached you first about this scheme, you didn't know they were Nazis and that you didn't know anyone would end up on ice. Other than that, you knew what you were doing from Day One."

She became quietly defiant. "You can't prove any of this."

"Keep telling yourself that. I hope it gives you some comfort when the cops are pushing your head against your desk and putting you in handcuffs," Le Pelleteur taunted as he left Nathalie Juneau's office. He stopped briefly to say goodbye to Claire, then marched down the outer hallway towards the elevator. He felt relieved, like he had just tak-en a sharp stone out of his shoe. Nathalie Juneau had been playing him

:or a chump from the second she hired him, which was not a particularly ıttractive feature in the detective's opinion. But for reasons he did not :ully comprehend, he still felt like he was going to miss that stone.

Nathalie ran to the door and watched Sam stride down the hall-vay. Although she knew she should be deciding whether to call her at-orney, she found herself starting to miss Sam. When she initially walked nto Sam's office, she shifted her feminine wiles into high gear, expect-ng to manipulate Sam as easily as she manipulated most other people in ıer life. She discovered that she could manipulate him only with great lifficulty and it became more difficult every time he found another hole n her story. Finding a man who is not so easily used was surprisingly ıttractive to her. She wondered if this was really the last time they would see each other, or if she could develop some stratagem to bring him back nto her life.

As Le Pelleteur left the elevator on the ground floor and walked hrough the department store back to the street, he noticed a white enve-ope fly up in a pneumatic tube. He stopped in his tracks and watched he envelope sail across the ceiling. It took him a moment to figure out why it was important, and then he struck his forehead with the palm of ıis hand and shouted, "Of course!"

Chapter LIV

Sophie walked into Sam's office at 8:00 the next morning and fell into her normal routine; starting the percolator, watering her philodendron forest and reviewing the textbook she had left on her desk, *Electromagnetic Fields: Theory and Practice*, right where she left off. Although the week she had been away felt like a year, the morning appeared to unfold like she had never been away, except she found herself repeating Charles Gautier's name in her mind, like the refrain in a Frank Sinatra song sung to a crowd of bobbysoxers. By the end of the day, she would decide to buy a shortwave radio set and learn Morse code.

Two hours later, a few minutes after Sophie finished reviewing her book and phoned *Père* O'Shaughnessy for a new one, Sam strolled in looking particularly groggy.

"Good morning," Sophie greeted Sam excitedly, eager to compare her adventures returning from St. Louis to his.

"Well, I'll agree with the 'morning' part, but it won't be 'good' until I get a cup of coffee. Any left?"

As Sophie pointed at the coffee pot, *Père* O'Shaughnessy came into the office carrying the galley proofs of the next textbook for Sophie to review: *Principles of Bovine Physiology*. "A week of carousing and debauchery," *Père* O'Shaughnessy lectured Sam. "That *is* excessive, even for you. When will you learn that the path you are following will not lead to true happiness?"

"I'm not on the path to true happiness?" Le Pelleteur queried, pretending to be shocked. "You could have fooled me, seeing how I'm so deliriously ecstatic all the time."

Père O'Shaughnessy shook his head, like the high hopes he once held for Le Pelleteur were crushed by an unnecessarily sarcastic remark. Le Pelleteur found this attitude more condescending and insulting than usual. He leaned down and glared into *Père* O'Shaughnessy's eyes like a wolf eyeing a particularly annoying rabbit. "You know, you should be very cognizant of the fact that, every time I see you, I need to find a way to refrain from driving my fist into your throat. This may come as something of a surprise to you, but the reason I have been successful up to now has very little to do with your inherent charm or winning personality. It is almost completely a function of my amazing, almost Job-like patience. You might want to think about that the next time you pity me, or lecture me, or judge me, because even Job got fed up after a while."

After the priest left, visibly shaken, Sophie warned, "Sam, I'm not sure he realized you were kidding. He's not that bad of a guy once you get to know him. You might want to give him a break once in a while."

"You want me to give him a break? How about I break his nose?" Sam then took a deep breath, concentrated like he was about to lift something heavy and changed the subject. He poured himself a cup of coffee and walked into his inner office, inviting Sophie to follow. "So, tell me about your trip home and explain what you did to my car."

As Sam sat and put his feet up on his wooden desk, Sophie settled down into the overstuffed and garish rose-patterned couch and provided a detailed account of her gunfight on Highway Q66 and how a cork in the gas tank enabled her to drive the car from the middle of no place in *Illinois* to Henri Druillette's repair shop. Sam pretended to criticize her for leaving all his gin on a stretch of pavement 600 kilometers away. He didn't tell Sophie how impressed he was with her quick thinking and resourcefulness. He also realized that, from then on, it would be difficult to justify limiting her to secretarial work.

Sam then regaled Sophie with his adventures, including his conversation with his Uncle Edouard. He also described his confrontation of Nathalie Juneau and a telephone conversation he had the previous afternoon with a claims investigator in the head office of the Mutual of Duluth Insurance Company, explaining Nathalie Juneau's fraud and what he found in George-Etienne Shapiro's files. Finally, Sam reported that, while he was walking across the main floor of the XY Department Store the previous morning, he suddenly realized who the mastermind was. Then he waited, to build the suspense, until Sophie playfully took a red pencil from behind her ear and threw it at him. "It was the operator," Sam eventually explained.

"What operator?"

"The telephone operator at the switchboard in the basement of the XY Building."

"How did you figure that out?"

"When I was leaving the building, I remembered talking to that operator last week. The more I thought about her, the more she made sense. If Little Miss Juneau was not the mastermind, then the operator was the only person who could have orchestrated this fraud. She fit Nathalie's description of old and crabby. Also, I realized that she must work with our favorite Nazi, Johan, because he made a gambling analogy in the casino almost identical to one the operator made when I talked to her last week. So, I went back to the switchboard to talk to her again and discovered that she's not there anymore. The regular operator was there. She told me she'd just gotten back from a trip to Miami Beach that she won in some kind of contest and that there must have been a temp working the switchboard last week. I went to the payroll department to get the temp's name and address and then I looked her up in the phone book. It turns out that the name was phony. The address she gave was in the middle of the Bay. Unless she lives in an ice shanty, that address is also phony."

"Well, congratulations."

"For what?" Sam asked incredulously.

"You cracked the case." Sophie explained.

"How d'you figure that?" Sophie's response seemed so absurd that Sam almost laughed at her. "Let's look at what we got. I could provide a description of the person we were hired to find and one known alias and I could corroborate Nathalie's statement that she is old and crabby. Not only is that not 'cracking the case,' I doubt it's even enough to justify the fee."

"How long did that switchboard operator work at that building?" She enquired innocently.

"I don't know, about a couple of weeks, give or take?"

"So, either she makes her living as a fill-in switchboard operator and she orchestrated this whole scheme from scratch on her first day on the job, or she's been planning this for a long time and she got rid of the regular girl when it was time to hire a private eye to spend a day making fake telephone calls. Which theory sounds more plausible to you?"

"I would have to guess that she'd been planning this for a while," Sam replied, like a straight man waiting for a punch line.

"So, if you wanted to get someone out of town for two weeks, how would you do it?"

Sam thought for two or three seconds and answered, "Send her two train tickets to Miami Beach, with a letter telling her she won a contest."

"And where would you get those train tickets?" Sophie asked, as if the answer was obvious.

"Let me guess where you're going with this. You think calling every travel agent in town is going to turn up a clue?"

"Sure, why not?"

Le Pelleteur thought of a few reasons not to bother. The trail was probably too cold. Although most working-class people couldn't afford a Miami Beach vacation, such trips were popular among Green Bay's wealthy and it seemed unlikely that any travel agent would remember one customer out of the dozens in that go to Miami Beach every year. In addition, the operator may not have purchased the tickets herself. If she did, she could have paid in cash, to avoid giving the travel agent a check with an address that could lead back to her. On the other hand, while it seemed like a long shot to Le Pelleteur, it didn't seem impossible. Besides, he didn't see any other lines of inquiry and couldn't see how calling a few travel agents would hurt anything. Also, he said to himself, if Sophie is right about this and she can turn up some useful information, it wouldn't be the first time she had proven him wrong about something.

Sam asked Sophie to look up travel agents in the Yellow Pages and to make a few calls, but not to let it interfere too much with her textbook-editing. As she left his office, almost skipping, Sam dug around in the top drawer of his desk and found a half a pack of Du Maurier cigarettes, the same half pack that Nathalie Juneau took a cigarette from when they met for the first time two weeks earlier. Although the case gave him the puzzle he was looking for when he agreed to take it, and a little bit of cash, this didn't feel like a happy ending. Unless Sophie hit the jackpot talking to travel agents, all he could give his uncle was a description of the person he was hired to find, one known alias and a verification that she is old and crabby. He doubted that handing over that information would constitute "doing his part" in his Uncle Edouard's eyes. He got burned doing his part once before, back in his Bunko Squad days. Le Pelleteur was sure that wouldn't make any difference to Uncle Edouard, however. He was also sure that his uncle would find another job for him and would find a way to make him feel duty-bound to take it, probably against his better judgment, even though he once thought that no one could make him feel duty-bound to do anything again.

In addition, not only was he still obligated to the Central Government of *La République Québécoise* in some way that he did not fully understand, he was still a target of a Nazi assassin. Johan Schmidt knew he lived in Green Bay and would probably track Sophie and him down in time. Worst of all, an insurance agent is dead and it was partly his fault. George-Etienne Shapiro would probably still be alive and cooking up new ways to gyp him out of money the insurance company owes him if he hadn't stopped by his office that day. Sam could not add it up in any way that made him come out ahead.

Samuel de Champlain le Pelleteur started to wax philosophical which he did often when he had too much time on his hands. He ruminated, not for the first time, about the original name of the city, *Le Baie des Puants*, Stinkwater Bay, and how well the name described his general state of existence. Like a sad song when you're on your fifth glass of gin. Like the nagging pain in the back of your head that makes you do the right thing even while it makes you feel stupid for thinking that such a thing exists. Like the bad break you get once you think it can't get any worse.

About the Author

Throughout his life, **Steve Rhinelander** has studied Wisconsin history, particularly the 1600s and 1700s, when fur traders and missionaries from Quebec began to make contact with the indigenous peoples of the region. A retired Washington DC attorney, he now lives in Michigan with his wonderfully supportive wife, Laurie. He keeps a bobble head doll of Milwaukee Brewer baseball great Robin Yount on his desk. In his spare time, he listens to 1950s rockabilly music. POUTINE AND GIN is his debut novel.

Consider these other fine books from Savant Books and Publications and its *avant garde* imprint, Aignos Publishing:

Essay, Essay, Essay by Yasuo Kobachi
Aloha from Coffee Island by Walter Miyanari
Footprints, Smiles and Little White Lies by Daniel S. Janik
The Illustrated Middle Earth by Daniel S. Janik
Last and Final Harvest by Daniel S. Janik
A Whale's Tale by Daniel S. Janik
Tropic of California by R. Page Kaufman
Tropic of California (the companion music CD) by R. Page Kaufman
The Village Curtain by Tony Tame
Dare to Love in Oz by William Maltese
The Interzone by Tatsuyuki Kobayashi
Today I Am a Man by Larry Rodness
The Bahrain Conspiracy by Bentley Gates
Called Home by Gloria Schumann
First Breath edited by Z. M. Oliver
The Jumper Chronicles by W. C. Peever
William Maltese's Flicker - #1 Book of Answers by William Maltese
My Unborn Child by Orest Stocco
Last Song of the Whales by Four Arrows
Perilous Panacea by Ronald Klueh
Falling but Fulfilled by Zachary M. Oliver
Mythical Voyage by Robin Ymer
Hello, Norma Jean by Sue Dolleris
Charlie No Face by David B. Seaburn
Number One Bestseller by Brian Morley
My Two Wives and Three Husbands by S. Stanley Gordon
In Dire Straits by Jim Currie
Wretched Land by Mila Komarnisky
Who's Killing All the Lawyers? by A. G. Hayes
Ammon's Horn by G. Amati
Wavelengths edited by Zachary M. Oliver
Communion by Jean Blasiar and Jonathan Marcantoni
The Oil Man by Leon Puissegur
Random Views of Asia from the Mid-Pacific by William E. Sharp
The Isla Vista Crucible by Reilly Ridgell
Blood Money by Scott Mastro
In the Himalayan Nights by Anoop Chandola

On My Behalf by Helen Doan
Chimney Bluffs by David B. Seaburn
The Loons by Sue Dolleris
Light Surfer by David Allan Williams
The Judas List by A. G. Hayes
Path of the Templar—Book 2 of The Jumper Chronicles by W. C. Peever
The Desperate Cycle by Tony Tame
Shutterbug by Buz Sawyer
Blessed are the Peacekeepers by Tom Donnelly and Mike Munger
Bellwether Messages edited by D. S. Janik
The Turtle Dances by Daniel S. Janik
The Lazarus Conspiracies by Richard Rose
Purple Haze by George B. Hudson
Imminent Danger by A. G. Hayes
Lullaby Moon (CD) by Malia Elliott of Leon & Malia
Volutions edited by Suzanne Langford
In the Eyes of the Son by Hans Brinckmann
The Hanging of Dr. Hanson by Bentley Gates
Flight of Destiny by Francis Powell
Elaine of Corbenic by Tima Z. Newman
Ballerina Birdies by Marina Yamamoto
More More Time by David B. Seabird
Crazy Like Me by Erin Lee
Cleopatra Unconquered by Helen R. Davis
Valedictory by Daniel Scott
The Chemical Factor by A. G. Hayes
Quantum Death by A. G. Hayes and Raymond Gaynor
Big Heaven by Charlotte Hebert
Captain Riddle's Treasure by GV Rama Rao
All Things Await by Seth Clabough
Tsunami Libido by Cate Burns
Finding Kate by A. G. Hayes
The Adventures of Purple Head, Buddha Monkey... by Erik/Forest Bracht
In the Shadows of My Mind by Andrew Massie
The Gumshoe by Richard Rose
In Search of Somatic Therapy by Setsuko Tsuchiya
Cereus by Z. Roux
The Solar Triangle by A. G. Hayes
Shadow and Light edited by Helen R. Davis
A Real Daughter by Lynne McKelvey
StoryTeller by Nicholas Bylotas
Bo Henry at Three Forks by Daniel Bradford
Kindred edited by Gary "Doc" Krinberg
Cleopatra Victorious by Helen R. Davis

Poutine and Gin

The Dark Side of Sunshine by Paul Guzzo
Cazadores de Libros Perdidos by German William Cabasssa Barber [Spanish]
The Desert and the City by Derek Bickerton
The Overnight Family Man by Paul Guzzo
There is No Cholera in Zimbabwe by Zachary M. Oliver
John Doe by Buz Sawyers
The Piano Tuner's Wife by Jean Yamasaki Toyama
An Aura of Greatness by Brendan P. Burns
Polonio Pass by Doc Krinberg
Iwana by Alvaro Leiva
University and King by Jeffrey Ryan Long
The Surreal Adventures of Dr. Mingus by Jesus Richard Felix Rodriguez
Letters by Buz Sawyers
In the Heart of the Country by Derek Bickerton
El Camino De Regreso by Maricruz Acuna [Spanish]
Prepositions by Jean Yamasaki Toyama
Deep Slumber of Dogs by Doc Krinberg
Navel of the Sea by Elizabeth McKague
Entwined edited by Gary "Doc" Krinberg
Critical Writing: Stories as Phenomena by Jamie Dela Cruz
Truth and Tell Travel the Solar System by Helen R. Davis
Saddam's Parrot by Jim Currie
Beneath Them by Natalie Roers
Chang the Magic Cat by A. G. Hayes
Illegal by E. M. Duesel
Island Wildlife: Exiles, Expats and Exotic Others by Robert Friedman
The Winter Spider by Doc Krinberg
The Princess in My Head by J. G. Matheny
Comic Crusaders by Richard Rose
I'll Remember by Clif McCrady
The City and the Desert by Derek Bickerton
The Edge of Madness by Raymond Gaynor
'Til Then Our Written Love Will Have to Do by Cheri Woods
Aloha La'a Kea edited by Robert "Uhene" Maikai
Hawaii Kids Music Vol 1 by Leon and Malia
William Maltese's Flicker - #2 Book of Ascendency by William Maltese
Honeymoon Forever by R. Page Kaufman
Shep's Adventures by George Hudson
Retribution by Richard Rose

Coming Soon

I Love Liking You A Lot by Greg Hatala
Lion's Way by Rita Ariyoshi
The Immigrant's Grandson by Vern Turner
Hot Night in Budapest by Keith Rees
The Power of Dance by Setsuko Tsuchiya

http://www.savantbooksandpublications.com
Enduring literary works for the twenty-first century

Made in the USA
Monee, IL
01 April 2022